WINGS ONCE CURSED & BOUND

PIPER J. DRAKE

sourcebooks
casablanca

Copyright © 2023 by Lalana Dararutana
Cover and internal design © 2023 by Sourcebooks
Cover illustration © Nekro
Internal design by Laura Boren/Sourcebooks

Sourcebooks and the colophon are registered trademarks of Sourcebooks.

Published by Sourcebooks Casablanca, an imprint of Sourcebooks
P.O. Box 4410, Naperville, Illinois 60567–4410
(630) 961-3900
sourcebooks.com

Cataloging-in-Publication Data is on file with the Library of Congress.

Printed and bound in the United States of America.
WOZ 10 9 8 7 6 5 4 3 2 1

To the first players in Chaotic NarrativeRPG—especially Katee, Jenny, Cooper, and Gabriel. Thank you for the joy and laughter, and all of the creative energy we generated together.

ONE

PEERAPHAN

Peeraphan Rahttana closed her eyes and exhaled slowly, letting her senses expand until she was aware of every dancer waiting in the wings, of every stage tech behind the backdrops. It was a part of her warm-up when she was onstage, a way for her to get a feel for the people and space around her and prepare for the performance to come. She bent at the hips and reached forward until her fingertips brushed her pointed toes, stretching her muscles as she extended her awareness in a way those around her couldn't— past the empty rows of seats and outward into the halls beyond until she was aware of every stir of air within the theater, of every warm breath taken and given back.

And sensed one presence entering the theatre that...wasn't drawing breath. A person, walking across the front hall who didn't need to breathe.

That couldn't be good.

"Punch! I have the perfect shoes for your performance!" Sirin's strident tone cut into Peeraphan's head more effectively than a physical strike, distracting her momentarily from the unnatural presence she'd sensed.

Of course, Sirin had that effect on Peeraphan—Punch for

short—whether the other woman screeched her childhood nick-name or not. They'd grown up in the same community and because their parents had been friends, the two of them were supposed to be friendly, too, which was why Punch gritted her teeth and smiled.

"Just look at these." Sirin opened a shoebox and shoved the contents forward, practically under Punch's nose. "A very important patron donated these to the production. I think they're antique or something? Either way, they *have* to be in the show."

Punch straightened from her forward stretch and took the box from Sirin's grasp before the other woman managed to actually whack her with it. She opened her mouth to respond, until the most glorious shade of red satin caught her eye and she inadvertently gasped, all irritation with Sirin evaporated, everything else forgotten. The red was luminous, spellbinding even, and she lost the whisper of control she had over her own power as she focused on the shoes.

It wasn't just the heart-stopping color of the shoes. The heels were the perfect height and shape: high and wide enough to accen-tuate a dancer's legs while still providing stability. They were elegant and sophisticated, tastefully decorated with fine crystal accents and bold enough to be noticed even onstage. They were designed to be a statement.

She needed to put them on. Right away.

Sirin was practically vibrating with excitement. "You have to wear these for the show."

Agreed. No argument there. She needed to put them on. Now.

"No one will be able to say the costumes were lacking when the main dancer has these on her feet," Sirin continued.

No one would be able to take their eyes away from those shoes.

"If they're vintage, they're in amazing condition. You didn't want to wear them?" Punch glanced at Sirin with an effort. Looking away from the shoes for even a moment almost hurt.

But it was odd for Sirin not to want to keep something so clearly special for herself. Throughout their childhood and into adulthood, Sirin did everything it took to be acknowledged as successful. Then she claimed the best of anything she could get her hands on as her reward.

It was a trait Punch admired about Sirin while kind of hating it at the same time—the ability to balance doing well and taking credit for her accomplishments.

Punch wasn't just Thai American—she was a full throwback to something most people in the United States wouldn't recognize. Hell, some Thai people, including Sirin, were barely aware of the old folklore.

Because Punch wanted to keep it that way, she had to be careful to hide what she was. It was all well and good to want to stand out from the crowd, shine a little, be unique. But in a lot of ways, that wasn't safe.

Sirin shrugged, crossing her arms over her chest, uncharacteristically chill. "It's obvious they're too small for me, and vintage isn't my style. Besides, my shoes were special ordered and dyed to match my costume. You were just going to wear nude-colored character shoes. These are better. You can practice today to get used to dancing in them."

The performance was intended to promote awareness of Southeast Asian culture and showcase a fusion of traditional dance and contemporary choreography, with all proceeds going to scholarships for students from marginalized groups. Punch's mother had asked Punch to be a part of the performance as a favor.

"Let's make sure they fit before we decide they're going with my costume." As amazing as the shoes were, Punch wasn't going to try to wear them if they were a bad fit. Her dance performance could suffer, or worse, she could end up injured. Not worth it, no matter how gorgeous the pair of shoes. "Thai dance, even with a contemporary flair, definitely comes across different with shoes on, especially high-heeled shoes."

She hoped they fit. She wanted them to fit. Almost *needed* them to fit.

Punch froze, realizing she had already kicked her other shoes off in her eagerness to try them on.

"What are you waiting for, Punch?" Sirin stressed the nickname again, making it sound obnoxious instead of fun.

It had to be on purpose.

The irony was that she liked her own nickname. She'd managed to mostly reclaim it as her own, until she'd agreed to do this performance with Sirin. Seattle was a big city, and yet, here they were, back on a stage together, and Punch was yet again wondering how she could shake off the feeling of continually returning to childhood patterns instead of actually making any kind of progress in life.

Do well, but don't show off. Study hard, but never be a know-it-all. Excel, but never brag. Bitterness spread through her mouth as she tasted those memories. All any of it had ever resulted in was a lifetime of unacknowledged accomplishments and second-guessing her own pride in herself. Humility had been drilled into Punch so deeply, daring to take pride in anything felt like a risky dive into arrogance and vanity.

She glanced at the shoes in her hands, so gorgeous. So *red*. She could put on the shoes and this performance could change her life. She felt so sure of it.

There was something wrong. She frowned. Now was not the time to be pondering every personal issue great and small, and her thoughts had been wandering all over the place. She'd sensed something before and hadn't followed up on it.

Other dancers were joining her on the stage, warm-ups complete.

Punch reached out with her senses again, scanning the nearly four-thousand-seat auditorium as she did. There were a few members of the production team sitting in the nearest rows. The air stirred with each exhale, and she could feel the minute changes in heat and pressure against her skin the way she imagined fish might sense vibrations in the water around them. There was nothing else, no other living thing in the building. If it moved, even only to breathe, she'd have sensed it. But she'd detected something earlier.

Stage lights caught on the crystals decorating the shoes she was holding. Glancing down, Punch admired the glorious red satin. She could see herself dancing inside her mind, wanted to make it real.

The sooner, the better.

She gave in to temptation and bent to slide her left foot into one. The shoe was warm, probably from her own hands, and practically hugged her foot like it'd been molded to fit her specifically. Her left foot was a touch larger than her right by less than half a size—which was why she always tried on the left first—so she might need an extra heel or gel pad. Doable. Better for a shoe to be a touch too big than too small. She put on the other shoe.

Perfect fit. That was weird.

Punch straightened and took a few experimental steps forward. They didn't pinch anywhere and her feet didn't shift or slide around inside the shoes. In fact, the arch support was fantastic.

She couldn't wait to start dancing.

BENNETT

Bennett Andrews studied the woman from his vantage point far to the back of the highest mezzanine. She seemed to have been looking out into the audience, searching. Perhaps she had been waiting for someone to come watch the rehearsal. Either way, he had prudently kept to the shadows and waited.

He would have come earlier, if he could have, before the red shoes had claimed a victim.

His consortium had received a tip the other day about the red shoes surfacing at Pike Place Market. Truly, one could find just about anything there, particularly if one knew where to shop in the deeper levels of the market. He'd tracked the seller down but had encountered complications following up with the buyer until he'd been forced to retire with the sunrise. The consortium's witch had managed to detect the presence of the red shoes in the meantime, pinpointing their location within this theater. He'd come as soon as he'd risen for the evening, sooner than any other of his brethren in the region could have.

It hadn't been quick enough.

He was not here to catch attention, and it would be best if the woman did not remember seeing anyone out of the ordinary—assuming she survived—so he hadn't used his enhanced abilities to reach her, instead moved into the theater at a normal *human* pace. As she joined the other dancers in formation and music began playing, he thought the chances of her living beyond the evening were low. Minuscule.

She had already put on the red shoes, after all.

At this point, there was nothing for it but to wait for the screams and chaos and panic, then choose a moment in all the confusion to remove the shoes from the corpse. Even if he'd failed to come in time to prevent the death of this victim, he could do his best to ensure there wouldn't be another.

The music started, and the dancer with the red shoes was quite good, actually. Based on his research, the shoes compelled the wearer to dance, but they did not augment their skill. This woman was talented, with a compelling presence that drew the eye wherever she was onstage, whether she was the principal or dancing in a supporting role. She was incredibly expressive, every line of her body projecting her interpretation of the music, and she was light on her feet, making challenging leaps and turns look easy.

She was so full of life, he scowled. It would take that much more time for the shoes to drive her past exhaustion and beyond collapse. Thomas would call him an asshole for thinking that way, but the longer it took, the worse it would be for her. He hoped, for her sake as well as his own, that this was quick.

The red shoes were particularly cruel, according to some versions of the fairy tale, with roots in the Nordic lands of Northern Europe. If allowed to pass from hand to hand, human to human, there would be a trail of deaths left in their wake. Better for him to stop them here, after this one last death, and take them so the fairy tale could fade back into nothing but a barely remembered story.

"Okay! Let's break for five!" The director clapped her hands.

The chaos would start soon, once the dancer with the red shoes realized she had no choice but to keep on dancing. The shoes would compel her to increase intensity and speed until she literally worked herself into oblivion.

There had been a time when he would have allowed himself more sympathy for the doomed human. He'd learned since then that the pain of such feelings wasn't within his capacity to endure. One could only witness death so many times without developing coping mechanisms to endure. He pulled his hands out of his coat pockets and prepared to move as soon as everyone was distracted.

But the dancer not only stopped, she walked over to what were presumably her belongings and sat down, reaching for a water bottle.

Surprise rippled through him, the unfamiliar sensation like a static shock. She wasn't even tapping her toes.

He frowned. Something wasn't right. There must be some mistake. Those shoes might not be the ones he was here for.

He would have to get closer to be sure.

Traveling the distance from the upper balcony past the carefully preserved artwork and furniture of the lobbies of three different floors to find his way backstage took seconds. He could move at speeds that were a blur to the human eye, and as the evening was deepening to full dark, his abilities woke even further. In full night, few things in the world were safe from him. His talents had evolved to make him one of the most efficient hunters on earth, among a host of beings whose existence humankind had forgotten. Humans were not the apex predators of the world.

As he found himself an out-of-the-way spot where he could look across the stage from the wings, he realized with another jolt that the woman wearing the red shoes was *aware* of him. Even more interesting, she was not staring. Her gaze was cast downward as she sipped her bottle of water, and she was sneaking furtive glances his way under the cover of lowered lashes.

Based on her body posture, she was not frightened, or at least not panicked. Her back was straight, shoulders relaxed. Her feet were drawn close under her but spread enough for her to launch in whatever direction might be necessary. He imagined she was on alert and ready to bolt, but she was, he thought, giving him the most epic side-eye he had ever had cast in his direction.

And vampires at their most arrogant made disapproval and scorn an art form.

He smiled; he couldn't help himself.

Unable to resist, he began noting details about her. She was petite, compared to him and most of the company he had been keeping lately. But then, they were mostly men of six feet in height or more. Even the women and nonbinary among his organization were closer to six feet in height. Among the other dancers, though, she was one of the larger built, with a robust frame and more generous curves. It wasn't just tits and ass, as the old Broadway musical put to song, but the curve of well-defined muscle over her shoulders and upper arms, over her thighs and calves. She reminded him more of a warrior, capable of delivering heavy strikes and devastating blows balanced by flexibility, agility, and grace. With training, he imagined her capable of quite the killing dance on a battlefield. But those times were long gone, by human standards. Humans had invented ways to wage war from a distance with massively destructive results.

She was dressed in comfortable athletic wear, with her dark brown hair twisted up into a bun and her feet trapped in a pair of brilliant red shoes that were definitely the pair he had come to acquire. They reeked of cursed magic, a blend of seductive suggestion and poisonous animosity. They'd been imbued centuries ago with a single intent: redemption of sins or the death of the wearer.

He had not taken more than a glance at her face. In fact, he refused to learn to recognize her, if at all possible. He had only met her across a distance, and he was already sure the memory of her dancing would haunt his nightmares despite every effort he'd made to keep up an icy wall of indifference once she died. And he had an eternity to wrestle with remembrance. He had learned the hard way it was wiser to maintain as much emotional distance as possible from the mortals he met.

So no, thank you, he did not plan to add her face to the other poor victims he had gotten to know before he had failed to save them.

But now he was confronted with an issue. The mythic items he had come to acquire were indeed here. He needed to take them into custody before someone else with greater malicious intent did. He couldn't just walk up and take them off her feet without attracting too much attention. She wasn't likely to believe him if he told her the shoes were trying to kill her, either. She was resisting them, somehow. Which also meant he could not assume she was doomed. It might simply be a matter of time, a quirk. Or it might be a chance for her—one in who knew how many—to survive.

"Break's over!" One of the other humans—the director—clapped her hands together. "Let's run the number from the top."

The woman in the red shoes shot him another glance, then put her water bottle aside and began to stand. She was going to dance again, and this time, she might not be able to stop. This was not as simple as acquiring the shoes anymore. He was in a position to prevent a tragedy.

If he cared about her life.

It was one thing to commit himself to a cause for the betterment of the world, but it was completely different when it came to saving a specific life. It required too much...humanity. And that was something he had been working to leave behind for too long.

She was on her feet, stepping toward the stage.

"Don't." The word was out of his mouth before he could stop himself.

TWO

PEERAPHAN

Punch froze, resisting the sudden urge to bolt.

The man, whoever he was, wasn't just some person who'd walked off the street and come backstage to watch rehearsal. Maybe he knew someone here, but if he did he wasn't actively looking for them. No, he'd tucked himself into a nook just offstage where he could watch without being immediately noticed.

Shady.

Only she wasn't getting a creepy vibe off him. Some rational part of her mind was yelling at her, sure. But the more instinctive part of her, the part she had grown accustomed to listening to first, thrilled at the proximity of this man. Call it gut instinct, or maybe intuition, or more accurately, the part of her that recognized what a normal logic-minded person might try to rationalize away.

Of all the people in the building—the dancers onstage, the production crew up in the booth managing lights and sound, and the few sitting in the first row or two of the audience—this man was the only one not breathing. She'd sensed him entering the building before and gotten distracted somehow by the unexpected allure of those shoes, but now that he was here, just a couple of yards away, she couldn't understand how she'd let his presence slip her mind.

Of course, that should be a bad sign. He was the kind of hand-some that stood out in a crowd, with a prominent brow and a look of intensity that made one stop and stare. On another person, such a rough-hewn facial structure could've given them a primitive look, unfinished. But for this man, his features came together like a sculptor's attempt to capture primal intensity and a hunter's patience in a human visage. So how could anyone forget he was there? How could he pass through any populated room unnoticed?

A tiny part of her thrilled with the excitement of encountering this man. He was different, like her. Someone who might look human, but was distinctly not.

He was watching her with a small, mysterious smile playing over his lips and he would've captured her with his gaze if she'd allowed eye contact. She was sure of it. The same intuition that had her excited about this man warned her to proceed with at least a little bit of caution.

It was like the desire to be near a wild animal, knowing it had the capacity to hurt her, but also knowing that if she remained calm and didn't provoke it, she would have the experience of a lifetime.

"Why?" She finally lifted her gaze to meet his. Why had he said anything at all?

Damn, he was a captivating man. He was immaculately dressed in a European-cut suit, sleek and fitted to his lanky frame that hinted at a fit physique. He exuded sophistication with an aristocratic air, and that alone would have—should have—turned heads. But no one else seemed to have noticed him, nor was he paying attention to anyone else but her. And that was exciting, too.

"You are in danger." He made the statement a simple fact. All seriousness, no wry humor.

She tilted her head. It was a line in any number of plays, movies, television shows, and probably in countless books. But his expression was completely neutral, and that unsettled her. Wouldn't someone trying to convince her of any kind of threat to her safety have at least a little bit of urgency in their tone? Wouldn't they at least sound like they cared if she believed them?

She raised an eyebrow. "Everyone in the theater, or just me?"

She thought the corner of his mouth quirked farther upward for a split second. "At the moment, just you."

The clarification was both reassuring and terrifying at the same time. She would probably sort out the feelings later. Currently, adrenaline was starting to kick in.

"I need a good reason or I'm going to call the police." Even if he wasn't creeping her out, the careful part of her brain said he should be. "Try to avoid saying anything resembling a quote from a movie."

He did smile then. "Those shoes will try to kill you."

Huh. She blinked. "Okay, I admit, no movie or television show comes to mind. Well done."

He was also some kind of fool if he thought she was going to believe a pair of shoes had the intent or ability to end her. Or...

The memory of a ballet she'd attended with an auntie decades ago tickled the edge of her mind.

"You don't believe me and you don't have any reason to, except you should." His tone had taken on a quiet urgency. "This is similar to standing on a ticking bomb. Listen to me now and ask questions after you are clear of the blast zone."

She took a step toward him.

"C'mon people!" Sirin's voice cut across the general chatter on the stage behind Punch. "Somebody go after the smokers who stepped outside for an air break. Rest periods can't run this long or we won't be taking any more until we get this right."

Punch shook her head. "I need to get back to rehearsal. You're running out of time to convince me here."

He lifted his hands, palms toward the ceiling. "I warned you. That is all you get. Remember this—after you begin rehearsal again, you had the chance to listen and survive. You decided to be too stupid to live."

"That's it?" She wasn't sure what she was expecting, but he wasn't making a whole lot of sense. "Who are you? How do you know me?"

"It does not matter who I am, and I don't know you." He shrugged. "This was already more than I would normally do to give warning, human."

Meaning he considered himself *not* a human.

Excitement shot through her veins, overtaking the adrenaline running through her.

"Don't leave." She stared at him, doing her best to memorize his face.

He crossed his arms over his chest. "I don't plan to." He paused. "You don't intend to listen to me, yet you don't want me to leave. Why? I will not rescue you from your own decisions."

"I have questions for you." She hesitated, then added, "For someone not human."

His scowl was impressive. Somehow, the way he drew his brows together until the intensity of his expression deepened made him even more attractive. She wasn't sure which of them was being more unreasonable at the moment. Neither of them was doing well with communication, admittedly, but seriously, she had questions and anyone who was willing to at least acknowledge there were humans—and not-humans who looked like everyone else—was a lot more than she'd managed to encounter in her life. She didn't want to lose this chance.

"Promise me you won't leave." Because if she thought he was going to disappear on her, Sirin and the rehearsal could wait. The worst Sirin could do was get her mother to complain to Punch's mother, like they were ten again. Punch had more important things to worry about.

He stared at her, or at least she thought he was staring at her. He'd ceased to move, standing with a perfect stillness. The effect was more than unnerving. She felt like a bird on a fence, frozen, sure the nearby predator would pounce if she so much as twitched a feather. After a long moment, he did smile, slow and irresistibly devilish. "No."

Anger flared up in her chest and heated her cheeks. She took another step toward him.

"Don't leave the stage, darling," a man said.

This new voice oozed charm. There was a pull to those words, compelling her to obey the command. This had real power behind it, not just charisma or strength of personality. It had nothing to do with tone or timbre of the speaker, didn't require volume, but carried intent all the same and urged Punch to do as she was told.

Punch took a step offstage, because she was feeling contrary and she was thankful for the streak of spite she had going for her. It might have been the only reason she'd been able to bring herself to ignore that new voice. As she stepped off the stage and into the wings, she turned to keep her back to the curtains gathered there so she could see both her new not-human acquaintance and the newcomer.

Who wasn't breathing, either.

"Two in one day," she muttered. What were the odds?

"You have extraordinarily bad luck," the man that was only a few minutes less a stranger said in a tone too flat to be anything but sarcastic.

She flicked her fingers at him as she looked toward the other speaker. The new person was standing next to Sirin, twirling a length of her hair around his finger as she stared up at him in a combination of smug pleasure and what seemed to be lust.

"We're about to run through the number again," Sirin said in an eager tone. "You can watch me perform from start to end."

"I've arrived at just the right time, then." The newcomer smiled down at Sirin, then lifted his gaze to Punch.

There was a desire there, intense enough to burn through her, but it wasn't the heated kind of *want* Punch had always hoped for. It didn't awaken any kind of answering attraction inside her. The look in his dark brown, almost black, eyes left her cold enough that bumps rose all along her arms.

"What does he want?" She asked the question in the barest whisper, guessing the other man could hear her. Maybe. If he couldn't, that was fine, too, because she wasn't sure she really wanted to know.

"Just the shoes." Apparently, the man in the wings could hear her after all, when no one else onstage could. He had some fairly amazing hearing, as good as her own when she leaned into her own strengths.

"Is he trying to save me, too?" Somehow, she didn't think so, but a woman could hope.

Her friend in the wings—or at least he was friendlier than the impression she was getting off the stranger with the fashion-model good looks and intoxicating charm down in the audience with Sirin—actually chuckled. "Neither of us were drawn here with the intent to save your life, to be honest. We *are* both here for those shoes, and we are not working together in this endeavor."

"I appreciate your transparency." Punch might have sounded a little salty when she'd said it, but she did appreciate his forthright response. She was inclined to believe him.

Sirin left the newcomer's side and headed to the steps at the far end of the stage. The intro music cued up and Punch felt an overwhelming urge to rush to her starting position. Her feet shifted of their own accord, startling her the same way she would wake out of a dream if she kicked in her sleep. It wasn't the tingling rush she experienced when she tried to use her own powers. This was sneaky, subtle, almost undetectable, until she was already moving with the impulse...to dance.

She stared down at the shoes. This was more than habit after years of dance training and performances. This was coercion.

"First come, first serve. Take the shoes," she whispered, afraid her voice would crack if she spoke any louder. Terror sang along her nerves as she admitted to herself she was truly in very real danger here.

"Come to me."

Aw, now, that didn't sound like a good idea at all.

She shivered, caught between fear and sudden desire. The man gave good voice. Very good. She decided to compromise and step offstage, farther into the wings and closer to him but not completely out of sight of the first few rows of the audience.

"Well, take them." It was hard to resist the music as other dancers began their opening steps. Her entrance was in another four counts of eight.

He was suddenly next to her, close enough to touch. "Take them off."

She tried to lift one foot and slip a shoe over her heel. It wouldn't budge. Neither would the other one. She gritted her teeth and stumbled to her previous seat as she tried to remove a shoe with both hands. "I can't. They won't come off."

"Ah." He leaned down to examine her feet, still not touching her or the shoes. "I had hoped with your resistance to the magic of the shoes, you would be able to remove them, too. This is a problem, then."

BENNETT

Bennett should never have looked her in the eyes.

They were a clear brown that let light in the way a deep pond held golden sunlight between the surface and the rich, earthy bottom.

There was so much more there than the fleeting moments of a mortal life. He'd seen sharp intelligence and dry wit, steady in the face of realized danger, and calm courage as she tried to take action on her own behalf. Now there was nothing she could do and she was afraid.

He wasn't a hero. Even if he wanted to try, this one time, he didn't know how to save her.

"Stop!" The director's voice cut across the music. "Punch missed her entrance. Start from the beginning."

"Wait." Francesco's voice made the director halt. She turned to look out into the audience, obviously compelled. Bennett wasn't close enough to see it in her eyes, but she moved a little too stiffly, like a puppet. That woman had a strong will and she was fighting the compulsion of a vampire. Not an easy thing to do.

This performance group was full of surprises.

"Bennett, is that you back there?" The man's voice sounded amused.

For his part, Bennett decided to focus on his objective, and the person currently wearing them. "I think we should go."

"Really, Bennett, I'm torn," Francesco said in a lazy drawl. "I was looking forward to witnessing a dance performance to die for, but the prospect of encountering you again is most amusing. How long has it been? Are you really going to attempt to spoil this fun?"

The woman, Punch, glanced out over the stage and then up at him. "You're not going to kill me, are you? You came for the shoes and you might've even let me die wearing them, but you weren't going to kill me yourself, right?"

"Correct." It was good that she hadn't asked him to promise that he wouldn't kill her at all.

She reached for her bag and slung it over her head so the strap lay across her body. Then she surged up so fast, he had to stand as well to avoid collision. He was far stronger than any human, so she would've bounced back into her seat or done herself worse harm. Neither of them had time for that kind of nonsense.

In fact, he was done with the patient approach. "Hold on."

"Wha—"

He scooped her into his arms—bag and all—cradling her against his chest. Then he darted out the emergency exit backstage before she could finish getting the word out.

"Leaving?" The other vampire's voice called out behind them, not far enough away.

Vampire speed was a species trait, and Bennett barely made it out the doors before he was struck from behind by someone with superhuman strength equal to his own. He cursed and twisted, just managing to take the corner of a building with his shoulder rather than allow the fragile human in his arms to be crushed between him and the brick wall, spilling them both into a narrow space between two buildings barely wide enough for a person to walk.

"Get to the end of the alley and out of sight," Bennett said to the woman. "Or run, if you prefer."

It wouldn't matter. Either he or Francesco could track her now that they'd gotten her scent. Running wouldn't save her, but it might make her feel better. He turned without waiting for her answer and faced the other vampire.

"Clever, Bennett." Francesco was practically hissing in his anger. "Always the fast thinker. There was a time when the two of us hunted in tandem."

"Only a brief time." Bennett did not need to feign nonchalance. It was unusual, but not unheard of, for two vampires as strong as they were to hunt together, but they had both been centuries younger.

Since then, Bennett had made the choice to restrict his hunting. He would not feed on helpless innocents, those who did no intentional harm to others and had no means to protect themselves.

Bennett had parted ways with Francesco then, thinking there were enough terrible human beings in the world to keep him not only well fed, but actively hunting in an effort to cull the population of the greedy and malicious. There was no need to spend lifetimes with a similarly toxic immortal.

Besides, there was power to be found in a vampiric feeding preference. The old knowledge was something handed down through Bennett's bloodline and not something Bennett had ever felt the need to share with another vampire, especially one as indiscriminately vicious as Francesco.

Francesco's dark hair, carefully styled, was barely disturbed by their earlier impact. Black eyes set deep into a sculpted face glared at him with barely contained eagerness. His olive brown skin was flushed. He'd fed very recently, perhaps more recently than Bennett, and that could have made the difference in this fight if they had been out in the open.

Francesco rushed forward, seeking to press his earlier advantage, but Bennett held his ground within the narrow space between the buildings. He intercepted Francesco's attack with a strike of his own, effectively stopping the other vampire and changing the flow of the fight. They traded blows, but for every one of Francesco's punches, Bennett parried and counterattacked simultaneously in efficient bursts.

"It's good to know you haven't let yourself go in all this time spent with your Consortium gathering dust in a library," Francesco said, sounding genuinely pleased, even if his words were meant to taunt Bennett. "But I never did understand why you do so much to protect all these mortals, especially humans. There's so damned many of them."

"Their numbers are precisely why you should have more care for what you do in front of them," Bennett responded as he stopped another punch and pressed Francesco's fist to the side to clear the way for his own strike.

Fights between vampires—or any supernaturals—out in public were frowned upon by every governing body of the various supernatural communities. The majority of the human population were blissfully unaware of the monsters living in the spaces humans were too self-absorbed or afraid to notice. It spoke to how much Francesco wanted those red shoes that the other vampire had persisted in a fight, risking exposure to humans—every one of them armed with a tiny computer and video recording function in their smartphones. Francesco might pretend he didn't care what humans witnessed or thought, but the other vampire understood what it took to survive and hunt successfully among them.

It was early in the night and there were many pedestrians on streets just a block over. Here, in a tight alley, Bennett had the advantage as he controlled the positioning and flow of their exchanges. Close-quarters fighting kept them relatively out of sight. Besides, giving Francesco room to maneuver would have resulted in wrecked cars and severely damaged buildings, most certainly guaranteeing a human body count. There was also the chance the other vampire would get past Bennett and catch the woman wearing the red shoes as prey.

Neither the red shoes nor the woman were Francesco's to take this night.

"It's more than that for you." Francesco continued to press Bennett, looking for an opening. "You were closer. You could have just killed the human and taken the shoes. Even now, you could've let her die and fought me for them. Where's she scurried off to? One of us is going to have to take the time to track her down now. How irritating. Why preserve her life at all?"

A good question. Bennett did not bother to formulate an answer, since he was not certain he understood himself. Besides, every verbal exchange had been an accompaniment to Francesco's efforts to escalate their fight. The other vampire was looking for even the slightest moment of distraction.

Both of them had trained in a variety of martial arts over the centuries. Their fight was a grab bag of styles, and they'd fought each other before—sometimes in friendly sparring, and in recent decades, more serious combat. Francesco employed more military styles of fighting now, harsh and brutally effective. Bennett preferred economy of motion and maximizing damage done within limited time, using stop hits to preempt Francesco's bigger attacks, simultaneously parrying the smaller attacks with punches of his own, and using low kicks to destabilize Francesco's footing.

They could've gone on like that for hours, days even, depending on when each of them had last fed. But they were still outdoors and the sun would rise eventually. Neither of them could survive the sun.

It was Francesco who changed the dynamic, pulling a ridiculously large combat knife from a hidden sheath within his black trench coat. In a normal human's hands, it would have been unwieldy and hard to use to good effect. But in the hands of a vampire, with his greater speed and strength, Francesco had tipped the scales to his advantage.

Damn. Bennett rarely traveled into human cities armed. He had no need against humans. Even most supernaturals posed little threat to a vampire as old and powerful as he was. Irritation crackled and he bared his teeth.

There weren't any convenient pipes or two-by-fours lying about to use in self-defense, either. Well, dignity meant nothing in combat. He launched into the air, flying where Francesco couldn't follow long enough to remove a shoe, then he came down at a new angle of attack. He used it to counter the blade and redirect it, looking for a way to disarm Francesco.

Francesco snarled, a sound of rage and frustration, and surged forward. His face stretched, his jaws pushing forward as his fangs extended, ripping into Bennett's forearm.

Bennett hissed, but didn't drop his shoe. Francesco managed to slip the knife under Bennett's guard though, and buried it in Bennett's abdomen. Bennett reached down with his other hand, gripping Francesco's wrist and trying to break his hold on the knife as Francesco twisted it and yanked upward.

Bennett wrenched his right arm, the arm Francesco was still chewing on, up and to the right. Francesco tore flesh and broke bone, but did not release Bennett's arm—which was exactly what Bennett needed. Bennett struck with his own fangs extended, ripping at Francesco's now-exposed throat and allowing blood to flow freely from the gaping wound.

In a flash, Francesco disengaged, backing away and clutching the side of his neck. Then he was gone. Bennett waited a full second, ready for another attack, but it was unlikely. The other vampire was in danger of bleeding out faster than he could heal.

The exhilaration of victory sang through him as he bared his teeth, tempted to let out a snarl of triumph. The searing pain of his injuries had been banished to the periphery of his awareness as he'd fought, and as he took stock of his surroundings, his mind began to catalogue and acknowledge the damage he'd taken. He might have won, for the moment, but he was not in a position to linger out in the open for much longer.

Bennett turned to see the woman peeking around the corner of the building at the far end of the alley. There was no way for him to feign health at this point, so he allowed himself to lean against a wall for support. "I told you to run."

She approached warily, not only studying him but looking beyond him and even upward. He approved of her attempt at situational awareness. It wouldn't have saved her if Francesco had still been a danger, but it was better than nothing.

She stopped an arm's length away, clutching the bag slung across her body as if she carried something delicate or precious.

"You told me to hide or run based on my preference." Her voice was steady. "I read once that it was a bad idea to run from anything immortal. It attracts their attention."

Wherever she had read such advice—and he thought he might know the novel she was referring to—it was true.

"We need to get you to safety." That particular next step felt very far away. He had come out of the fight in worse shape than he cared to admit, and he could not afford to hunt here in order to hasten his healing. He needed to get her and the red shoes someplace more secure.

Suddenly, her arms were around his waist, supporting him as she tucked herself under his uninjured arm. "Where can we get you help?"

Who was she, that she could step to his side without his reacting? What was she? Or was it because he was injured so badly?

"Good questions," she responded. "I'm going to go with the last one as the likeliest possibility. You're injured that bad and I'm not even sure you realize you're talking out loud."

He decided to focus on next steps, rather than worry about his rapidly deteriorating condition. "Pier 66 at the waterfront. Help is there. We must get you to Duncan. Then I will leave you with him and go feed."

It would be necessary, for him to survive his wounds. But he needed to get her and the red shoes to his colleague first.

"It's a good thing you're wearing black. It hides the blood at night, as long as we stay off Pine and any of the other really well-lit streets." She didn't waste time with questions, only started them walking. He found his steps weaving more than he'd like and the echoes of their footsteps in the alleyway assaulted his hearing. Her hand gripped his sleeve and tugged at him. "If you'll wrap your arm around me, we can be a cute couple on a date."

Not a bad idea, but he found he had tilted into her until she stumbled under his weight. She was, he thought, quite a bit shorter than him.

"Maybe you're just ridiculously tall, dark, and not completely lucid," she quipped.

A fair assessment.

It was a long trip down to the pier. Partway, the woman used an app on her phone to activate an electric scooter to hasten their trip. The vehicles were not intended for use by more than one person, but he was not able to ride one on his own and he felt better able to protect her with his body riding behind her, his arms bracketing her as they both held the handles. She took them directly across the pedestrian bridge to the edge of the stairs leading down to the pier.

He would not feed on a victim. He would not draw in air to catch her scent or give in to the temptation to taste her skin. He would not sink his teeth into her until her blood flowed.

He would not.

"To the boats." Words had become harder and his vision was narrowing. "Just...get to the boats. There is help. Duncan can keep you safe."

From me.

Seemingly oblivious to the danger he represented, she steadied him against the railing and used it to practically slide him down the steps. A figure stepped out of the shadows of one of the boats and moved towards them. Bennett bared his teeth until he caught the flash of silver hair and the scent of fae.

Ah. Relief washed through him. She would be safe. He wouldn't break his oath.

He managed to give her a shove toward Duncan before he fell to the ground, satisfied.

THREE

PEERAPHAN

"We've arrived." The man—Duncan, she assumed, though they hadn't exchanged introductions yet—was simply dressed in dark gray. He was older, with long gray hair gathered neatly at the nape of his neck and tied off with a simple black cord. The way he held himself with perfect posture and moved about with an air of competence had lulled her into resting in his presence over the last couple of hours.

Punch looked up blearily at his calm statement, but couldn't see much outside the boat's main cabin. Dark had fallen and they were far from the city lights she was used to. The man driving the boat hadn't said much on the journey. She was holding on to a very thin lifeline of trust, at the moment. There was a man who'd fought to keep her safe and the man they had fled to for help.

She didn't know her rescuer's name and he had gotten hurt for her. And there had been the thing their attacker had said back in the alley.

I never did understand why you do so much to protect all these mortals.

Her protector lay on a bench in the cabin, still and possibly dead. The whisper of magic she had was only really enough to tell her he wasn't breathing. She'd experienced how fast he could move, got an idea of the damage he could do in a fight. If he had wanted to hurt her to get the shoes she was wearing, he could have. And he hadn't. The person he'd guided her to had treated her with cautious care, too.

She couldn't be sure either of them wouldn't kill her at any moment. And thoughts kept popping into her head, inconsequential and distracting. Did one drive a boat, or pilot one, or what? There was a motor, so she didn't think the correct verb was *sailing* for this particular vessel. But none of those things actually mattered. It was just easier, tempting, to let her mind dodge the scarier realities she'd encountered tonight.

She struggled to pull her deteriorating thoughts to something that mattered.

"Wouldn't it have been better to get him medical help?" A hospital might not be the right place for Bennett. He was hurt and bleeding, yes, but he was also not human, and everything she'd learned from mythology or modern media indicated taking a nonhuman to a hospital was a bad idea. Very bad. Depending on what kind of nonhuman, it could be catastrophic.

"A hospital would be a dangerous place to take Bennett, both for him and for the patients there. We will do our best to help him here." The man approached, taking Bennett's wrist and pulling the unconscious man up until he could get a supporting arm around his employer's waist. "Please follow me, Miss..."

"Punch. Just Punch." She didn't have the energy to go through proper introductions and name pronunciation at the moment, and her name wasn't a familiar one to most people in the United States. Nicknames weren't her favorite with new acquaintances, but they made things easier.

"You can call me Duncan. I'm Bennett's personal assistant."

"It's nice to meet you, Duncan." The pleasantry came out automatically, comforting and normal.

He hadn't said his name was Duncan, only that it was the name she could call him by. It seemed like an important detail, one she ought to remember, even if she couldn't quite retrieve the why from her jumbled thoughts. Then again, she'd given him her nickname and not her real name, so she'd set the tone. A flash of guilt jabbed at her. Perhaps she'd started off on the wrong foot with Duncan.

Ah, it was too much to try to think through and she couldn't manage it. She pulled her bag close, cradling it in her arms, and got to her feet.

If nothing else, it said something positive about Bennett if he was the type of employer on a first-name basis with his employee. She had never found an employer that insisted on the formality of surnames to be the kind of person she respected in the long run.

"It's a pleasure to meet you, too, Punch." There might have been an undercurrent of amusement to Duncan's words, but she wasn't absolutely sure. "Just this way."

Well, he sounded pleasant enough, so if she had messed up on introductions, there seemed to be some hope to repair the damage later. If there was a later. She was pretty focused on taking one step at a time currently.

There were people outside, including two men in dark uniforms, one tying up the boat and the other remaining in a compact structure attached to the small pier where they had docked. Neither did more than exchange nods with Duncan. Punch was too tired to register any other details. From the pier, she followed Duncan as he hurried up a path, supporting Bennett as they went.

Even in the darkness, her eyesight was good enough to make out the looming silhouettes of towering evergreens. Stars, so many stars, spread across the night sky over the treetops, visible only

because they were far from the light pollution of the city and surrounding suburbs. Shadows gathered thick around the trunks of the
evergreens, an array of shrubs and lush ferns and smaller deciduous
saplings.

Dim lights lined the way up the path, and under other circumstances, Punch might have slowed down to appreciate the nighttime
ambience. Not now though. Not with the man who'd saved her
leaving a bloody trail on the paving stones along the pathway. She
wasn't sure how he was surviving.

Whatever survival entailed for a being like him.

Uncertainty nibbled at her calm, making her anxious. There
wasn't a lot she was sure about, really, and she tried to anchor herself in what she did know.

She was here because she felt responsible. Bennett wouldn't have
been hurt if he hadn't been protecting her. She also didn't want to
be in the city, or go home alone, when Francesco was out there. He
could come after the shoes, and her, again. Her chances were better
with Bennett.

And beyond that, she wanted—desperately needed, if she was
being honest—to know more about Bennett. Hope sparked and
chased away the uncertainty eating at her. He was the first not-
human person she'd truly met. Someone who could help her learn
about things everyone else in her life thought were just myths and
legends and stories. Things she was sure were real.

Her feet felt heavier than usual, prone to catching on the ground
no matter how careful she was.

The fleeting image of her dancing and twirling on her toes across
the flagstones rose up in her mind. She'd feel lighter, more sure of her
footing if she could dance. Wouldn't she?

No. She shivered. No, she wouldn't.

Duncan didn't seem to notice her wrapping her arms around

herself as he hauled Bennett up wide steps to the front door of a large home. Mansion. Manor. Castle?

The front doors opened on their own and she followed Duncan and Bennett inside to a vaulted entryway.

"Asamoah!" Duncan called out to the household in general as he laid Bennett down on the floor and began opening his coat and shirt to get a good look.

A large man burst through a swinging door and stopped short, taking in the scene with deep brown eyes. He filled the doorway, his shoulders almost brushing either side, and he was drying his big hands with a soft-looking red-checkered hand towel. He flipped the towel over his left shoulder and set his hands on his hips. "We'll be needing something stronger than the usual to make this right."

"Yes." Duncan leaned over Bennett, studying the wounds.

"What does he need?" Maybe there wasn't much she could do, but she had to at least offer. Anything but simply stand there.

"Blood," the big man in the doorway answered simply, shaking his head. His skin was a mellow brown, the color of freshly turned earth after it had some time to warm in the sun. His voice was hearty, with a musical quality to it like the resonant sound of a viola or a cello.

Asamoah had a steadiness about him without losing any sense of urgency. He gave off an air of competence, that everything was going to be all right. Asamoah, and Duncan, too, were different. Somehow.

And currently, Asamoah was considering Bennett's wounds with a remarkable calm for someone watching another person die. "There isn't a tisane, tea, or tincture that can help a vampire more. We've human blood set aside in bags for his normal needs, but wounds this bad will require blood fresh from the artery and even that might not be enough to save him."

Bennett was a vampire.

Well, that explained the not breathing. Punch had guessed, but having never met any actual vampires, she hadn't been absolutely sure. It was possible she'd gone into shock, way back at the theater, when Francesco had attacked them.

Images flashed in her mind of their faces, the way their jaws had come forward and fangs had extended. They'd ripped into each other and torn through flesh and bone.

"No." Bennett stirred.

Her attention snapped back to him, her heartbeat pounding in her ears. How was this man arguing with anyone when he'd lost enough blood to be in a coma by now? Not that she was any kind of medical professional, but there had been a lot of blood between Seattle and here. Vampire or not, this just didn't seem to be the time to be arguing with anyone on how to save his life.

"What happens if he doesn't get blood fresh from the artery?" Punch asked and immediately regretted it. In her experience, a person should only ask a question if they really wanted the answer.

Asamoah fixed Punch in place with a hard look. "He dies."

Bennett lifted his chin and opened his eyes. "I am already dead, by human terms."

Asamoah sighed. "His existence comes to an end."

Despite his brisk commentary, Asamoah's lips pressed into a thin line and his arched brows were drawn together. He was worried. "He's taken an oath not to feed from any member of this household. I cannot help him. Neither can Duncan or anyone else who makes this place their home. Even with our consent, his oath would prevent him. It isn't a conscious choice."

Of course not.

Punch kneeled down next to Bennett, looking from Duncan to Asamoah. "So what do I do, just wave my wrist in front of him?"

Bennett reached up a hand to ward her off. "I do not feed on innocent humans. Ever."

"Define innocent." Then again, she didn't particularly want to have a conversation about what his concept of innocent might be. Ever. "You know what? Don't bother, because I am not precisely human anyway. Bite me."

She shoved her wrist into his face.

He glared at her, his mouth remaining stubbornly shut.

Duncan took hold of her wrist and turned it upward so the inside of her forearm was exposed. His gray eyes were full of storm clouds when she met his gaze, and any argument she had for him stayed inside her head. His grip tightened on her. "You're sure you want to make this offering?"

Punch put every ounce of stubborn courage she had into her eyes as she held his gaze. This was one thing of which she was absolutely certain. "He saved my life."

She hated owing anyone.

A nod. Then there was a flash of silver and the sweet, metallic scent of blood filled the air. Her blood. She stared down at her forearm, her body only just beginning to send pain signals to her brain as blood welled from the deep cut on the inside of her arm just below her elbow. The blade Duncan had used was still in his hand, hovering over her arm. It must've been really sharp.

Bennett groaned as her blood ran down the side of her forearm and dripped onto his lips. Suddenly, he struck, his mouth fastened over the cut as the searing pain spiked.

The sound of her own blood rushing through her veins roared up until the sounds of anyone else in the room disappeared. She swallowed any gasp or yelp she might've made. If she let him know she was hurting, he might stop. His eyes snapped open, a deep red, and she felt like she fell forward, into them.

Fear screamed through her as power—his, she was sure—threatened to tumble her mind and she wrestled with it, falling. Falling. Falling into Bennett.

His power lulled her into a sense of security, of safety, if only she'd let him hold her. If she struggled, he might rip her apart. She'd seen what vampires could do just hours ago. But no, he wouldn't. His power whispered with a different promise. He promised to be gentle, to give her peace.

But he could rip and tear and break her.

Images of the fight between Bennett and Francesco flashed through the space around her. Everything beyond them was a blur of light and shadows, a maelstrom. Bennett's power might murmur promises, but it couldn't make her forget what she knew.

Still, she had volunteered for this, she reminded herself. He hadn't wanted to. He wouldn't kill her. But she was afraid and the storm continued to spin around them both.

A double beat interrupted the rushing noise around her, like a drum. *Lub dub.* Then again. *Lub dub.* She took another steadying breath. The double beat came again, slower. It was the sound of her own heartbeat.

There was an echo out there somewhere in the rushing sound of wind. The wind was hers, her power. As the chambers of her heart contracted in their double beat, the flow of her blood gave another heart the power to beat somewhere else, in someone else's body.

Bennett.

Yes. She'd chosen to do this to save him. It was her promise to take care of him, give him life. She reached out with her power, the winds around them slowing and swirling as they wrapped his presence. She had the impression of white feathers, of wings curving around them both to envelop them in sheltered quiet. And then there was only the sound of her heartbeat, then his.

The world came back into focus as Bennett disengaged, lifting his mouth from her arm and sitting up. She watched him, her thoughts sluggish, and found herself being gathered into his arms until she was cradled in his lap. Ah. She should've argued or whatever, but the thought of the effort it would take to struggle upright was more than she could manage.

She looked up at him. "You keep doing this."

There was blood smeared across the lower half of his face, and he had fangs. Definitely fangs. Those were very prominent for sure, now that he had them bared at her. His pupils had become so large, the whites of his eyes were gone. Had they been red a moment ago? Maybe. There was something in his gaze though, something desperate. Like hope.

"What are you?" he asked, and she wondered if his voice cracked with emotion or exhaustion from his ordeal.

She was fascinated, probably should be horrified, but again with the too-exhausted-for-extreme-reactions situation. Clear thinking was not her forte at the moment. "It's a long story."

Her bag started rustling and a zipper finally gave way and unzipped. Punch struggled to try to say something, but she was so tired. A little furry form wiggled through the open zipper and climbed up her arm to her shoulder, lifting tiny clawed hands toward Bennett as the electric pencil sharpener sound started up again full force. A second flying squirrel joined the first.

"Tobi. Cory. Shh," Punch whispered faintly. "I'm here. It's okay. He's done now."

She seemed to still have the capacity for fear, because a new spike of worry poked her. She really hoped no one here would hurt her friends.

"What are those?" Bennett asked.

"Perhaps if you let the girl have a sip of this juice, she could gather her wits enough to answer both questions." Asamoah's voice had an exasperated edge to it, and a cool glass pressed against Punch's lips, despite Tobi's continued crabbing.

Punch sipped, and cool, sweet liquid burst over her tongue. Fruity sugar rush for the win.

"Here. Have a slice of apple." Asamoah's voice was back to brisk and Cory chirped out surprise, then fell silent. A moment later, Punch could hear the sound of tiny teeth chewing.

Punch smiled. "Sugar gliders can't resist a fresh apple."

"We will assume the sugar gliders are the tiny guardians," Bennett said, his tone dry. "You still haven't answered me about what you are."

Punch looked up at him through her lashes. The blood—her blood—drying on his face seemed surreal. It was also fading as she watched, absorbed into his skin. Vampire. He might be older than he looked. He might know more than normal humans would. He might have heard of her kind, when her own family couldn't tell her more than a folktale. "Have you ever heard of a kinnaree?"

FOUR

BENNETT

I have the means to find out." Bennett cleared his throat. He hadn't intended for the statement to come out as a growl. Fury sang in his heart as he glared at this woman. She had goaded him into doing a terrible thing.

"I'm sure you do." The woman in his arms smiled, her voice faint but steady, face still pale beneath the golden tan of her complexion. "Or you could ask nicely and I could tell you."

He waited.

She blinked rapidly. "As much as I know, in any case."

He bit back a snarl. She was fighting against disorientation. The rapid blinking was likely a futile attempt to clear her vision. All she had done was further incite the killing urge in him. He had struck prey in the past, drained them beyond their ability to recover enough to escape on their own, and watched them struggle in much the same way as they attempted to survive. She was in his arms and had no chance of evading him if he decided to drink from her again. The taste of her blood still lingered on his tongue, sweet and tart, with a bright quality to it he had never before encountered.

"You are not human." He'd tasted humans, many, over the long years he had lived. And yes, he experienced some remorse, but not as much as a few others of his kind might. He was not the sympathetic, tortured soul made popular in human books and movies. Predatory and powerful, he took pride in the simple fact that he was one of the most dangerous creatures in existence, even among his own kind.

And she was something new to him.

"Probably not completely human, no. I've never been absolutely sure, so your opinion sort of confirms it for me." She breathed deep. "It's hard to say, when generations of my family always thought they were human, seemed perfectly mundane, and poof, I turned out to be some sort of throwback. Depending on your resources, which I'm guessing are more extensive than mine, you may be able to learn more about kinnaree than I have to date."

Ah. "Is this where you offer to share what you know in exchange for whatever my research may reveal?" It would be a clumsy bargaining attempt at best. Vampires were not only predators in the most primal sense, they were also intellectual and emotional hunters. They relished political intrigue, enjoyed manipulating entire empires from behind the scenes. He had been introduced to such amusements when humans were still crossing continents on horseback.

He'd played every game through the course of centuries, and he'd lost interest in any of it anymore.

She huffed out a laugh. "Would love to. I don't think it's important enough for you to care, though. Look, the kinnaree I know come from the legend and folklore of Thailand. They're bird people, one of many magical creatures who are supposed to be from the Himmapan, deep forests at the foot of mystical mountains nobody can find anymore."

She took a deep breath and let it out slowly, then continued. "But I haven't met any kinnaree, much less any descendants like me. My parents haven't. My grandparents, who were born and lived all their lives in Thailand, hadn't. I don't know where my heritage came from or how I have some of the powers of one myself. I don't know if there are others like me. Honestly, today was the first time I met anyone as clearly supernatural as I am. And you seem to have an entire household. So that's all I've got."

She was regaining clarity of thought quite quickly, considering the blood loss she had experienced because of him. He was amused, and mildly ashamed for being so. He should still be horrified with the harm he had done her. But he watched her carefully, because from what he understood, such improvements could be brief. She would need real rest to truly recover.

He also doubted she had shared all she knew. "I am sure you have touched on the salient points, but there may be more detail to explore."

She opened her mouth to respond, but he gathered her more securely in his arms and stood. Whatever she had intended to say was lost on a surprised squeak and one of her tiny guardians dropped a piece of apple. It clutched her shirt and gave a short bark of surprise. The other rushed up her sleeve, taking shelter in the hair close to the nape of her neck and gave him a bark of its own. He quashed an unfamiliar urge to grin. All three of them had far more courage than was wise for their own survival in this world.

He turned to Duncan, drawing his brows together and reaching for an appropriately severe tone. "I am taking our *guest* upstairs. She requires rest."

Duncan nodded, composed as ever. "Will Lady Punch be with us for more than one night? I can look into acquiring some necessities."

"Just Punch, please. Adding 'Lady' to a tomboy's nickname sounds awkward, even to me." Her voice was warm and held a tinge of what might be embarrassment, but her words were starting to slow and run into each other. Fatigue was setting in.

Bennett had missed the exchange of names somewhere along the

way as well. Irritation scratched at him and he flicked the emotion
to the back of his mind. Of course Duncan would have determined
how to address her—he was both competent and thorough. It was
why Bennett retained Duncan's services. There was no reason to be
irritated with the sidhe for doing his job.

Asamoah, on the other hand, was observing them all with a slight
smile playing at the corner of his mouth. Considering Asamoah's
unique position as one of the only advisors Bennett paid any attention to, his silence was somewhat suspect. There was no telling what
Asamoah might be thinking and the man would only share in his
own good time, without regard for Bennett's temper.

The woman wriggled in Bennett's arms. "I can walk."

"If you tried, you would struggle on the stairs and we would
have to help you anyway." Even now, her feet were twitching ever
so slightly as they dangled. She might not realize it, but whatever
resistance she had was waning and the power of the red shoes was
taking hold. Whatever ability she had to deny them was finite. "I
would prefer you conserve what energy you have left."

He strode through the entryway and into the main hall. It was
shaped like an octagon with a series of doors or arches leading into
other rooms or hallways. He turned sharply and took one of the
stairways bracketing the archway of the entry, climbing up to the
second level.

"I didn't say I was staying." The woman struggled again, and this
time, she did it with enough strength to break a normal human's hold.

"You need to recover." He reached the top of the stairs and
proceeded around the balcony overlooking the main hall, bypassing
the two nearest guest rooms. He didn't want her to be so accessible
from the entrance of the manor. "After your...donation, I am not
sending you stumbling out into the night. Who knows what would
prey on you."

The thought of Francesco tasting her sparked a burning anger deep in his chest. Francesco was a merciless killer, known to play with his prey and even torture his victims before feeding. More than once, Francesco had deliberately slaughtered a human Bennett had allowed to live, even extended his protection to. If a victim survived Francesco, they often bore terrible scars, visible and otherwise. More often than not, Francesco enjoyed taking a human to spite Bennett or other vampires.

It had happened too many times for Bennett to not take it personally.

Bennett had an inkling of why Francesco had interest in acquiring the red shoes. The kind of shock, panic, and confusion the shoes could cause as they killed their victim was just the kind of chaotic disturbance Francesco loved to inflict on humankind. It wouldn't surprise Bennett if Francesco had acquired the red shoes simply to be able to put them out into the human world over and over again, then insert himself among the onlookers to enjoy the havoc before retrieving the cursed shoes in the uproar. Bennett was not inclined to allow Francesco to acquire either the shoes or their current wearer.

She glared at him. "I could have recovered on a bench downstairs. I even saw a dining room off the main room down there. I could've had a meal to replenish my energy and then left you to your evening. Or do you people not stock your pantry with solid food around here?"

Whether her bravado was out of a desire to hide the weakness she felt or outright brash foolishness, he wasn't sure yet, but she did have spunk. If she was truly panicked, though, he would smell more fear coming off her, and of that, there was very little. Surprise and unease, yes. But she was not afraid of him.

Her little sugar gliders perched on her shoulder, staring at him.

He glanced at them and decided they would be far more agitated if she had any residual fear.

"You will feel better after a hot shower and a true sleep." He carried her into the last room at the end of the hallway, where the least amount of noise from the hall would travel.

Setting her on her feet, he flicked a hand toward a door to the right. "This room has a private bath. Go ahead and clean up."

Her blood had clotted on her arm, a side benefit of his bite, but traces of it were smeared over her skin. A fresh pang of guilt stabbed at him. He had not been gentle.

She stood, looking around the room, scanning each door and window. She seemed steady for now.

"We are on the second floor, and while you could leave out a window, I wouldn't recommend it."

"Are you going to force me to stay here?" Her voice held a slight tremor. He wasn't certain if it was emotion or fatigue. She had ample reason for either.

He considered. The red shoes were his priority, and knowing Francesco had found them as well, Bennett was not inclined to let them out of his sight. Beyond that, he wanted to make her stay put, where he could watch over her and satisfy this growing need to understand what she was. But he didn't want her to hate him for it.

"I should." He decided to be frank with her, because she had responded well to the truth earlier. "Those shoes are still a problem. While you wear them, Francesco will hunt you, and it would not be safe to give any items of magic into his possession. If you can remove them, you can leave. I will not force you. But I cannot allow those shoes to fall into the wrong hands."

An odd look passed over her face, there for a brief second and gone. "I had questions for you."

Indeed. She had mentioned it and he was still considering how many he would be willing to entertain. "If you stay, I will listen to your questions."

Answers were a different story.

She sighed and bent to remove the shoes again. He reached out to steady her as she almost toppled over trying.

She cursed. "It's going to be interesting, trying to take a shower with shoes on."

He had to force himself to let her go so she could walk to the bathroom on her own. At the door, she turned and glared at him. "You can go now. I won't try to run away."

He decided to give her his best enigmatic smile. Too creepy? No. Not for this woman. She had a bit of steel to her. "I will be listening to make sure you do not collapse in the shower, for your safety."

She narrowed her eyes.

"You did just tip over trying to touch your toes."

Her cheeks flushed an attractive rose. He allowed his lips to curve in a hint of a smirk.

She firmly shut the bathroom door in his face.

He chuckled, wondering whether her supernatural senses included better hearing than humans. Yes, he wanted to know more about kinnaree, these bird people, and this woman specifically. He was bitterly amused with himself for it, too.

FIVE

PEERAPHAN

P unch pondered the doorknob. No lock. Well, considering what she'd seen this vampire do over the course of the last several hours, a locked door wouldn't have stopped him if he'd decided to walk in on her. But turning a lock and hearing it click into place would've made her feel better.

She sighed and studied the inside of her arm. It ached but didn't hurt nearly as much as it probably should.

A tremor ran through her. He had fed on her.

Yes, she was freaked out. But she had offered herself willingly and at no time had she really feared for her life. Worried, yes. But in no way did she believe he would have intended to kill her.

Which honestly did not reflect well on her survival skills. He had been on the brink of death and not in full control of his mental faculties. Killing her, however unintentionally or accidentally, would still leave her permanently dead.

She swallowed hard against the sudden dryness in her mouth. She didn't want to die.

Shaking her head, she stared at her reflection in the mirror. She was way out of her depth in this situation. No matter how she tried to clamp down on the trembling fear rising up from the pit of her stomach, she couldn't completely dismiss it to some back corner of her mind. Every logical thought and rational argument she used to try to seal it all away helped, but no amount of reasoning could counter the fact that she had about as much chance of surviving beings like Bennett and Francesco as a baby bird fallen out of its nest.

She'd spent years looking for others like her. Intellectually, she'd understood being different meant evolved abilities setting them apart from humans. Like her. She'd convinced herself that other species had claws and fangs and other evolutionary traits for defense and survival. She thought she'd been prepared to face the fact that humans weren't the apex predators of the world. She hadn't expected that the first she'd meet would be so incredibly attractive.

The ridiculousness of that thought stopped her spiral before she tipped fully over the precipice of her fear.

"Ha." She breathed out the laugh.

Her taste in men was bad, too, if her dating history was anything to go by. Great. No chance of blaming it on the legendary charisma of vampires, either, because the other vampire they'd encountered tonight had been repulsive to her, despite the polished glory of the man's handsome face.

She glanced down as Tobi scampered across the front of her shirt, checking out their surroundings. Automatically, Punch looked for the toilet. Finding it tucked behind a discreet room divider, she put the lid down over the seat. Sugar gliders were incredibly curious and sometimes fell into places they couldn't get back out of. Drowning in fish tanks, ponds, pools, and bathrooms happened if an owner wasn't careful.

Taking precautions to ensure the safety of those in her care helped her feel a little bit less vulnerable herself.

Just a little.

That precaution taken, she studied the private bath. It was beautiful. Actually, everything she'd seen about this place was lovely, so far. The building had an old European feel to it, with pale creams and warm wood accented by deep, rich colors. This bathroom had ivory tiles and sage fabrics. There was a teak bench with a small basket of washcloths. Thick towels hung from the rack and there was a very modern showerhead installed in the clawfoot tub. Hope sparked in her chest as she turned the taps.

Steaming hot water instantly erupted from the showerhead, with more water pressure than she'd enjoyed since she'd left the college dorms years and years ago. Hurriedly, she placed Tobi and Cory on the counter and pulled off her shirt, arranging it in a nest for them to curl up in, then stripped the rest of her clothing off. Luckily, the pants she'd been wearing to rehearsal were designed for dance and yoga—very stretchy—so she was able to get them over the damned shoes without too much problem. Stepping into a bathtub wearing high heels was begging to break her neck or leg, however. She glanced at the washcloths and figured it would be safer to wipe down than risk a fall. All that wonderful water pressure, though. Her apartment just outside of downtown Seattle was older and the water pressure was less than half this. She wanted to cry at the thought of missing out.

Then she took another look at the teak stool the washcloth basket was sitting on. It had slip-resistant rubber caps over the end of each leg. Aha! She moved the basket onto the counter and placed the teak stool in the tub, then very carefully got in and sat down on it. Hot water immediately soaked her in the best way.

Tobi chirped at her, but otherwise, the sugar gliders tucked themselves into the shirt she'd left on the counter to wait.

Punch studied the red shoes. The water from either the shower spray or splashing in the tub did nothing to diminish the glorious red of the satin. Wetting her skin around the edges of the shoes did nothing to loosen them, either. She still couldn't get them off.

And she felt the impulse to keep wiggling her feet, maybe get up and do a little dance under the fall of the water.

Oh no. Nope. She wasn't going to entertain those thoughts. It seemed they popped up more frequently when she admired the shoes. Very deliberately, she looked away.

There was a lovely shower curtain of fabric with a waterproof liner to pull all the way around the tub. Once Punch pulled it from both sides to meet at the other end of the tub, she was enveloped in wonderful steam and delighted to note that the drain was keeping up with the volume of the water.

Someone had thought out this bathroom with an excellent balance of style and practicality. There'd been a small shelf on the wall behind the curtain with a selection of shampoo, conditioner, and bath gel. She tried each of them in succession, spreading some along the edge of the shoe, trying to work each substance in against her skin. None of them helped her remove the shoes.

They would have been fantastic onstage. No chance of one slipping off at the wrong moment. She could have danced with confidence in them, a whole show and more.

She bit her lip in frustration and decided to use the toiletries as they were meant while she was in there anyway. Better to think about taking care of herself. After she got clean, she turned her back to the showerhead to let the water pound some of the tension out of her shoulders as she studied the inside of her arm again.

The cut Duncan had made was clean but not terribly deep, and there was a ragged edge where Bennett had bitten into the flesh of her arm. She had gotten her share of cuts and bruises as a kid and she didn't think she'd need stitches, but blood was starting to well up again now that she'd washed herself clean and the scabs had loosened. She should probably see if they had a first aid kit, maybe some butterfly bandages to help hold her skin together for a better line. This was probably going to scar.

Shutting off the water, she pulled the curtain aside and reached for towels. She tossed the first one on the floor, spreading it as best she could from her seat, then lifted her leg over the edge of the tub and stepped down on the towel as carefully as possible. Once she was safely standing, she wrapped the towel around her body and considered the lotion and body oil on the counter. Might as well try each of them.

It took less than a minute. Neither had made any difference. The red shoes were stuck to her feet. Frustrated and worried and exhausted, she looked at Tobi and Cory curled up and asleep in her shirt. Getting back into her clothing was not appealing, either. She'd been rehearsing for hours before she'd put the red shoes on and she'd sweated in those clothes. There'd been a lot of fear and distress going on shortly after, plus some of Bennett's blood—was any of the blood coming out of him actually *his* if he took it from others? She wasn't sure how it worked—and at least a bit of hers on her clothes, too.

A light knock on the bathroom door made her jump.

"I have fresh clothes for you, if you are willing to come out." Bennett's voice had a resonant quality to it, allowing it to carry without him having to make any effort at volume.

Punch tugged the towel tighter around herself, ignoring the way her nipples were tightening. Briefly, she imagined what his expression might be if she stepped out and dropped her towel. A naked woman in striking red heels had to be a temptation, right?

The impulse to dance for him slid through her thoughts. That seemed uncharacteristically daring, but she wasn't absolutely sure she wouldn't have thought of it herself. She wasn't sure she could blame this idea on the red shoes.

She took the impulse and stuffed it way, way to the back of her mind and told her imagination to focus on creative ways to solve the problem of getting the heels off. She should be more concerned about what these shoes were doing to her and trying harder to get away from them.

Damn it. And damn the shoes, too.

Before her libido could argue on her imagination's behalf, she cracked open the bathroom door and peeked out.

"Any chance you'll hand over the clothes so I can dress in here?"

Folded cloth appeared in front of her and Bennett harrumphed. "Put this on for now and we'll get you settled in for the night. Perhaps once you've rested, we will have a better chance of getting the shoes off. Duncan is working on getting you clothes more suitable for going out in the morning."

She took the cloth from him and shut the door. It turned out to be a nightgown, the fabric a soft, opaque weave unlike anything she'd encountered. It wasn't silk or cotton or any synthetic she knew of, just a wonderful combination of comfortable and luxurious. It slid over her skin and settled into place, a simple sleeveless sheath covering her to her knees and flowing over her form like water.

"Come on, Tobi, Cory, we'll need your carry pouch." She reached out and gathered them into her palm. Their little claws would go right through this fabric and she'd end up scratched all over if she let them run loose over her clothing at the moment. Tobi and Cory only chirped at her and held on to her thumb like a guardrail.

Punch took a deep breath, squared her shoulders, and opened the door to face the vampire waiting in the bedroom.

Other room.

Best not to think about Bennett and a bedroom in the same context.

Too late.

Said vampire was standing there, holding out a robe at arm's length. She flushed, happy to have the added layer of coverage. "You couldn't hand that to me in the first place?"

"You are unsteady from blood loss and also attempting to navigate a bathroom in footwear that is untrustworthy in the best of circumstances." His tone could be patronizing if she thought he'd care enough to patronize her in the first place. His expression gave the impression of clinical detachment. "Add the magical nature of said footwear and it seemed best to encourage you to focus on one task at a time."

He wasn't wrong, just infuriating. She wasn't going to give him any kind of gratification by letting him know he was pushing her buttons. Any of her buttons.

She started to reach for the robe, but his eyes lowered a fraction and he shifted his stance, taking the robe in both hands and holding it open for her.

"Thank you." It was easier to slide her arms into the robe while he was holding it for her, and juggling Tobi and Cory would have made it harder. Tobi barked and ran up her sleeve once she had the robe on.

"I heard you mention a carry pouch. If you prepare to rest now, I will retrieve it for you." Bennett gestured toward the huge bed set against the wall between two windows. There was a low bench at the foot of the bed, her duffel already on it.

She headed for her duffel. "I can get it myself, it's just in h—"

"Please." There was a punch to the word. "I am already uncomfortable allowing you to walk to the bed on your own power. Please settle yourself before I attempt to…tuck you in myself."

Uncomfortable? How? She paused and looked at him, really saw him. He was tense and could've passed for a statue, he was holding himself so rigid. There was a whole lot of self-control being exerted.

A small part of her wanted to remain right where she was, frozen in place until the dangerous thing went away. Another part of her wanted to run. And then there was the really unwise part of her that wanted to go to him and run her fingertips over his collarbone and down his chest.

She stepped sideways and climbed onto the bed. "Their carry pouch should be right on top, if you look inside the duffel."

He retrieved the sugar gliders' carry pouch with concise, efficient movements and practically threw it at her. Well, if he was going to make so much effort to stay at a distance now, there might be a good reason for it. "Thank you."

He nodded. "Do you need anything else?"

She considered. "I'm not going to turn into a vampire later, am I?"

"No. Not from just a bite." His answer was clipped.

Best to back away with just that much reassurance for the moment. Food might be good, but the thought of trying to eat anything substantial made her stomach twist. Maybe not now. Exhaustion was starting to set in, and the heat of the shower had sapped any remaining energy she'd had. If anything, she was starting to feel shaky. "No. I appreciate the chance to rest."

He nodded again and turned, striding toward the door to the hallway. At the last moment, he stopped short. "You may know this already, but just in case, it is unwise to thank any fae. It will imply a debt owed and the fae have a different set of values than others as to what appropriate repayment would be. There are many supernaturals who either live in or visit this house. Some are fae and some are not. It's not always obvious what any of us are. If it is easier, don't thank any being on this island. I will not take offense, nor will others who are not fae. Your unspoken appreciation is sufficient."

Which of the people downstairs had been fae? What kind?

She pressed her lips closed on those questions and on the thanks she wanted to give him. She hadn't avoided thanking the others on purpose. Maybe it had been instinct or just pure luck. But now that she was thinking about it, she was sure to mess up if she let herself respond automatically. It'd be better not to say anything without thinking.

Not her forte.

Instead, she held open the carry pouch and coaxed Tobi and Cory inside, then placed it on the nightstand. Tugging at the comforter, she slid beneath it, then met his gaze again. "All tucked in. We're good here."

His expression didn't change, but she still got the impression of a hint of a smile. "Good night. You can turn off the lamp at your bedside if you wish for darkness."

Because she might sleep better with the light on, having realized she was in a house with a vampire. She stared at him for a minute and decided he'd left a dare hanging in the air, unspoken.

She turned off the light.

He stood there silhouetted by the light from the hallway. "If you don't need anything else, I'll let you get some slee—"

"Half a glass of fruit juice isn't enough for humans who voluntarily donate a pint of blood, vampire, much less however much you drained from her," a new voice shouted down the hallway. "Don't you close that door."

Six

Bennett

Bennett allowed his lips to curl in a silent snarl as he turned to face Thomas. The werewolf came down the hallway, his long legs closing the distance in a ground-eating stride. Thomas was long-limbed and lean, rangy in build rather than slight. He was of Asian descent, with the same golden tan skin as their guest and thick black hair. Perhaps they were from the same region, Southeast Asia, if Bennett was going to continue guessing.

His and Thomas's working relationship included a mutual respect for the other's privacy. They only shared history when it was pertinent to the work ahead of them. Such instances were rare.

Just behind Thomas, Duncan carried a tray loaded with covered dishes. Someone must have pulled something together in a hurry.

Bennett had wanted to leave the woman alone before his control fractured, but he would be beyond damned if he was going to leave her with the werewolf.

"She declined any other aid." Bennett reached for calm. He could be reasonable. Rational, even.

Thomas halted just outside of arm's reach—not that either of them couldn't reach the other in an instant—and glared at Bennett. "I get that you bloodsuckers are loners more often than my kind, and you chose to be a solitary soldier, but even you must have been taught somewhere in your centuries of sad existence to properly take care of those under your protection."

There was real anger in the other man's posture and a flash of moon-driven madness in his eyes. The moon was waxing, not far from full, and the werewolf's instincts were riding him hard.

Bennett pressed his lips together, rather than continue to bare his fangs at the werewolf. "Are you canine or avian? You haven't even met the woman yet and you are already set to sit on her and brood like a hen."

Thomas bared his own teeth and growled. Bennett waited. As tempting as it was to taunt the other man further, theirs was a delicate balance. It would be ill-advised to push Thomas over the edge into real rage. Perhaps someday, they'd find out which of them would survive a true fight to the finish, but it would have to be over a better reason than Bennett's transgression this evening. He wasn't going to admit it to the wolf, though.

The lamp flicked back on behind him. Duncan skirted around both of them, slipping into the guest room without even a nod to Bennett.

Fine. He should have insisted on feeding their visitor. He had asked and she had assured him she needed nothing else, but he should have known she required additional sustenance to recover from the blood loss.

He had been angry, seeing the ragged incision on her arm. Blood had still trickled over her skin, and he'd intended to ask Duncan to come in while she was sleeping and properly bandage the wound. He had intended to see to it that she would be cared for, just not by him.

He couldn't. He'd done her harm and he couldn't undo what he had done. In retrospect, any of them tending to her while she was sleeping was not a good idea if they wanted her to feel any amount of security. He was not thinking things through enough and it only served to prove he should not be the one to tend to her at this moment. Perhaps later, he would ask himself why he cared. But for now he set the question aside.

Instead, maintaining eye contact with Thomas, he stepped back and tipped his head to indicate the werewolf should proceed into the room.

Thomas stopped growling and studied him for a long moment, then went into the room without another word. Whatever the werewolf had seen, Bennett would have to wait to find out later. If the werewolf decided to share at all. In his own way, Thomas was as annoying as any vampire.

"Oh, I'm not hungry." The woman's voice did sound tired and Bennett closed his hands into fists.

"Couldn't we tempt you with just a few bites, Punch?" Duncan was very good at coaxing. Bennett gritted his teeth. "Asamoah is a talented chef in addition to his official capacity as an advisor to our organization, and he put together a light repast designed to aid you in a speedy recovery. There's a dish for your small companions as well."

Bennett knew the name she'd given to Duncan, but he hadn't been invited to call her by it and he would wait until she did, even inside his own head. It mattered to him and again, he did not want to think about why immediately.

"It does smell good." A pause. "Thomas?"

Everyone froze.

"I'm sorry," she whispered, staring at Thomas. "You remind me of someone I knew as a kid. I don't think we've met yet."

The change in her tone from warmth to absolute neutral brought a smile to Bennett's lips. He took a moment to get his expression back under control, then stepped inside the room to see how Thomas handled someone who apparently knew him.

Certainly, Thomas had not been present when Bennett and

Duncan had arrived. Thomas had probably run up, literally, from his cabin near the manor.

Bennett took up a position to be closer to her than Thomas. However they had known each other in the past, she was Bennett's guest and responsibility now.

"Since you aren't going to get any rest until my colleagues satisfy their curiosity," he said, noting that Duncan had placed a tray with legs extended to position it over her lap, "may I introduce Thomas? He and I, and everyone you've met tonight, are part of an organization called the Darke Consortium."

She stared at Thomas.

After a long moment, Thomas spoke almost reluctantly. "Phee eng ja."

Bennett wasn't familiar with the language.

"Khidtheung jahng ley ka." She shook herself and smiled, wide and bright. "Well, this might answer a few questions I've had for the longest time."

"You never run out of questions." Thomas gave her a grin and started to sit on the edge of the bed.

Bennett narrowed his eyes. Thomas was a flirt and convinced his charm was irresistible. However, this interaction was both more familiar and had absolutely no seduction in it. This was a side of Thomas he had never encountered to date. Bennett did not like the instant familiarity between the two of them.

The moment Thomas's rear end touched the comforter, dual sharp grinding sounds rose up from the nightstand.

Thomas shot back to his feet, and she laughed. "Tobi and Cory would prefer you kept your distance."

Good.

"Who—"

Even as Thomas asked, she reached over and unzipped the small

WINGS ONCE CURSED & BOUND   57

carry pouch on the nightstand. "Tobi and Cory are nocturnal anyway, so they probably wouldn't have wanted to go to sleep so early."

The woman tipped her head to one side, focusing on the tray in front of her with a curiosity matching her little friends' as the sugar gliders first leaped from the nightstand to the bedcovers, then ran up her sleeve to perch on her shoulder.

"As an FYI, I grew up knowing Thomas as my older cousin. He went away on deployment with the military before I graduated from high school." As she explained, she lifted the cover off the smaller plate first, revealing a dish of cold poached chicken breast sliced thin and fanned out in a tempting arrangement. The sugar gliders both chirped and literally pounced, landing with separate thumps on the covers before stalking the dish and snagging a slice of chicken each.

Tiny they might be, but those two were not simple rodents. They were predators in their own right.

"It's been about two decades, give or take a year, and here he is looking exactly the same. Maybe grumpier. Obviously, I have a lot of questions." Apparently not urgent ones, because she continued to investigate the food on her tray, setting the cover to the side and lifting the larger one to reveal a clear teacup filled with light broth. Tiny slices of carrots carved into flowers had settled at the bottom alongside half-moon slivers of celery and onion. Crisp, thin crackers were stacked like a deck of playing cards next to the teacup.

"This is lovely!" She lifted a cracker, nibbled at the edge first, then picked up the teacup and took a sip. Her eyes closed, face full of blissful joy.

Bennett had seen many creatures in this world enjoy both the hunt and the consumption of their prey, but this—this was joy on a level that was almost blinding. All for a sip of soup.

Duncan cleared his throat. "Asamoah thought a restorative soup would be helpful without being too heavy."

"This is perfect." She gifted Duncan with a bright smile. "I love chicken soup and I've never had it served to me this way. It's as fun to look at as it is to eat."

While she focused on food, Bennett considered her interaction with Thomas. Bennett spoke quite a few languages, but the words she and Thomas had shared between them weren't ones he knew. A fair guess would be Thai, considering her earlier discussion of Thai mythology and kinnaree.

Thomas shifted his weight from foot to foot, and if Bennett could have guessed, he'd say the werewolf was feeling very awkward right now. Good.

"So you are all a part of the Darke Consortium." She set down the teacup and lifted a cracker to nibble. "Is that a private club of some kind or a job?"

"Neither..."

"Both..."

Bennett glared at Thomas as the werewolf turned and curled his lip to show his teeth. Punch looked from one to the other and lifted her teacup of soup again.

"This broth is clearer than your answers," she said, and sipped.

Duncan coughed, obviously covering a chuckle.

"To clarify," Bennett started quickly to preempt Thomas, "the members of the Darke Consortium have a common goal to locate and retrieve objects of myth, imbued with magic. We place them in sanctuaries around the world for safekeeping. Joining our organization is currently by invitation only."

Thomas groaned. "Don't make it all out to be completely altruistic. You might not need the salary, but some of us do. The Darke Consortium provides a yearly salary and covers expenses related to each mission."

Bennett glowered. "You are relatively young. Those of us who've learned to survive over the centuries have amassed a certain amount of wealth."

"Survive comfortably," Thomas shot back. "I do just fine. Money is about math, and for someone making my way through my second lifetime, so to speak, I'm just getting started. But you can't make the Consortium out to be this higher purpose without full disclosure that there are incentives for what we do."

"Do they do this a lot?" Their guest looked askance at Duncan.

Duncan's expression was markedly bland, but he lifted a shoulder in a slight shrug.

"Got it. You two have a sort of bromance thing going on."

Duncan made a choking noise.

Bennett closed his eyes, reaching for patience.

Thomas growled. "Look, we work together. We don't even like each other."

"Thus the common goal," she said, nodding wisely. "I can think of several Asian dramas where lead characters share a similar friendship dynamic. It's very entertaining. I'm here for it."

"This is not a drama," Thomas growled.

She sipped soup from her teacup again.

"Our priorities, currently, are for you to rest and recover from the trauma of our arrival." Bennett was experiencing a certain amount of desperation to get them all focused on the real issue at hand. He was also uncharacteristically concerned about her well-being. She had perked up considerably, which was all well and good, but her shoulders were slumping, and she was undoubtedly tired. He continued, "While we look for a way to remove the red shoes before your resistance to them fades."

"I think I remember a ballet about the red shoes." Her voice was somber as she set down the teacup finally. "It didn't have a happy ending."

"No," Bennett confirmed.

"I'm assuming everyone's tried the obvious to get those off so far." Thomas tapped the bedcovers near her feet.

Both sugar gliders reared up and lifted itty bitty clawed paws as they issued their tiny grinder growls.

"Tried force, tried everything slippery you can find in that bathroom over there, from soap to lotion to oil," she said. Her frustration was clear in every statement.

"What did they try in the original fairy tale?" Thomas asked.

Duncan shook his head as he took the now finished tray and stepped back from the bed. "These specific shoes are not of fae making."

Bennett gave Thomas a sharp look. "A woodcutter or blacksmith, depending on the version of the folk tale, cut off the wearer's feet above the ankle."

Thomas grunted in surprise.

"Pass." She was still markedly calm, her sugar gliders playing with each other in her lap now that Thomas had backed off again.

"It didn't work anyway," Bennett conceded. "The shoes continued to make the feet dance, blocking the victim's way."

Any color she had regained leached away and she seemed to shrink back into the pillows supporting her.

"There's an image." Thomas crossed his arms over his chest.

The werewolf's few centuries were relatively short in comparison to Bennett's. But Thomas had seen many things in those years, of that Bennett was certain. Thomas had been a soldier for the U.S. military and had deployed several times. Add those experiences to life as a werewolf and a few detached limbs should not be a surprise. It did not mean the image was pleasant.

"In at least one version of the ballet, she dances to her death, I think." She bit her lip.

Thomas stilled, bracing for something. It didn't matter who one was, impending death wasn't an easy thing to face.

But it was Bennett she looked to and held his gaze. "I don't want to die."

This was why he had not wanted to know anything about her once she put on the red shoes. He should not give her any kind of reassurance. He could not. "We do not know how to save you."

"Yet." Thomas's voice was almost completely obscured by his growl at this point.

She only nodded. Her eyes held sadness, a touch of fear, a spark of courage, and a resolution to try. Try to survive to the very last moment.

He gave her the only promise he could. "I will search for a solution."

SEVEN

BENNETT

S o you're not explaining. No. There's too much." Thomas was
actively searching the index of a large volume on Thai folktales on the library's second floor. "You won't even sum up."

Bennett sat in a comfortable armchair on the first floor, scanning
through one of the only other books they had on the topic. "No."

He refused to give Thomas any ammunition with which to poke
at him. Besides, Thomas seemed to be curious about their new guest,
and Bennett was not inclined to give the werewolf any more information than what could be gleaned from the general household. After
all, Thomas had knowledge of her from being a childhood relation.

A fact that did not bother Bennett in the slightest.

She did have a rather memorable skeptical expression, though.
The image came to him of her face with a single eyebrow lifted, lips
pressed together. He fought to keep the corners of his mouth from
twitching upward.

"Seems to me a lot happened today." Thomas sounded more
amused than angry.

"And it is apparent to me that you already have a grasp of
the pertinent details." Bennett checked the bibliography at the back
of the book, then leaned forward to glower at the general search

results on the wafer-thin digital tablet resting on an end table next to his chair.

There were actually a handful of computer tablets in the library. It prevented either of them wasting time fighting over possession of a particular item. Asamoah had suggested the idea not long after Thomas had joined the Consortium, having pointed out that Bennett and Thomas would never actually work together if they did not make certain accommodations for their respective predatory natures.

Asamoah was an old, old being. Over the rise and fall of civilizations, Asamoah had been there. He was a being who not only offered ideas, but inspired innovation and creativity. It was foolish to dismiss an inspiration offered by Asamoah, and Bennett was not a fool. "Duncan is discreet and gives facts, not juicy context." Thomas ignored the spiral stairs leading from the second floor down to the first and simply vaulted the railing to land neatly next to Bennett's chair. "Asamoah had the more fun rendition, but could only tell me what happened once you got here to the manor. I want to know how you went out for an easy win, a fairly low-risk retrieval, and managed to come back from the brink of true death in the space of one evening."

Bennett looked up at Thomas over the wire rims of his glasses. Bennett didn't need the glasses, being a vampire with supernaturally acute senses including sight, but he found the effect satisfying. Besides, it deepened the contrast between him and the werewolf. Thomas became a werewolf at the beginning of the prime age for humans, early thirties, and he wasn't very old as werewolves go, with only two centuries to his actual age. Bennett was well past his third century.

There were vampires and werewolves far older than either he or Thomas, but not many. Being of a supernatural species with the potential for long life was no guarantee of survival, which still required certain amounts of skill and intelligence, neither of which were particularly common. If they were, the world would have been overrun and humans, however quickly they reproduced or tenacious they were as a species, would have been hunted to extinction.

"What matters is how to address the situation as it stands now." Bennett lifted his tablet and waved it under Thomas's nose.

Thomas barked out a short laugh. "The situation is currently lying down upstairs, asleep in one of the guest rooms. She grew up quick-thinking, and pretty."

That last observation ended on a growl, and if Bennett had had any previous doubts regarding Thomas's attitude toward his "cousin," it was clear now that Thomas was not pleased at the thought of how others might be attracted to her.

Insufficient to call her simply pretty, in any case. But then, Thomas might be picturing a child or awkward youth from his memory and hadn't seen the adult, current version of her moving. Dancing.

She had powerful leaps and that extra snap to her spins that took her from good to excellent, yet she had a grace that lent elegance to her movements. No matter how many times she rose up to balance or left the stage completely in her jumps, she connected back to earth with a surety of someone who always knew where she would land.

She was like a bird, lovely when perched. But the truth of her beauty came out when she was in motion, and it stole one's breath away.

If one had any need to breathe, which he did not.

"Her appearance isn't pertinent."

As if his heart wasn't trying to beat inside his cold chest at the memory of her dancing.

Thomas grinned. "Are you sure? I saw the way that look she

gave you melted even your frigid vampiric heart. As an older cousin, I ought to express a sort of familial concern regarding your intentions. That's why we're here digging through the library, isn't it?"

Bennett wouldn't bother to deny that particular point, but he could add to it. "Her resistance to the compulsion of the red shoes is unprecedented, and the answer could lie in her nature. If she can resist, perhaps she can escape intact. It's worth the effort to research what we can about kinnaree to find a solution."

"True." Thomas rubbed his jaw. "I'm Thai, too, and I know close to nothing about Thai folklore and mythology. I would never have disappeared on her family if I'd known she would need a guardian." He scowled and lifted the book. "There's not a lot written about it and what there is is generally written by someone who isn't Thai. There's still a lot of cultures in this world who have traditionally relied on oral history to pass folktales and mythology from person to person and haven't gathered those into print. Any compilations done by some scholarly type from a Western university tend to be presented through the lens of a first world context. I remember a few random comments from my grandmother, but never heard the full stories from any of my grandparents or my parents."

Bennett grunted, distracted. He was accumulating a list of things he was not ready to think about regarding her, especially when he wasn't certain he could save her. The red shoes had to take priority. And he was not ready to dig up old feelings he had long since buried with the memory of someone else.

"There's statues of kinnaree guarding ancient palaces and temples." Thomas took the tablet from Bennett and enlarged a few images from the search results. "They're featured in artwork, too. I've even seen the murals at Wat Phra Kao, the ancient royal palace in Bangkok. They're not major players in the epic those murals depict, but the kinnaree are there along with giants and mermaids and other legends. There's one epic tale about a kinnaree that's performed as a series of dances set to music. I saw one portion during one of those touristy dinner dance shows a few years ago when I was on leave in Bangkok. They didn't explain much about it and that sort of thing hasn't ever been something in which I had any real interest."

Well, that left them with English translations of foreign interpretations of a Thai folktale. It was like the scholar's version of the telephone game. It would be funny, if a life wasn't threatened. Bennett wasn't fooled by the werewolf's calm discourse. The room was charged with tension and frustration.

"Well, we can gather that kinnaree have a certain amount of magic, or she wouldn't be resisting the compulsion of the red shoes. This gives us time, but we don't know how much. We can also assume she had the ability to recognize me as not-human." Bennett remembered her expression as she met him. The lack of surprise.

"Not-human?" Thomas chuckled. "That's one of the politest ways I've heard it put. You mean she didn't just call you a monster outright?"

The last question had a bitter note to it that Bennett was certain Thomas didn't ever bother to hide.

Bennett snarled quietly. "Wouldn't that mean she was a monster, too? No. She didn't even know precisely what I was when she met me. She was only certain of what I was not."

She'd been excited to meet him. Hopeful.

And he'd been moved to reach out, steal her from impending death. Because he didn't want her light extinguished. Whatever else that meant to him could wait until he figured out how.

"And you fed on her." Thomas made the statement quietly. There was more than anger there: real rage held chained.

"With her consent." Bennett did not attempt to defend himself further.

Asamoah and Duncan would have made an effort to provide such detail to Thomas. He was a vampire, Born, not Made. He required blood. He could feed on animals to survive, but human blood enabled him to thrive. Feeding on a very specific type of human enhanced his power, and his oath prevented him from taking from those innocent of such evils. That she had found a loophole to get around the binding of his own oath in order to save him was astonishing. He had done her harm and he was determined to invest whatever time and effort it took to repay her. He owed Thomas no similar debt.

After a long moment, Thomas turned away. The tension in the space eased back to what passed for normal between them.

"She did not taste human." It might antagonize Thomas more to pursue this line of thought, but Bennett felt it necessary to analyze all the information he had. "Her blood gave me a boost in energy I've never experienced before."

The closest experience he could describe was the rush of power from feeding off a fae or another vampire. An immortal.

"What? Like drinking a sports drink? Or like having a quadruple-shot iced latte?" Thomas looked up from the tablet and the searches he was actively running.

The werewolf was quick to anger, but once he chose to let something go, it really was done. Usually. Apparently, this was one of those times when he was ready to analyze the situation without the heat of his temper putting an edge on everything.

"Neither has an effect on either vampires or werewolves, so I don't know why you enjoy them, but I got an overall sense of rejuvenation that is only just beginning to taper down to my more usual sense of normalcy." Hardly a sufficient description for the surge he'd felt as her blood had trickled over his lips. Energy had spread through him, kicked his brain into high gear, and he'd not only managed to heal himself but had felt warmth rush through his veins. It had been beyond the warmth of fresh feeding, a tingling effervescence of liquid joie de vivre.

Thomas stilled, then asked, "You're not thinking of feeding from her again, are you?"

Despite the light tone of the question, an edge had returned to Thomas's words. Bennett waved his hand. "Hunger for power is not one of my afflictions."

Not quite a lie. He could control his thirst for her because he did not desire power from her.

He removed his glasses for a moment and pinched the bridge of his nose. "But we should know it's the case, because if she survives and is the only one of her kind, she has no seethe or pack or coven to protect her. She will be in more danger than she ever was as an anonymous human living out her life in the oblivious world. Energy drinks are popular for a reason."

Thomas raised an eyebrow. "Look at you caring for a person other than yourself."

Bennett curled his lip. He might be able to say the same in regard to the werewolf, but then he would be forced to acknowledge how his reactions to her were different from Thomas's.

"Ridiculous," he scoffed instead. "My consideration for what becomes of her is the same as any athlete considering what edge a rival might achieve if they are making use of a nutritional supplement I am not. The supply is limited. Best if she is not used by anyone."

Her life would last only as long as the self-control of the vampire who managed to capture her, and few vampires were moved to exercise even a modicum of self-control. That's why few managed to live beyond a century or two. They eventually killed and killed until they had to be eliminated by their brethren to avoid exposure.

"Noted. Also, you know you're an elitist, self-centered asshole, right? Humans shouldn't be considered walking blood supplies. And Punch is—" Thomas seemed as if he was going to say more, but apparently changed his mind and with a disgusted grunt, he settled for leaning back on a table, glancing down at the large volume he'd retrieved from the second floor. "Well, not a lot going with the internet searching. I might as well read this version of a folktale about Manora, the bird princess, and figure out what we can get from it."

A window burst open and a small light zipped into the room. "Bennett! Thomas! Hey! Listen!"

The brightly glowing ball of light resolved into a winged man, lean and dressed sparingly in armor that seemed fashioned of pine cone seeds and birchbark. His skin had tints of the greens and yellows of spring growth. His eyes sparked with the iridescent, deeper green of gemstones, and his hair was a shock of unruly white fluff.

"Ashke." Bennett put down the tablet he had been using.

"She arrived with you and Duncan, so I told my teams not to shoot her down." Ashke zipped in the air, his flight pattern erratic in his excitement. "I thought she was human, but this is the first time we've had a guest with wings. What is she? Not an angel, their wings are different."

Bennett surged to his feet and was at the window in an instant. Thomas threw open the next window over. There, above the back garden, was their guest, floating just above the tree line closest to the manor and glowing with a soft golden light of her own. Her dark hair was flowing around her shoulders in loose waves stirred by the night breeze. The robe he had given her was gone and the simple nightgown was gathered high up to accommodate snowy white wings extending from her hips. The wings were massive, shaped much like a swan's, and partially spread at the moment. Her legs were bare except for the red shoes and she was literally dancing on air, eyes open but not focused on anything.

Her movements were slow and spoke of a gentle spirit, not weak, but like a candle flame in the midst of a storm, a soft light in the dark. Her arms were gracefully bent as she lifted first one hand, then the other, in accentuated hand gestures. She angled the upper part of her body to complement the movement of each hand gesture, even tipping her head just so. It was as if she was telling herself a story through dance, ready to step lightly through the clouds as she did.

She was so beautiful she would have stolen his breath away if he had been breathing at all.

"I flew around her twice," Ashke was saying. "Didn't touch and didn't speak to her, but she didn't react to me. I don't think she's aware. Sleepwalking, maybe, or bespelled."

"A little of both, perhaps," Bennett murmured as he watched her. "She was tired and we left her to sleep. Perhaps in her sleep, she was not able to resist the red shoes."

"Sleepwalking is a human thing," Thomas commented. "Generally, you don't want to startle them awake. Best not to shout or bring her down by force."

Thomas paused, then added, "She's high enough now that I'd need to wait for her to pass near the roof and jump for her, if I was the one to bring her down."

"I won't risk touching her. I'll have to shoot her to wake her." Ashke readied a bow and drew an arrow from a quiver at his back. "It's a bad idea to have her up there. The glamour protecting the manor isn't going to hide her the way it does the buildings and the grounds. She'll draw attention from anyone keeping surveillance on the island for unusual activity."

Bennett snarled. "No shooting her down. I'll get her."

He planted one foot on the windowsill and launched himself upward out the window, letting his vampiric power rise as he did.

Above and ahead of him, the woman was slowly gaining altitude as she continued her elegant dance. Each gesture was detailed and graceful, where every movement of every finger mattered and even the tilt of her head was just so. This wasn't Western ballet or modern or lyrical, not any of the styles he had seen on theater stages in the United States. Even the sample of Chinese or Polynesian dances that occasionally came through the theaters in the Seattle area were nothing like this.

He slowed his flight as he approached her while she extended her right palm outward until her arm was straight, fingertips together and pointed up. Her nails had extended significantly, into talons of a sort, and if she'd wanted to, she could have defended herself with them. Her left arm was bent and flexed inward at the wrist, her index finger and thumb touching as the rest of the fingers on her left hand splayed out in a fan shape. Her wings swept back. Taking advantage of the opening, he gently took hold of her right hand in his left and slipped his other arm around her waist above where her wings met her hips.

Air whispered over his skin, different from the ocean winds. It smelled of jasmine and mango trees, of sweet-scented flowers he did not know the name of and luscious fruits he might have tasted in his travels through the centuries. But her skin smelled of morning dew, clean and simple. Her magic didn't disperse at his touch or hide beneath her skin—it surrounded him and enveloped him the way mist took him in when he walked the night after a hot day and the microscopic droplets hung heavy in the air.

Her face had been tilted up toward the moon, her eyes looking out at something far away. He took hold of her, pulling her to him. Those brown eyes full of silver moonlight focused and her gaze found his as he took her into a dance for two instead of one. Her left hand fell to his shoulder and the fingers of her right curled around his. She was a good follow, actually, her body instinctively bending in response to his lead. Her heart beat strong and steady, slower than any human's. And she was warm, vibrant, so alive and vital in an unhurried way that made human lives pale in comparison. She was a swan, gliding through the sky among a world full of hummingbirds.

Her breath hitched and her body jerked in his hold, hands clutching. He had to tighten his arm around her waist as her body weight began to fall. Her heart rate sped up to the pitter-patter of normal mortals. She was awake. She turned her head to look over their arms and down to the ground. "What—?"

"I have you." He continued their dance because she was still following his lead and because it pleased him. "You were sleepwalking and the shoes took over."

Though they either had not been able to force her to dance the steps they were designed to take or the shoes hadn't cared what dance she performed so long as she *danced*. It was hard to tell.

"We're dancing. On air." Her smile was brilliant, bright with delight.

"It was the gentlest way I could think of to wake you." His chest tightened and he spun her out, then brought her back to him. She laughed. He did not know why he did it. Ashke would be down there having fits over security.

"Thank you, Bennett." Her lashes lowered as she said his name, her tone turning shy.

"You have not told me what you want me to call you." It shouldn't matter, but he wanted to know, wanted to hear it from her.

Her brows came together in consternation. "Everyone calls me Punch."

He raised his brows in response. "Everyone? I will call you Punch if you ask me to, but I have seen you dance and the nickname doesn't quite fit your grace."

A soft rose flush spread over her cheeks. "My given name is Peeraphan."

She pronounced it like a musical phrase, lilting through the first syllable and rolling the soft "rr" into the "ah" of the second. The last syllable was something between "p-aah-n" and "pun" with a stress on the ending consonant, and he could understand how that syllable led to Punch as a shortened nickname.

"Peeraphan." He repeated her name three times, slowly, getting a feel for the sounds as he shaped them, trying to match the tonal inflections she added. English did not make use of the nuance, whereas apparently Thai was a tonal language. "Beautiful. May I call you Peeraphan?"

She nodded, blushing even harder.

It was not her true name. If it had been, calling her by it three times would have invoked a certain amount of power over her. But it was a part of her name, much more a part of her than Punch. It was enough to make a connection with her, of sorts. At the very least, it was a second thread to add to the one already between them from his feeding. Perhaps the connections would never be necessary, but for now, they were an appropriate precaution.

Especially if she had the ability to take flight at any moment.

"We're soaring." She didn't seem afraid, now that she had gotten past the initial waking moment. And she may have grown uncomfortable with the silence between them.

"You were first." He clarified, "I only came out to retrieve you. You seem surprised."

"Flying is a surprise. The wings aren't new. They first appeared when I hit puberty. I only managed to make them disappear and reappear at will." She glanced back. "Seeing them doesn't get old though. I figured I might be able to fly if I could manifest wings, but I just didn't know how."

Obviously, her subconscious had. Either that or the compulsion to dance had triggered the knowledge. A victim could dance much farther across the sky than inside a closed room.

Her wings swept forward and down, brushing his thighs but not hitting him, the sensation teasing him in ways that weren't for here and now. Her body, pressed against him, was lithe and he started thinking of other ways they might move together. As her wings lifted back and up, her weight lightened in his arms and he tightened his hold on her. She was enjoying herself, and he didn't begrudge her the joy of exploring her first flight, but she was also giving in to the compulsion and the shoes were draining her as they pushed her to dance, even with him.

The magic of the red shoes was insidious.

"Do you think you could fly on your own if I released you?" He had an idea.

She was busy looking out over the waters of Puget Sound, as they had flown beyond the shores of the island. "I'm not sure. I probably need more practice."

"That might be for the best."

"Why?" She turned her head to look up at him.

He smiled and dropped her.

EIGHT

PEERAPHAN

P unch screamed as she fell, reaching out for anything she could grab hold of. It took her a long second, too long, to remember her wings and concentrate enough to bring them forward into a powerful downbeat, attempting to gain any kind of altitude. Her fall slowed, enough for her to take a deep breath, but she still splashed into the ocean.

Cold enveloped her, shocking her to her core. She reached up, kicking instinctively, sure she hadn't gone deep. Her wings moved in coordination with her arms, pulling her up through the water in powerful sweeps. She broke the surface in moments, the waves around her moving in big swells. Calm, she needed to stay calm.

She'd been working with air and water in small ways for years now. Most of that had been reaching out with her senses. If she could use those elements to sense and gently influence flow, maybe she could work with them enough to save herself from hypothermia.

It was possible because she thought it was. She could handle this. Survive this.

She gathered her magic to her with each breath, reached for more than she'd ever dared before, centering herself and slowing her breathing in spite of the adrenaline rush. Air was hers more than water, so it seemed wisest to go for small magic, like not freezing in the dangerously cold ocean. She also didn't need to boil an ocean, only raise the temperature of the water around her skin just enough to not steal her own body heat.

Along the same line of reasoning, she probably shouldn't try to do anything more dramatic with water. Swimming was likely to get her to safety faster.

"Bennett! Hey! Look! She's here." A new voice zipped around her as a glowing ball of magic resolved into a tiny winged person.

"I know where she is." Bennett came into view, immaculately put together in a fresh dress shirt and slacks, with his hands in his pants pockets, looking like he was just casually standing there. On air. Above the ocean.

"You're an asshole." As she tossed the words up at him, she didn't bother to shout. She focused on treading water with hands and wings and feet.

"Yes." He looked down at her, eyes narrowing slightly. "Did the shoes come off?"

She paused. "No." She tried to curl her toes. Then she tried to kick them off. "Still on."

He *tsk*ed. "It occurred to me that some magic items lose their power in running water and others lose their power to salt. It seemed to me this was a way to test both."

"Are there sharks out here?" She was furious.

"Mostly skittish dogfish sharks. Larger sharks would be swimming in deeper waters where there are colder, stronger currents. There is a higher risk of hypothermia, or possibly a pod of orcas." He seemed unconcerned. "The most dangerous predator in the waters near here is a toss-up between a mermaid and a selkie. Neither of them is nearby, to my knowledge."

"The mermaid has a pet, though," said the winged fairy, "a big one. It was eating killer whales in Puget Sound before we helped her feed it."

Funny how Punch's most recent visit to the aquarium in downtown Seattle had left her with memories of cute sea otters and sweet-faced seals. The closest thing resembling a sea monster had been the giant Pacific octopus, and the one there had been adorably mischievous, collecting feeding poles in his tank once his caretakers ran out of shrimp for the day.

"Test is over—get me out of here." She reached up to Bennett.

Her magic responded, gathering the water around her and pushing her upward on the swells. Oh, that was unintended, but she'd take it. Her wings broke the surface and began flapping, but she couldn't get enough lift for her body.

Warmth surrounded her uplifted wrist as strong fingers gripped her. She yelped as she was yanked upward, free of the water. Desperately, she pulled her magic around her as she spread her wings outward and managed to hang suspended in the air.

Punch stretched her arms out to her sides, trying to hold herself there. "Hah!"

She looked down at herself and grinned, elated.

"That's enough for this evening." Bennett was suddenly there, wrapping his arms around her waist and pulling her against him. "Fold your wings close."

Pressing her palms against the hard planes of his chest, she considered pushing him away, then thought better of it. She could hover. Punch hadn't reliably figured out the whole flying thing yet, and there'd been a fairly strong current pulling her away from the island. She didn't want to try to figure out flying when she didn't know how long she could manage to stay up in the air. Abruptly, she realized the only heartbeat she was feeling was the pounding in her own chest. Where a heartbeat should have been beneath her palms, there was nothing.

"How are you warm when you have no heartbeat, no blood flow?" She asked quietly. She wasn't sure if he'd hear her with the wind and crashing waves as they flew over the shoreline, back toward the manor.

"My heart beats for a short time after I drink," he answered, his head bent so his lips brushed her ear. "The warmth and life energy fades over the course of a day or more, then I have to feed again. My body temperature is still a few degrees cooler than most humans', but you are cold from exposure to the ocean despite your magic."

Ah. Well, she'd managed to prevent hypothermia at least. Besides, her cheeks were flushing hot in response to his touch and his fit body pressed against hers. He was very well built. They hadn't been pressed close like this when he'd been leading her in a dance earlier. This was more.

"No disturbances detected." The winged fae was back, keeping pace with Bennett. "I notified my security teams of the situation."

"Noted," Bennett responded, his voice considerably cooler than it had been a few moments prior.

The winged fae zipped in close enough for her to see his grinning face. He waved. "Good evening, my lady! Beautiful night."

She laughed, feeling lighter, because what could she do besides laugh at this point? "It is."

"I am called Ashke." He executed a neat bow, midflight.

Bennett's arms tightened around her, so she settled for a nod in return. "You can call me Punch."

"Lady Punch!"

She shook her head, smiling. "Just Punch will do."

She had let Bennett use her given name and she wasn't quite ready to explore what it might mean. It did feel good to have someone ask the way he did, though. Like he wasn't asking for an easy way to think of her, but rather, wanted to know more of who she was.

"Okay, Punch!" Ashke drew a sword from a sheath at his hip and brandished it in a jaunty salute. "I am the head of security for the Darke Consortium and this island. I command both the human teams and the supernaturals assigned to security duty. I also maintain the glamour around the island to hide us from unwanted visitors. If you have need of anything, just whisper my name to the island and I will know you are looking for me."

He hadn't said he'd come when called though. She was going to need to read up on fae and fairies. She'd studied some of the mythology in primary school but had been more interested in Greek and Roman gods in high school or the folklore and legends from Southeast and East Asia during her undergraduate studies. The only stories she could recall from her younger days were all cautionary tales to avoid the fae and beware angering them.

She wasn't the type to avoid much of anything, especially when people were as interesting as those she'd met this evening—Ashke included.

"Inform Duncan and Thomas that I'm taking her in the sea entrance and directly to the lair," Bennett said.

Ashke didn't say anything more, only zoomed off into the night.

"Talking over me isn't the best way to keep me in the loop here. I appreciate your help, truly, but I also have a choice about where you're taking me." She didn't make it a question and tapped her fingertips on Bennett's chest to make sure he realized she was talking to him.

"I told you I would search for a solution." He shrugged. "This is the next step I could think of, considering the urgency of the situation."

She had to make an effort to unclench her jaw. "Let's try deliberating together before experimenting with possible solutions from here on out."

"It's more expedient to move from one possibility to the next."
He seemed oblivious to her growing ire. Or maybe he didn't care.
"Explaining everything in detail to you could eat up precious time
that you do not have. You are still in a ticking bomb situation."

Perhaps, but she could only go for so long without knowing
what would happen next. "This is not okay."

He didn't have a right to take her anywhere without her say-so,
and she was prepared to spread her wings and do everything in her
not insignificant power to fight her way free.

They slowed, the air not quite rushing by, and Bennett's jaw
tightened. "I had thought the expedient thing to do was to take you
directly to the next logical source of information."

"So tell me about this source and I probably won't put up a
fight." She was all for reasonable conversation. "I like to make
informed decisions, especially when they involve allowing myself to
be taken to someone's *lair* barely dressed and soaking wet."

Because that had all sorts of connotations. For example, was
it Bennett's lair? Punch wasn't absolutely against it, if he asked
nicely. But she wasn't going to stay tucked conveniently against
him if he was just dragging her off, assuming she'd be all for it.
On the flip side, she also didn't want him to regret the possibly
more expedient solution of just killing her to get the shoes in the
first place.

"You had sufficient clothing to cover yourself when I left you to
your sleep earlier this evening." There was amusement in his voice,
but he had also pulled them up so they were standing on air.

"We already established I was not aware while I was sleep-
dancing, thank you very much. That's never happened before, so
I'm guessing the curse played a part in that, which is freaking me
out a little." Her temper boiled up. "And I wouldn't be wet if you
hadn't dropped me into the ocean without any kind of warning. I

don't know how old you are, but you need to bring yourself out of whatever misogynistic, patriarchal dark age your mindset is stuck in and include me in decisions having to do with me!"

She glared at him, her wings half extended behind her, ready to break away from him and deal with the fall to the ground far below if she had to. Yes, she'd hoped for his help. But she wasn't going to beg him for whatever aid he saw fit to give and she wasn't going to just blindly let him do whatever with her.

He stared at her for a long moment, then cleared his throat. "You make a valid point. More than one, actually. I appreciate your directness."

He smiled at her then.

Just the upward curve of his lips changed his entire expression from severe to disarming, and her anger seeped away at alarming speed. The entire situation was something out of a dream, and none of her ancient folktales or well-loved myths had given her any good ideas for what to do in this situation.

As her anger left her, a taut awareness of him remained and plenty of bad ideas started bouncing around in her mind. Naughty ideas. Between the mischief she could visit on him to take his arrogant ass down a notch or two and the saucy fun she hadn't ever had the actual nerve to instigate in real life, her mind was definitely disqualifying her for sainthood.

She cleared her throat. "So what is this lair? Who does it belong to? And why do you want to take me there?"

"It's the only place I have left to take you in search of a solution. Alternatively, I can take you back to the manor and you can remain a guest until the red shoes compel you to dance to death. Either way, I get what I need." His smile widened and his eyes gleamed red in the night. A flash of ruby, there and gone again.

That was downright unsettling. She should have been terrified.

Instead, she narrowed her eyes. There was a glint of mischief in his gaze and she thought he might be teasing her.

Or maybe she'd imagined it. She wasn't too stupid to live, she had been taken off guard. She'd absolutely felt a shock of fear, for a whole fraction of a second. But wow, she hadn't thought such eyes would be so attractive.

There was a thought.

"Are vampires able to play mind games with people?" Perhaps she shouldn't be making eye contact as readily as she was.

He wasn't looking away. "Yes. We can confuse weaker-willed beings, like humans."

"Ah." Interesting, and also not clear as to whether he was actively messing with her head or not. "But not strong-willed beings, humans or...otherwise?"

"If I was able to blur your reason, I'd be sorely tempted to facilitate quicker decision-making."

She jerked back, spreading her wings. She could take her chances at figuring out hovering at least.

But his arms tightened around her and his chuckle wrapped around her, too, sending delicious shivers down her spine. "I said *if*. It would be dishonest to say I hadn't thought about it. But I give you my word, I will not use my abilities to influence you."

Punch glared at him and he waited, loosening his hold but not letting go. Thinking back, she realized he could have overridden her thought process several times tonight. He hadn't. Now she had his word, and she had the impression he took that seriously. Studying his expression, she decided he liked verbally sparring with her. Which was fine. Maybe this was the vampire version of flirting, the extreme edition.

She wasn't sure what to make of it, but she didn't hate it.

"The lair is the home of my sponsor. It's situated beneath the manor. Once we ask our questions, we can go directly back up into the manor and you will hopefully be able to rest for what remains of the night. I'll watch over you, so you can sleep." He sounded so damned amused. "When the dawn comes, the others will be in the manor."

Well, that sounded nowhere near as reassuring as she figured it would have. Should have? This whole evening was some kind of emotional roller coaster.

"Can I trust you?" She met his gaze again, searching for some kind of anchor. Trust would be a good start.

His eyes flared ruby red, like gemstones lit from within, as he stared back at her. "Not in all things. Never."

The honesty in his answer caused a tightness in her chest. It wasn't reassuring, but she liked it. Liked it a lot.

He continued, "But in this moment, at least, I'm doing everything in my power to help you."

That would have to be enough. "Let's go."

NINE

BENNETT

ennett was caught in a moment without words, a rare
occurrence. Peeraphan was looking at him expectantly, her
upturned face illuminated by moonlight, her jaw set with a
determined expression. Admiration and amusement spun through
him in equal measure. She was a force to be reckoned with, both
because she was so decisive and because it seemed little could deter
her once she had made up her mind. He also found her courage very
attractive.

Any words he could think to say in response to her decision to
trust him were bound to come out wrong. Rather than ruin the light-
ness he felt, he chose not to say anything at all. Instead, he gathered
her closer than was strictly necessary, and directed their flight with a
whisper of a thought through the darkness.

The tide was going out, so the entrance to the sea cave was easier
to find. It would still be difficult to locate even for low-flying sea-
planes, and Bennett had the advantage of both knowing where he
was going and having better vision than a human pilot might. Even
at low tide, the entrance was partially submerged, and it was easier
to swim in than fly. At high tide, there would be no choice but to
take a dive.

Peeraphan's body tensed as they approached the rocky cliff. Perhaps she hadn't spotted the entrance yet. Giving in to a perverse sense of mischief he had thought long smothered, he increased their speed until they were barreling through the air toward the side of the island. Rather than duck her head or cry out, her chest pressed hard against his as she took in a deep breath and her body relaxed against him.

Trust. She had decided to place so much trust in him so quickly once she had the information she'd asked of him. Or at least, she had trust that he wouldn't do something to harm the both of them.

Though the entrance to the sea cave was small, it opened up quickly inside in every direction, and he took them upward until they hung suspended at the top of the dome-like interior. Below them, a deep tidal pool formed an almost perfect natural circle, with shallow edges and a center so deep the bottom remained a mystery even when the tide had receded. There were underwater caverns below the island, unmapped by humans and largely unexplored. The sea was not Bennett's domain, so he left those mysteries to others, with assurance from his sponsor that no threats to the manor could approach using the underwater route.

"This is amazing," Peeraphan whispered, her words carrying through the cavern. "Why did we come here?"

"I do not have the answers we need to help you." Bennett bit back frustration so it only became a rumble in his chest and did not break loose as a growl. "Nothing turned up in the library or via the various information databases we have access to online. We are here for a primary source of knowledge—my sponsor."

She looked up at him through long, dark lashes. "In a cave."

"A cave, yes." He nodded toward the edge of the pool, where stairs were carved into the side of the cavern heading downward. "This is simply the entrance to the lair. Those stairs will take us to her. The others lead up to the manor."

Peeraphan craned her neck to look at the stairs curving downward into darkness, then leaned to the other side of him to get a good look at the ones heading upward. "Are we landing soon, or do you plan to dive straight down there?"

He chuckled. Not that he hadn't considered it, in other times, when his temper had gotten the better of him. "It is not a good idea to enter her domain so abruptly."

"Her." Curiosity ruled her tone, though there was a hint of caution, too. "Any hints as to who she is, or am I going to have to figure it out on the fly?"

It was not his intent to tease her with breadcrumbs of information, provided bit by bit, but he was feeling his way along. He did not want to unintentionally set any expectations or push her too fast beyond her comfort zones. Peeraphan had demonstrated herself to be very open to the existence of the supernatural, but she was likely to hit a limit somewhere. "I'd intended to do as much research as possible using our library and the internet, in order to ask her specific questions. She has limited patience for us, and we risk learning only what we could have easily looked up if we do not do our best to narrow the focus of our questions. She is patient, for one of her kind, but it is best not to rely on her patience. She is a dragon, after all, and unpredictability is a species trait for her kind."

"A—" She blinked. Then she shook her head and lifted a gaze full of sparkling excitement. "Seriously? You promise—you're not teasing me?"

He stared down at her, taking in the joyful excitement suffusing her expression and her brilliant smile. He spread his hands, turning his hold on her into a more intimate embrace. "I am not teasing you, not on this particular topic, Peeraphan, but I am very tempted now."

Her breath caught and she stilled in his arms, not stiff and not pulling away, but seemingly suddenly very aware. Rose flushed over her cheeks and her bright smile melted into parted lips that might have been an invitation.

Someone cleared his throat.

She let out a squeak and reflexively pushed at his chest.

Bennett released her, ready to catch her again rather than allow her to fall back into the water if her own magic did not keep her in the air. The pool below was more than deep enough, but the waters were cold. Testing a theory was one thing, but he would not subject her to repeated dunking. She managed to stay aloft though, her wings spread as if holding her in the air on an updraft of magic when there was no wind.

Duncan spoke in a dry, neutral tone, his words rising up from the edge of the pool. "I brought dry clothes for the lady, since Ashke mentioned she'd been exposed to the elements."

Oh, there was judgment beneath those words, and no small amount of disapproval. Bennett wondered when Duncan had become so concerned with a human. But then again, she was a guest and the sidhe took guests very seriously.

Either way, Duncan was justified. Bennett extended a hand to Peeraphan. She was still new to flight, and in his experience, the landing part of it all posed the greatest risk.

She was smiling as she placed her hand in his, her gesture elegant while allowing them to create a firm contact. He started their descent, heading toward a spot near Duncan with plenty of room to either side. She hovered momentarily until he gently tugged at her hand and she managed to follow him, her wings arched the way a swan's would be as it came to land on the surface of any lake. His feet touched ground a moment before hers and as they did, she still had some forward momentum, causing her to stumble. He turned and caught her against his chest before she fell forward.

"Oof." Her forehead made contact with his sternum, and she

looked up at him with wide eyes. "Sorry. Thanks. That was probably not the best way to come back to firm ground."

He fought to keep his expression neutral despite the amusement tugging at the corners of his mouth. "As first landings go, yours was one of the better ones I've witnessed."

She extricated herself from his arms to stand on her own. "Well, here's hoping I get better from here on out."

"I am happy to be of assistance as you practice." The offer came out before he had a chance to consider it more carefully. She was here for a specific reason and they had best focus on it, or any talk of future endeavors was folly. He cleared his throat. "Why don't you change into the clothes Duncan has for you, before he holds me any more accountable. Then we should hurry down to speak with my sponsor."

Peeraphan glanced at the stairway leading down and nodded, then made her way carefully across the cavern floor to Duncan. The red shoes shone a sullen satin, not quite glowing in the dimly lit cave but still more noticeable than regular fabric would be.

"I apologize, Lady Punch, but we don't have spare clothing specific for a lady of your specific measurements at the moment. I think you'll find this shirt and pant combination will accommodate your wings for the time being." Duncan produced a large blanket and held it up so Peeraphan could change with relative privacy.

Bennett opted to turn his back anyway, for good measure. The nightgown had been fine when she had been dry and in a guest bed, but outside and wet? Well, it was a sight worth keeping tucked away in his store of good memories. It had been thin enough to dry reasonably quickly, too, but the clothes Duncan provided would probably be more comfortable for her. Her comfort was far more important than Bennett's opinion and he had best keep his reactions to her—however she was dressed—to himself. There was no room for his errant impulses with her life in jeopardy.

"If you are ready, we can proceed."

Peeraphan moved toward the stairway and placed a hand on the wall as she took the first step down. Bennett moved quicker than he intended, at her side fast enough for her to glance up at him with eyes wide, lips parted. "I know you can move that fast," she laughed softly, "but it takes some getting used to."

She took the next step and her ankle turned, causing her knee to buckle and throwing her forward.

He caught her, steadying her at the elbow and other hand at her waist. "The stairs are somewhat uneven."

Her heart was pounding and the scent of fear rose up from her. That could have been the kind of fall to send her tumbling down the stairs, into unknown darkness. Her wings were pressed tightly against the sides of her thighs and her fingernails had extended into talons again with her panic.

She looked up at him, brows drawn together in a slight frown. "The stairs aren't so bad and I'm generally comfortable in this heel height. It felt more like my shoe pivoted as I stepped down. I turned my ankle too fast to catch myself."

He froze, considering. "So it is not limited to dance."

Her mouth twisted into a wry half smile. "Well, a pivot into a turn is a dance step in the right context. At the wrong moment, though, a dancer's career is over."

It had not occurred to him that the shoes would push a dancer to step into an injury which could potentially lead them to an untimely death. If Peeraphan had fallen down the stairs, which curved downward to the caverns below, she could have broken her back or her neck. Her death would have come abruptly and violently. He was no stranger to either, but the thought of this woman's bright smile suddenly gone was a pain so acute, he acted before thinking, scooping her into his arms and cradling her against his chest.

She squeaked in surprise.

"There is no guardrail to hold on to as you descend." He started down. "It seems wiser to take you down any stairs without giving the red shoes the opportunity to influence how you get there."

"Yeah." She still sounded shaken, but she looped her arms around his neck loosely. "I appreciate the lift."

"It is no hardship." He traversed the stairs at a normal human speed, taking extra care.

The influence of the red shoes should be limited to the wearer, but there had been enough unexpected effects for him not to be wary. He would not be surprised if the shoes extended their compulsion to anyone touching the wearer. Some magical artifacts could do so; why not the red shoes? He had not come across the possibility in his prior research, but folktales and historical references may not have captured all there was to know. Certainly, something could have been lost along the way, either in transcription or translation, or simply creative license. He made a point of updating his own notes about such discoveries for any magic items he retrieved for the Darke Consortium.

Peeraphan's head was turned, taking in the subtle lighting around them as they descended. "This place is amazing. Is that bioluminescent moss?"

"And larva, of a type of insect." He nodded. "The organisms are slightly different from those found in caverns frequented by humans around the world. These are evolved to be a part of the ambient magic of the dragon living here."

She was silent for a moment. "Am I correct to assume your sponsor and the dragon are the same being?"

"Yes."

"A magic being. That lives underground, in a cave."

He was amused by this progression in questions and commentary. "A rather extensive system of caverns, actually."

"And by sponsor, you mean this dragon is your boss?" She sounded hopeful.

He paused, considering, then continued his descent. "Our relationship is complex, but in very simple terms, yes. She makes me aware of magic items awakening or surfacing in the region, and I work with the rest of the Consortium to research and retrieve them. She then helps us to contain them here or in other appropriate places around the world, preferably nearest their origin, if possible. She uses the wealth accumulated over the course of millennia to fund the Darke Consortium and those who are a part of it."

She shook her head and a wisp of her hair brushed his jaw along with the scent of tropical flowers and sea. "Vampires, werewolves, fae, and dragons. Wow. Even better, you're not the über-powerful, gorgeous, billionaire philanthropist. You actually work for a dragon."

"I apologize if I have fallen short of your expectations." In truth, he felt he qualified for all of her descriptors, but if she liked him even more for acknowledging his sponsor, he would not press the point.

"So is the Consortium named after her? The dragon? Like a play on the word 'drake'?"

Warmth and amusement fled, leaving him cold in a wash of painful memories. "No."

"Ah." She looked away.

There was more. He hesitated. It was personal. A wound that would never heal and a weakness he didn't want known. But he did not feel right cutting short the conversation, not when she had been so earnest and opened up to him as she had. She had saved his life a few hours ago. And so he offered her a bit of himself because he owed that much to her.

"Victoria Darke was my lover, my partner. It was she who made the original pact with the dragon to establish this consortium, here on this island." He paused, not wanting to delve too far into the past. "There are other consortiums around the world, each with a similarly powerful, benevolent sponsor. There are also other private interests emerging in comparatively recent times, some supernatural and others completely human-run, with their own intentions for such items of power."

It was likely Francesco had joined one of the latter. Francesco had issues with authority, unless bending to someone else's will temporarily would serve his purposes in a longer game. Even then, the Francesco Bennett had known would still only take an action that was in alignment with what Francesco would have done on his own anyway.

"I see." Peeraphan was silent for a long moment, then she took a deep breath and spoke again. "Where is Ms. Darke now?"

"She was human. She died of old age." He did not want to continue and he also did not want their conversation to fall into awkward silence. "The dragon, on the other hand, is immortal and also one of the oldest of her kind. She is rare. Powerful. And she understands the loneliness of the immortal. Do you want to ask me anything about her before you meet her?"

"Hmm. I think it'll be better to find out if we're meeting her soon, rather than ask and build an impression in my mind ahead of time." Peeraphan seemed to be willing to move on with their conversation, for which he was grateful. "I don't think I'd be disappointed, per se, but I'd be caught up in the guess and the reality, if that makes sense. I'd rather just follow curiosity and find out what there is to discover."

He chuckled. "Wise."

She grinned at him, her face very close to his. "Not always. Maybe not even often. In this case, I guess so."

Her excitement—her wonder in experiencing the new—was

refreshing. Not in the light spritz of a carbonated drink way, but more like diving into cool water after decades of walking through a desert. He could not remember when he had last paid attention to the path down below and taken in the beauty of it the way he was now.

The stairway curved gently as it led them downward, and the tiny bioluminescent organisms were scattered above them like galaxies of stars, providing a soft, glowing light.

The cavern opened up here and there to reveal smaller tunnels and overhangs. As a vampire, he would always see more than others, more colors in less light with greater intensity. He heard and smelled more as well. He could not remember the last time he had cared what another person could sense, but he wanted to know more about what she was experiencing. He wanted to experience more, through her. Right here, right now, with her in his arms and her face close to his, he was as close to seeing things in her perspective as he could get.

"How much can you see?" he asked her.

TEN

PEERAPHAN

I t's like wandering under a night sky with a full moon, only there's no moon." Peeraphan kept her volume low, almost a whisper. There was a weight to the feel of the place as they traveled farther down. "Everything is cast in silvers and blues and the shadows are deep, but not scary. Just quiet."

She looked deeper into the shadows. Her memory and imagination popped suggestions into her brain, just to prove her wrong. A shiver swept through her as a particularly unhelpful thought jumped into her overactive mind's eye.

Bennett's arms tightened, steadying her. "Something is upsetting you."

His voice had a hint of a growl behind it and she thought she caught a glint of fang between his lips. She stared, wondering whether it hurt when his face changed the way it had back in the alley as he was fighting the other vampire. It hadn't happened the way some television and movies portrayed vampires, making them look more like demons. Instead, his upper and lower jaws had pushed outward and lengthened, giving his extending fangs better advantage to bite and rip and tear. She had been horrified when she'd seen first the other vampire change, then him, and fascinated at the same time. It might have been shock, but she remembered thinking sort of clinically about how it made more sense than the way she had always thought vampires might be.

When he had fed on her, she'd been scared, too, but even more fascinated. He could have ripped up her arm, the way the other vampire had ripped up his, but even on the brink of dying, he hadn't left much more damage than had already been done by Duncan's knife. At this point, the wound on her arm barely even ached and Bennett still appeared human, for the most part.

Of course, one didn't have to appear monstrous to be an asshole. He had dropped her into Puget Sound. She should have more trust issues with him. But he'd actually seemed to listen when she'd said her piece about discussing things with her and keeping her informed. Better yet, his attitude and behavior changed for the better—at least a *bit* better.

More importantly, the feel of his strength wrapped around her as he carried her was comforting. When he'd caught her at the top of the stairs, relief had washed through her like a balm smoothing over jangling nerves.

Right from the beginning, everything had happened so quickly— she'd been buffeted left and right and up and down, and when he held her, she felt she had the chance to catch her breath. He was dangerous, yes, and unpredictable for sure. But her body, at least, was associating him with a shelter from the storm even while her mind was busy cataloging all the impressions she was getting of him.

Fear was becoming barely even a thing in his presence, and she found herself wanting to know more about him.

The ruby red of his eyes smoldered, the way coals burned red when air blew across them. Her mind jerked back to his earlier statement and she realized he was ready to take action to address whatever was upsetting her.

"Just my imagination being super not-helpful," she attempted to reassure him. "I'm a very image-oriented person and I tend to remember a lot from movies I've watched, sort of like snapshots or clips inside my head. A while back, there were a handful of horror movies set in caves. Monsters attacking human explorers."

She shuddered, unable to suppress her response. He shifted her in his arms, pulling her closer so her head was tucked under his chin. But not before she caught a glimpse of even more fang.

"I will keep you safe."

More comfort. Safety. The concepts weren't words in her head. They were feelings, warm and soothing, accumulating in thin layers and wrapping her in a cocoon.

He hadn't said there was nothing dangerous down here. Which, to be fair, would've been a lie. There was him and the dragon, at least. And he wasn't promising her safety from his sponsor. But whether he said it to her or not, she felt sure she was safe with him.

He'd saved her life once already, and when he could've drained every bit of blood in her body, he hadn't. Yes, he'd dropped her in the ocean, but there was a touch of mischief there she could relate to. As if she had never pushed a friend into a pool or splashed someone while swimming in the ocean. What he'd done was a bigger deal, but maybe for supernaturals, everything was a different relative scale.

He also could've left her there, but everything he'd done tonight only made her more and more sure he was doing what he could to help her and keep her from harm.

He might not be able to save her, though. He specifically hadn't promised her that. She needed to remember. It wouldn't be fair to hold him accountable if they didn't find a solution, and she really didn't want to hate him.

But she didn't think it would make either of them feel better to say so, so she only said, "Thank you."

They both fell silent for a while and Peeraphan almost wished for a natural continuation of the conversation. When her mind wasn't coming up with words, her thoughts were running wild with other things. Since Bennett had assured her he'd protect her—and she believed him—she was no longer distracted by imagined movie monsters hiding in the crevices.

Instead, she was very aware of his broad shoulders, which she was literally hanging on to, and the strength of his arms. Plus, she had been intensely aware of his hands earlier, especially when he'd spread his fingers as he'd held her. He'd sent delicious sensations running through her in waves of warmth and she wondered how it'd feel to have him run his hands over her bare skin. Heady thoughts, there.

He was the most attractive person she had ever encountered, without a doubt. She didn't think it was a part of his power as a vampire. To be fair, his being a predator had to have some part to play in how she was reacting to him. But she didn't think he was clouding her mind the way some stories indicated vampires could.

Yes, he could be carrying her down to some terrible doom. She wasn't too stupid to live. She could admit there was that possibility.

But she honestly didn't think he would waste the effort in doing that. He'd have just brought her down here to begin with, rather than having seen to her comfort earlier and letting her rest. He wouldn't have let Thomas know she was there.

No matter how little she and her family had ever known about Thomas, she was certain of his affection when she'd been little. He'd been her favorite cousin. Thomas wouldn't let Bennett lure her into an illusion of safety only to bring her down here and kill her.

And apparently, nobody could've predicted her little jaunt out into the night. Flying. None of them had known she could do that, not even her.

So no, she didn't think this was all part of any plan. Instead, she was in his arms, able to look right up into his very handsome face and wonder what it'd be like to kiss him.

Did his fangs nip when he kissed?

She'd dated her fair share of men once she'd gone to college, graduated, started living the life of an independent adult. She didn't exactly call home and keep her parents up-to-date on her adventures, but she also didn't make it a secret if they asked her. She liked kissing. First kisses were moments of held breath and imaginary butterflies.

Kissing was a taste of how other things could be.

If she'd had any leftover chills from her impromptu dive into the Sound, they were banished by her current thoughts. He was still warm, actually, and she wondered what it would be like to be near him as his body lost the heat of having been recently fed. She wasn't turned off or disgusted, but she wasn't sure how she'd react if she had the chance to find out.

"Are you excited by dalliances in wild places?" His quiet question zinged through her, almost electrifying.

"Pardon?"

"You're warmer now and your cheeks are flushed a most attractive peachy rose. Your heart rate is elevated and your scent has a delectable spice. You are excited, and most paranormals couldn't miss it." His tone was gentle and didn't sound patronizing or judgmental. If anything, there was a slightly apologetic note in there.

She was excruciatingly embarrassed anyway. "I'm so—"

"Please do not apologize." He sounded contrite now. "I did not comment to embarrass you. I… I thought it prudent to let you know I was aware of your emotional state based on those cues. You're deep within the supernatural world now. Leaving you ignorant of the tells that give the predators insight about you would be criminal."

"Ah." She wasn't sure what to say next. She didn't feel as bad now, but she was still cringing inside.

He turned his head until his lips brushed her forehead. "I find myself also interested in knowing whether it is your surroundings or the present company that have brought about your response."

Her heart just about stopped in her chest. It was him, definitely him. Especially when he was so eloquently asking her if he was turning her on. Eloquence was hot. And she wasn't sure she had the courage to answer him in this very moment.

Well, the worst he could do was drop her and make her walk the rest of the way down. Not something he was likely to do. Or she was reading the situation wrong and he could simply turn her down now. No problem. It would just be incredibly awkward hanging out in his arms as he continued to carry her like a romance novel-level gentleman.

She decided to be forthright, because nothing ventured, nothing experienced—whether it was awkward or wonderful. "To be honest, this cavern is breathtaking, but I'm mostly focused on you."

She risked a peek up to get an idea of how he was taking her confession. His gaze was on the way ahead, but a faint smile played across his lips. That was good. Right?

A gentle laugh echoed around them, seeming to come from every direction because of the cavern's acoustics.

"It is refreshing to find I am not the center of attention for this visit." The voice had a mellow tone with resonant depth, like listening to a cello.

Bennett came to a stop and lowered Peeraphan slowly so she could get her feet under her. He leaned close for a moment, his lips brushing the upper shell of her ear. "Just a few more steps. We'll resume this conversation later, hmm?"

Sure. Fantastic. Peeraphan wasn't certain how much

embarrassment she could survive in a single night, but hey, no time like the present to find out. Maybe she should switch to the Thai word for "embarrassed" even when she was thinking in English, because at least the Thai word had fewer syllables and sounded closer to the way she felt. "*Aiy.*"

Bennett slipped his left hand under her right, lifting it so her forearm rested on his, and led her forward. The treacherous shoes made her feel like she was walking over gravel and marbles. Maybe they could get her ankle braces until this whole thing was solved.

Or would that just let her dance longer, exhaust her more, bringing her that much closer to her death?

Morbid thoughts needed to be shoved into yet another compartment of her brain. She needed solutions. Not despair.

The narrower stairway opened into another cavern. This one didn't have as much height as the one above, but it still had the feeling of a vaulted ceiling. A ceiling of deep grays and blues speckled in bioluminescent lights like stardust was reflected in pools and underground streams with stalactites and stalagmites reaching toward each other, some meeting in great columns veined in glowing light. Wound around a grouping of several stalactites directly above them was a figure out of legend.

"Oh?" The voice still echoed from every direction. "I can't remember the last time a child of humans cast their gaze upward the moment they entered one of my domains. So often, adventurers and explorers are busy looking far forward or down at where they are putting their feet. I think you found me even sooner than Bennett did the first time he came to visit me."

The dragon had a long body, serpentine, with two pairs of short legs. Fragments of memory scampered through Peeraphan's mind. Everything she'd heard about dragons compared them to animals of the everyday world: some resources claimed the body of a snake, the face of a crocodile, mane of a lion, antlers of a deer, claws of a hawk or eagle, and pads of a tiger. The thing was, those were only ways to piece together the whole and in no way did justice to this fantastic being.

She was deep blue in color, the intensity of the night sky just before the light of dawn touched the horizon. Her scales shimmered, one moment deepening in color to almost matte black so she almost disappeared, a shadow against the bioluminescence. The next moment, her scales flared iridescent and azure, lighting her long silhouette as she flowed from the ceiling to the floor. A mane surrounded her face, silky and longer than any lion's, and as she approached, Peeraphan realized the dragon's head was twice her own height. It was huge, longer than an anaconda, with a broader girth more than capable of swallowing a human whole.

"I will not eat you." When the dragon spoke, her lips moved, shaping the words. She shook her head, her mane flaring silver and her scales shimmering in silver and blue and green and every color the sea ever was in an ever-changing progression of color.

Peeraphan decided it would be the understatement of the decade to say the scholars describing dragons hadn't done her justice at all. "You don't have the jaws of the crocodile."

The dragon dropped her jaw open and grinned. "You don't think so, little one?"

Peeraphan swallowed hard. Those were some impressive teeth, though. "No. Your mouth is dangerous, yeah, but the lines of your jaw are more elegant in my opinion. Everything about you is."

Laughter filled the cavern, wrapping around Peeraphan in kind warmth. "Your sincerity is as appreciated as your flattery. Thank you, little bird."

The dragon settled herself somehow in a curving pose, her forelegs in front of her as she lay mostly on her belly and extended her head forward until her eye was even with Bennett. "While I'm enjoying this visit, I'm certain you've a reason beyond light conversation in gentle company."

"The red shoes." Bennett tipped his head to indicate Peeraphan's feet. "The recorded stories only give warning of what the shoes do, not how to remove them before the wearer is changed beyond all recognition."

"Hmm." The dragon's exhaled breath blew Bennett's hair back and Peeraphan stifled a giggle.

It wasn't the time to be silly, but honestly, if Peeraphan didn't hold on to the wonder of everything happening around her, fear of imminent death was going to drown her. So damn it, she was going to find the silver lining in all this and soak in every drop of dream worthy experience while she still could.

"You've changed, my steward." The dragon sounded thoughtful, though it was hard to tell based on expression when one wasn't used to reading the expressions of creatures of myth.

Still, Peeraphan got an overall impression of kindness from the dragon's countenance. It was a little like a certain luck dragon, though the resemblance was only barely there. Mostly, Peeraphan thought it was in the eyes. This dragon had very kind eyes, round and deep with feeling—a lot like looking into a horse's or dog's or rabbit's eyes, or maybe a whale's. Peeraphan had never been close enough to a whale to know personally, but she'd seen pictures. A whale was closer in size, that was for sure.

"Not so long ago, you'd have felt some small pity for the victim of such magic but would have waited to collect the item from the corpse. Perhaps a year ago, perhaps yesterday. Time is an odd thing for those of us who've lived so long. I'd have thought you might even deliver the mercy of death to one trapped in such magic." The dragon blinked slowly, one huge eye focusing on Peeraphan. "But for a vampire as old and as jaded as you, Bennett, to seek another way? This is unexpected."

"Well, he did try to stay back and wait. I sort of made the unexpected happen. For which I'm not sorry. Sorry to interrupt, though. Anyway, please excuse me, but—" There was too much Peeraphan didn't know and it had been a damned long evening already. She took a steadying breath. "I'm new to a lot of this and I have a list, no, several lists of questions I'd like to ask and would love the time to take it all in. But time is something I'm not sure I have. I'm the person trapped in this particular magic and I'm hoping for a way out that doesn't involve me dying, either a slow and exhausting death or a quick and merciful one. I get that you and Bennett both may have a bigger picture to be concerned with, but he was pretty focused in the scope of his question. Do you have the answer we need?"

Damn it. She'd intended to bring the conversation back to target, but even her commentary felt long-winded. Somehow, she had lost the concept of *concise* in this place.

The dragon lifted its head and turned so it could look at her with both of its eyes. That required it to back up some. Peeraphan hoped it was only for that reason and not so it could rear back and strike at her.

"The red shoes are a curse, little bird. Curses so old are not easily broken. But magic is always evolving, changing." The dragon's voice held a bit of exasperation, maybe, but there was compassion, too. "It is most important to understand the intent behind the magic. The shoes will stay on and compel the wearer to dance, not only as a punishment for the wearer, but also as a warning to others against pride and vanity. That has been their purpose. But they are not sentient, not capable of nuance. When is anyone without any pride or some vanity? And who has not committed some small sin in their lives? The shoes are a trap because no one is perfect. Therein lies your doom and also your hope."

Peeraphan didn't have any illusions of being able to understand what the dragon was telling her right away. Instead, she listened and repeated key phrases inside her mind, committing what the dragon was saying to memory so she could think it through later, when anxiety wasn't trying to strangle her. "How?"

"The creator of this trap did not account for the possibility of perfect honesty, when pride and vanity are cast away and the person strips themselves bare." The dragon canted its head to one side. "The wearer might be doomed, but at the same time, only the wearer has the chance to break the curse of the red shoes with a true acknowledgment of everything they are, everything they have ever done, everything they have the potential to do. Such honesty would counter pride and vanity and set you free."

"There is a phrase among humans, of a person being honest to a fault." Bennett stood rigid, his hands in his trouser pockets, his face impassive. "Others will claim to be brutally honest. Honesty doesn't seem to be entirely missing from the human race. But perfect honesty might as well be a completely different thing."

He sounded detached, objective. Maybe he did it to think more clearly. Peeraphan tried to similarly compartmentalize her emotions from her rational mind. It did help.

But Peeraphan wasn't thrilled. "I'm guessing you would be telling me to sit right here and be honest with myself if you thought I could just do it and be free of these shoes. There's a catch. I get the need to think through this problem carefully, and intellectually, I absolutely understand that objectivity is necessary. But I'm afraid and on the edge of panic every time I try to take a step anywhere, so my sense of urgency seems to be a lot more intense than the academic discussion we've got going on here."

Silence. Then the dragon lowered its head to rest on the ground close to Peeraphan. "Well said. My apologies, little bird. You are right to cite the urgency of the situation. My sense of time is different from yours, and I suspect my steward may also have a different sense of time relative to your own. We have both lived a very long time, me longer than him, and our natures are not serving you well at the moment."

"I am sorry," Bennett offered from where he stood. "As I said, perfection is a category on its own. Almost no creature in this world is ever *absolutely* honest. Therein lies the catch, as you call it. We are all influenced by wants and needs, social constructs of our eras, and more. Absolute honesty is outside our ability without the aid of some other force."

The dragon lifted its head and addressed both Peeraphan and Bennett. "Look and listen for a moment."

Peeraphan pressed her lips together and did as the dragon instructed, lifting her gaze up to the ceiling, where motes of light seemed to flow over the surface and gather in thin streams and rivulets in a network of gentle light. The cavern sighed with the faraway murmur of the ocean waves. This place was saturated with old magic, primal and elemental, and it thrummed around her, indistinct and without form, but ever-present.

"This cavern is imbued with magics," the dragon said. "They encourage a sense of comfort, of peace, to coax all within to be forthcoming about their thoughts and feelings, perhaps share more than they would on their own. It is excellent to facilitate conversation and brainstorming. But it isn't the same as personal truth."

Peeraphan rubbed her forehead with the heel of her palm. "Okay, brainstorming is good. Let's keep brainstorming."

"There are items that compel truth, scattered around the world, making appearances throughout the history of each age, but there are none in the sanctuaries we have access to at the moment."

Peeraphan added sanctuaries to her list of things to ask Bennett later, right alongside his title of steward and more about the consortium. "How do we locate one?"

She didn't think it'd help to ask if they could find one in time. They had to. She had no other choice.

"I think a different option would serve you better." The dragon tapped huge, curving claws against the cavern floor. "There are places, just a few, imbued with the magic that require a state of being, such as truth. I know of one cave that might be accessible to you."

"A cave of truth. Seriously?" Peeraphan wanted to sit, hug her knees up to her chest, and maybe rock back and forth for a little while as she tried to grasp the situation. She forced herself to remain standing. "I don't mean to sound ungrateful. It's just a lot."

The dragon chuckled. "It is what it is. If I was making this up, I would come up with something more impressive in nature. I promise. Or at least, I would have made the cave sound more mysterious. But truly, you can travel to this cave, with help. You can enter and be compelled to absolute truth."

"We have a course of action, then," Bennett said briskly.

"The curse of the red shoes should break, but in the process, you will have to make your peace with the truth you have faced to be free of them." The dragon reached out with a foreleg and touched the tip of a claw to Peeraphan's chest. "That is no small consequence. Many humans could not survive it and most mythic beings and paranormals could not remain sane. Too often, those of us who live in the mortal world live a life of lies to exist. Facing absolute truth is likely to destroy most beings, at least in part. It is what you need to do and I will not insult your determination by asking you to consider if it is worth the risk. But I warn you so you know what it means to ask anyone else to accompany you."

Peeraphan swallowed and nodded.

Bennett stepped to her side before she could say anything. "Perhaps she will enter the cave alone, but she will at least have help getting there. Where do we find it?"

She'd have liked to think his statement was unexpected, but if she would have to be completely honest to save herself, she might as well start practicing now. She had very much hoped he'd be willing to help her. Otherwise, he could've just suggested they all wait comfortably at the manor above until she lost her battle with the shoes and died. He'd still have the shoes.

She needed help to save her own life. The decision wasn't hers alone. And that was a bitter taste in her mouth.

"Please tell me how to get to this cave." Peeraphan met the dragon's gaze. There was an ageless sort of patience there, like it was watching Peeraphan's internal struggles and waiting for her prompts to give her the information in bite-sized pieces at a rate she could handle. Peeraphan was grateful, even though she'd been frustrated and rushed just a short while ago.

"There are layers to this world you live in, just as you can use your smartphone device to view a map in a number of formats to find your way to a desired destination." The dragon gestured upward toward the ceiling and the outside world. The delicate network of bioluminescence above them flared in stages, first one layer, then another brightening and fading in succession, the magic fluctuating as if demonstrating the dragon's point. "With such a tool, you have a flat visual representation prioritizing human-made roads for you to travel. You can touch a place on your screen and change the map to show you elevations. Another touch will show you what a satellite sees from orbit. But if you were to stand here, looking at what is in front of you, could you imagine finding your way to someplace distant without such perspective to aid you?"

"No." She wasn't even sure she could find her way back to Seattle and her own home without a map.

"Now think of the nuances of the world we interact with as another layer. A world suffused with magic, traversed by supernaturals. We are a part of your world, and perhaps humans encounter us, but they do not recognize us for what we are." The dragon tipped its head toward Bennett. He bared his fangs in response. Yeah, Peeraphan could guess at how many humans actually realized Bennett was a vampire and lived to tell. "Or perhaps, like you, they are aware. This view of the world, with an awareness for the supernatural, is just one more added layer. There are places protected by magic that any might explore, once they become aware and know to search for them. The Under Hill of the fae or the pocket domains of the *kitsune* are extensions of this world. Humans simply don't know how to find their way into these places, bar a few rare accidents or when they had help."

"I'm guessing this cave isn't a place I can get to by plane, train, or automobile." Peeraphan didn't actually know where her smartphone was—probably back in the guest room with Tobi and Cory. But it wasn't like she was going to be able to open up a map app and type in an address. "Are we able to at least get defined coordinates?"

The dragon chuckled again. Fine. That was a little too much to hope for, apparently.

"This cavern of truth is indeed one of those tucked-away places. It does not require crossing land or sea or traversing distance geographically. Instead, those who seek must traverse magic to reach this place, walk through mists having no connection to time or space, only reality." The dragon gathered its forelegs under it, settling somewhat like a cat with its paws tucked under its chest. "Bennett. The Consortium's witch knows how to traverse the mists. She obtains certain herbs and plants in this way. Go with her, and the caverns will be near where she forages. Be ready, though, because I am not the only one with this knowledge and you are not the only one seeking possession of the red shoes."

Witch. Peeraphan turned to Bennett. "Is Thomas a witch?"

"No." Bennett's response was dry and concise. "He's a werewolf. I realize we were remiss in specifying earlier this evening."

Well, werewolves and vampires didn't exactly get along in most of the movies and books Peeraphan remembered. "Do you have an org chart or something? If it's something you're willing to share, it might help me process all the surprises. The way this night is going, they just keep coming. I'm not really sure when my brain is just going to shut down and decide I need a reboot, but until it does, I'm doing my best to just take things as they come."

Bennett stared at her with his ruby red eyes. She stared back. Vampire. Sidhe. Little flying fae. Werewolf. She had no idea what Asamoah was—maybe Asamoah was the witch. Or there was someone else she hadn't met yet.

"A more detailed overview of the Darke Consortium seems appropriate," the dragon interjected. "I am open to new members, assuming you survive, little bird. I do hope for the best. Keeping in mind the urgency you rightly raised earlier, the both of you should return to the manor and get rest before heading out. You will need it. Oh, and another thing—as hard as a place is to get to, it is sometimes even more difficult to get back. Even once you manage to return, if you do, you will be forever changed. There is no more hiding once you've faced the full truth of yourself."

ELEVEN

BENNETT

"Dawn is close." Bennett opened the door to the guest room for Peeraphan. "I understand you want to set out as soon as possible, but we were warned to get what rest we could. I also literally cannot be of help to you during the majority of the day. I will send Duncan to watch over your rest while I retire."

Peeraphan had entered and headed toward the nightstand, where two tiny faces peeked out from their pouch. The two sugar gliders burst out of the pouch and reached the edge of the nightstand. Then, one after the other, they each leaped to her, their tiny legs outstretched so they resembled furry squares with heads and tails. They each landed on her forearm, more or less, and climbed their way up her arm to sit on her shoulders.

"I really need to fix the zipper so it closes properly." She had a sweet smile for her companions, one that called to him.

Again a pang tapped the long forgotten heart deep inside him and he did not want to address what it meant. As she picked up the pouch and fiddled with the closure, he decided to take his leave.

But as he stepped back, she looked up. "Wait."

An edge of panic to her voice stopped him when he might have otherwise gone before she could move to prevent him from leaving.

"You arrived at the theater yesterday at dusk, before the sunset..." Her observation tapered off, open ended—an invitation for added information. As if she had not been given far more than most could digest in less than a complete day.

"Most vampires cannot walk in daylight, you are correct. As a general rule, we are...inactive while the sun is up. But with age and power, usually a combination of the two, a very few vampires can rise earlier and stand in the dying light. In contrast, I know of only one or two in existence who could linger to watch the dawn. And of those, only one still survives."

"So you are a combination of old and powerful." She sat on the edge of the bed, looking petite and tempting in his dress shirt. He was not sure if Duncan had informed her whose clothes she was wearing, but Bennett experienced a certain satisfaction seeing her in them.

"Do you have a coffin you have to return to for your rest?"

He smiled. "I do not require a coffin, no. But I do find a certain security in my own space, safe from sunlight."

She glanced around the guest room, with its several large windows. "These drapes are as thick as blackout curtains."

His attention sharpened. "They are. We occasionally host other vampires as guests. Rarely. Our guest rooms are intended to accommodate a variety of supernatural needs. Is this line of discussion leading to an invitation?"

Her eyes shone a deeper brown in the soft light of the lamps, her regard a mix of emotions he could not define. He wondered if she could. After a long moment, she said simply, "I don't want to do anything, but... I would feel safer if you stayed."

"When I retire for the day, I am unresponsive." He did his best to make sure she understood. She was allowing him to see a vulnerable side to her, and he did not wish to mislead her in any way. "It would be like sharing the presence of the dead."

The tiny muscles along her jaw tightened under her skin, but she only nodded. "Everyone I've met tonight, they've all been kind. I just... you...we've been through a lot in a really short amount of time and I don't think I could settle my nerves around anyone else right now. Maybe if I got to know them better. Maybe later. But not right now."

He did not want to tax her further by arguing with her. Instead, he moved to each window and drew the drapes securely to guard against the light. He also pressed a button on the control panel by the door, changing the opacity of the window glass to further ensure his safety. The manor was built in a classic style, but he had been investing in up-to-date technology as part of his management of the property. He turned to her. "To be clear, you're certain you want my presence, even if I'm a corpse?"

She bit her lip. "It's not like I'm going to ask you to curl up in the closet or on a chair."

He gave her a half smile. "I could lie on the floor. Perhaps under the bed, even."

"Oh no." She laughed, her shoulders finally relaxing. "That doesn't sound comfortable at all. Would you be, though? I mean, even if you had to be in a dark place to protect yourself from the sun, is comfort a consideration if you're unresponsive?"

He shook his head in the negative. "No. I wouldn't be aware to care."

She hesitated, then seemed to make a decision to press forward. "I apologize if this is too private, but you've had a partner in the past, a lover. If you shared a room, maybe you had a sensible arrangement for daytime?"

He and Victoria had, in fact. Addressing memories seemed inevitable tonight—this morning—so he ceased mentally dodging them. "Victoria slept in her own suite. I would go to her when I rose each evening. She rarely stayed with me during the day."

His chest was tight. His skin felt chilled. Sorrow had been locked away and he wondered if there was truly no time limit to grieving. Of course not. Even a vampire had a soul with which to mourn a mate.

"I see." Peeraphan nodded. "Thank you for sharing with me."

Though she had not asked, he continued, giving himself over to the end of this past story. Needing to speak and let it out. "Our nights together were happy, working with the Consortium and sharing time together. Those nights ran into one another until years went by without my noticing them. But I am immortal and she was human. I retired with the dawn one morning, and she passed peacefully of old age while taking a nap in the afternoon, when I could not be there to listen to her heart beat for the last time."

The mournful music of his memories rose up in a crescendo and broke inside him. All at once, his muscles relaxed and he took in a breath, not because he needed the air but because his body needed to expand and create space in his chest.

"I'm sorry," Peeraphan whispered.

He shook his head, giving himself over to remembered fragments before the sun had risen on that day, and also the moment he had risen and looked for Victoria as he always did. And then he had found her, at peace. "I had offered her immortality with me long before, and she declined for her own reasons. So she lived with me, and left me, in the space of a few decades. It was her choice, the right thing for her. I am content to have shared happiness with her in those years."

Not a lie, though close. He was more conscious than usual of how many of them skirted the edges of truth and lies to keep moving forward through each night. Of course he would have preferred to have spent eternity with Victoria, but only if she had chosen the same. She had not, and he respected her choice. He had been bereft with her passing, had locked away the emotions and refused to dwell on the memories, avoided connecting with individual mortals. Time had worn away the jagged edges for him, though. Speaking with Peeraphan had offered him a way to truly lay those memories to rest, in a way he could not have done speaking to anyone else who knew him and her.

In any case, Peeraphan stood before him now, not Victoria, and he was not tempted to compare the two. Thankfully. Both deserved better.

He gave Peeraphan a half smile, wanting to lift the mood and tease her charming curiosity back to life.

"When I retire for the day, it is not simply sleeping like the dead. I am dead." He wanted badly to reach out and touch her in some reassuring way, but she might not welcome it. He slipped his hands into his trouser pockets to better resist the urge. "It is a reality of who and what I am. Vampires might be immortal, but we are not living in the way mortal humans live and breathe. The difference might not be as apparent at night when we are active, but during the day it is much harder to ignore. We might be more than animated corpses, or the walking dead, but there is a distinct difference between my body and that of the living partner. I'll ask again: Are you certain you are comfortable resting next to a corpse?"

She didn't respond immediately, the way some hopeful humans had in the past with their impulsive assurances that they indeed knew exactly what they were requesting when they asked to stay with him. Too often, those people had kept the romanticized view of what it would be like to be with the supernatural. But she did not look away, either, the way some did when they were offering themselves to him unwillingly. Instead, she studied him, and for once, he found himself without any theories of what might be going through her mind.

Finally, she spoke. "I am definitely a little freaked out at the idea of sharing a bed with a corpse."

He lifted his hands out of his pockets and spread them wide, intending to indicate he respected her wishes. No harm, no foul. "It is okay to change your mind. That is a good start in speaking truths."

She reached out and caught one of his hands in hers. "Both of us need rest, you're right. Truthfully, I'm frightened of how all of this is going to catch up with me the minute I'm alone. So I asked you to stay. But I'm taking my request back for two reasons."

He nodded, giving her the chance to continue.

"The first, because even with your love, the two of you didn't share space while you were at rest during the day. Out of respect for you, I don't want to ask for that. It wouldn't be right. Second, even if I don't want to process through what's happening to me, I should. I can. And...and third, I'm very attracted to you, so I want to take a step back and make sure I'm feeling this way for the right reasons and not as some potentially harmful misdirection."

There were so many layers to her reasoning, he found himself mentally racing to try to catch up. Oh, it wasn't as if he was unaware of the attraction between them. Quite the opposite. Perhaps he had been too busy attempting to hold himself in check so he would not be taking advantage of her when she had need of his help. He had been focused on the immediate issues at hand without considering how much was new to her, full of possibilities. She was incredibly optimistic and positive about making the most of these new experiences.

And he was thinking entirely too hard. Keeping it simple, he agreed with her in every way. He could take a small step forward to meet her honesty with some of his own.

He curled his fingers around her hand and gently tugged until she stood. Moving slowly so she had plenty of time to decline or step away if she wanted, he leaned forward until their foreheads almost touched. "I'm going to kiss you now. If you don't want me to, say stop, and I will."

She closed her eyes and tilted her face up toward him in invitation. "Don't stop."

He brushed his lips over hers and groaned. So soft. He pressed a kiss at the corner of her mouth and when she opened for him, he settled his mouth over hers and tasted her. She was both sweet and hot, and desire swept through him faster than he was prepared for.

She was not passive or waiting for him, either. As their kiss deepened, she had closed the space between them, her hands against his chest balling up the fabric of his shirt as her body melded against his. He closed his arms around her, encouraging her with one hand at the small of her back. He coasted the other up her spine and into her silken hair so he could cup the back of her head.

An alarmed bark caused her to jerk back a few inches and gasp. He didn't let her go, because she was already leaning back enough that she might fall without his support.

Glaring out at him over one shoulder from beneath her hair were her two sugar gliders.

"Oh wow." She pulled away from him and he let her go once he was sure she was steady on her feet. "I'm sorry."

He wasn't certain whether her apology was directed at him or her two little companions. "There is no need to apologize to me. You always have the right to let me know when you no longer want things to continue."

She gathered the two sugar gliders into her hands and gave them each a nuzzle before placing them back into their carry pouch and zipping it closed. "Thank you."

Rather than leaving the pouch on the nightstand, she picked it up and glanced around.

He had no idea what she was looking for, so he raised an eyebrow at her.

She bit her lip. "At home, they have an enclosure in my sitting area, outside my bedroom. It's tucked into a corner to protect them from direct daylight. I think I mentioned before that they're nocturnal, too. I was thinking that a closet or something might help them feel more secure."

He lifted a corner of his mouth and stepped back so she could pass by him and get to the closet at the opposite end of the room. "By all means."

A light, teasing sensation tickled him deep inside his chest, warm and effervescent, an emotion he didn't have a name for and couldn't remember if he'd ever experienced. She was so easy to read, and yet so many unpredictable things happened when it came to her. He found himself off balance even as he was tempted to pounce on her.

Seemingly oblivious, she slipped past him and picked up her bag on her way to the closet. She looked inside, studying the walls and ceiling before placing her bag on the floor and the pouch on top. "Doesn't look like there's any vents or crevices for them to run off through on an adventure. I figure the familiar scent of my stuff will help them settle down, too, and hopefully they'll snooze for the day."

"It seems reasonable. If we need to put together some other solution for them, I think Duncan and Thomas will enjoy the mental exercise." He remained where he'd been standing as she closed the closet door.

When she returned, her gaze shone with curiosity and, he thought, heated interest. An interest he returned, perhaps more intensely than either of them were prepared for, so he was acutely conflicted as he sensed the impending sunrise beyond the blackout curtains. He gave her an apologetic smile, wincing at the sudden hurt in her eyes. "I sincerely wish we had more time to explore this... development between us."

Her steps slowed as she hesitated. She came to a stop just out of arm's reach, and he wanted to curse the distance she left between them.

"I only have enough time to help you into bed," he said as he tipped his head to catch her downcast gaze. When he had eye contact from her again, he continued hurriedly, "I would stay if I could. Perhaps you've heard those words before, but I imagine the circumstances were somewhat different. I can only ask you with utmost sincerity to allow me to settle you for rest before I return to my rooms for the day."

She didn't answer, but she edged past him to the side of the guest bed. He reached past her and pulled back the covers, placing a hand on the small of her back to gently urge her into the bed. She lay down on her back, looking up at him with her fingers curled over the top of the blanket. There was awareness in her gaze, and a stillness, the kind of patience of a soul much older than her physical years.

He wanted to be sure she knew his thoughts. "I am conflicted. You make me consider options I wouldn't normally want."

"I've done a complete pendulum swing on what I thought I wanted, and I'm still confused," she whispered. "I think it would be good for us both to think through things on our own some more, then come to a better understanding. We can talk about it tonight, if you want."

"I do." Her words took the edge off the anxiety he had begun to experience. Still, he wanted to leave her with some sense of security. "Ashke placed wards around your room. Duncan and Thomas will be alerted if you sleepwalk again and will help to make sure you don't come to harm. There is also now magic in the weave of the comforter to help keep you safely tucked in this bed. It is nothing you cannot consciously overcome if you exert your will, but I think it will be harder for you to get up and wander in your sleep. The day members of the Consortium are in the manor and ready to help you. It is my hope your rest will be more peaceful with this knowledge."

"And you?" Her question was the barest whisper. A human would not have heard it.

"I will be in my suite." The sun had almost risen. If he lingered any longer, she would find herself with no company but his dead body.

She nodded, her fingers tightening over the covers as she maintained eye contact with him.

Much about her perception of reality had been changed in the space of less than a day. All things considered, she was doing very well.

He smiled gently at her. He could not remember when he had expressed such a range of emotions toward another being in such a short space of time. "Today is not the day to manage it all at once. You have your life to prioritize and you need your strength. Have a good rest."

"Thank you, Bennett."

He left her, then, closing the door quietly behind him.

TWELVE

THOMAS

Thomas waited, propped up against a windowsill at the far end of the hall so he had a clear line of sight past Punch's guest room and down to the stairway at the other end. The manor had been built by humans and while the Consortium had added magical safety measures, soundproofing hadn't been one of the features deemed necessary for the guest rooms. He could hear the conversation going on inside the room.

The sky was just beginning to lighten with the oncoming dawn. He did a lot of waiting in his line of work, but it wouldn't be long now.

Bennett shot out of the guest room, still managing to close the door gently behind him despite the impetus daybreak lent to his retreat. Thomas straightened, making sure he caught the vampire's attention.

"Cutting it close," Thomas said, keeping his voice low enough for Bennett's ears only, even in a manor full of supernaturals.

Bennett's upper lip curled into a snarl, but he faced Thomas. It said something that the vampire was willing to pause on his way to his own rooms despite the rising sun. Another few minutes and Bennett would fall wherever he stood, his body at the mercy of whoever might be nearby.

Thomas would keep it quick. "Punch is family to me, vampire. Keep that in mind."

Bennett blinked slowly, letting his lip relax and his features smooth. "Noted." He paused, then continued. "For what it's worth, I do not have plans and I have no desire to cause her pain. I find myself honestly making decisions moment to moment, without any certainty about what will happen next. She brings with her an unsettling amount of unpredictability."

Thomas grunted. He wouldn't know. The Punch he remembered was a little girl, years from puberty. She'd had a quiet, steady personality for a child. He would have to get to know the adult she had become. "I'll take over guarding her for now."

Bennett nodded sharply, then left. It was hard to track the vampire's movement, faster than a werewolf's. Fortunately, vampires couldn't maintain such speeds for long. Werewolves might be a fraction slower, but they could maintain their pace longer.

Thomas sighed and settled in on the wide windowsill. The child Punch had been probably would have curled into a ledge like the ones in this hallway, sitting and reading, half hidden by the curtains. She'd been different from her cousins, requiring little to no attention from the adults and desiring it even less from the other children. She had always had a thick novel or even two in her backpack and had a knack for finding quiet nooks and crannies.

More often than not, she could be found tucked under a piano in someone's living room or a dining-room table while others were in the kitchen or living room watching television or playing games together. Because she was quiet, if there was a household pet, it would curl up next to her. He had started to keep tabs on her because she was vulnerable away from the rest of the family, the rest of the pack.

And here she was again, away from the safety of family.

"Thomas?" Ashke appeared, floating at eye level. "I've put

more glamours around the property. If we have another unantici-pated flight, no one will see from outside the property."

"Good." Thomas nodded and glanced out the window, his gaze sweeping over the grounds. He'd made certain there was no land-scaping close to the manor, minimizing any dead zones or blind spots in the surveillance systems he and Ashke had established. The uncer-tain light at dawn and dusk were the times to be extra wary, though. He would know, they were his favorite times to hunt. "Why don't you go get some rest?"

"You're not going to sleep at all?" the fairy asked.

Thomas shrugged. "A werewolf my age can go a few nights without sleep."

He'd been turned centuries ago, on a different continent and far away from his home village in what was now considered Thailand. It had taken him a long time to find his way back, and even longer to control who and what he had become—a werewolf. But he had stayed near his family through the generations, always known as a distant cousin or an estranged uncle. Coming and going as his rela-tives lived their lives and passed away, doing what he could to ensure his family thrived through the changing times. He even migrated to the United States with them.

"Okay." Ashke did a reverse flip in the air. "It's been an exciting night. I'm tempted to stay up, too. Wouldn't want to miss anything. You said you know her?"

Thomas scowled for a moment, then forced himself to relax. If he was going to declare Punch family to Bennett, Ashke's ques-tion was also fair. "To Punch and her parents, I'm sort of a distant cousin."

"Is that close?" Ashke tipped his head to one side. "I find humans are very inconsistent in how they define family."

Thomas chuckled. "That's not a bad thing. There are a lot of

definitions for family. Among the people I was born to and spent my
time with, family was family no matter how many steps removed or
how distant the relation."

When it came to Thai communities that he and Punch were a
part of, it sometimes seemed everyone was an uncle or an aunt or
a cousin, whether they were actual blood relations or not. Thomas
couldn't remember whether that had been a mentality carried with
them from Thailand or if it had been a natural attitude developed
as Thai Americans who gathered as communities here in the States.
Either way, Punch was one of many cousins, and he'd been mildly
interested in all of them, the way anyone finds pups cute as long as
they belong to someone else.

She'd never asked much of him. There were no demands to play
or help in some way. She did smile at him, though, and offer to share
her snacks if she had them. She wasn't afraid of him, the way some
of the other children were if he got surly. She just gave him space, so
it got comfortable for him to linger at the edge of hers.

If he'd had a favorite, it probably cost little to admit now that
she had been his. She had been the closest one he had ever come to
thinking of as a sibling.

"Did you part ways for a while?" Ashke's curiosity wasn't
anywhere near sated. "Seems like her arrival was a surprise for
everyone."

"Yeah." Thomas hesitated, but he was thinking along the same
lines as Ashke's questions anyway. It didn't hurt to think out loud for
once. "I'm long-lived. Maybe not as long as you fae, or Asamoah,
or even Bennett, but werewolves live much longer than humans. The
hard part about being near extended family was that none of them
knew I wasn't like them. I had to leave before they noticed I wasn't
aging."

"Ah." There was a lot of understanding packed into that one

syllable. For all his lighthearted chatter, Ashke had lived twice, maybe three times Thomas's lifetime. Once somebody could claim they were centuries old, it wasn't particularly interesting to count how many centuries.

Thomas had planned to come back after a few decades, when memories faded, and the one family member who had known his secret would welcome him back as a nephew. Then for a few years, he would have family again.

He was a lone wolf. Always had been. Those few years, every few decades, were enough to fulfill his need for anything resembling a pack.

"Punch grew up while I was away. We lost touch," Thomas finished. Suddenly, he didn't feel talkative anymore.

Ashke seemed to sense the change in mood. "All right. I'll be around later, then."

Thomas nodded as the fae slipped out the window and flew into the first rays of sunlight over the treetops. It was hours before the sound of blankets rustling let him know Punch had woken. Took her a bit longer to emerge, but when she did, her face still showed signs of fatigue. "Did you get enough rest?" he asked.

Punch let out a surprised squeak and two pencil-sharpener growls sounded in response from somewhere on her person. Thomas fought to keep a smile from his face. He hadn't meant to startle her and didn't want her to think he'd done it on purpose for his own amusement. He lifted both his hands, palms out, signaling that he meant no harm.

She relaxed after a moment and gave him what seemed like a self-conscious smile. "I slept enough."

He scowled. "It's only just noon. You slept for about five or six hours. Last I remember, humans require eight or nine."

"No one I know gets a full eight hours on a regular basis."

Punch shook her head, sounding amused. She was pale under her complexion and the delicate skin under her eyes was so dark, she looked bruised. "Back in college, I could go an entire semester on four hours or less a night. These days, I wake up pretty naturally after about six hours."

If that was the case, the red shoes were continuing to drain her. Thomas didn't like that. Not at all.

"How about lunch?" He tried to pitch his voice to tempt her, the way he remembered was effective when they'd been children and he realized she'd been reading for so long, she'd missed a meal. "Asamoah is cooking today and there's always a lot of interesting things to try."

"I could eat." She perked up a bit at his suggestion. Then she glanced down at her rumpled clothes. "Oh..."

"We're casual here," Thomas assured her.

"Okay. Food sounds like a great idea," Punch agreed, giving him a shy smile. It was familiar and he found himself returning it.

He jerked his head to indicate she should accompany him down the hallway and they walked together. Or rather, he walked. The shoes were influencing her and he wasn't sure she was aware, but she was weaving as she walked, unsteady. He nudged her with his elbow after she stumbled again and she took his arm.

He was relieved when they entered the kitchen, where he could encourage her to take a seat and stay off her treacherous feet. They were subtle, those shoes. They seemed to lull her into a false sense of confidence in her walk, then caused her to slip or stumble at the worst possible moment.

Asamoah greeted them both with a wide smile. "There's a lemon and basil pesto to go with a grilled peach and sliced prosciutto salad of baby spinach and other leafy greens. There's also Ghanaian-style jollof rice with cubed beef brisket and a seafood coconut curry. I wasn't certain what flavors you liked best, so I prepared a variety. These dishes get a good amount of love here, so take what appeals to you and don't worry about what doesn't suit you—it won't go to waste."

Peeraphan gave him a nod and smiled quickly at Ellery, who was washing dishes at the sink.

Ellery was another fae, slight of build and with a rich, earthy-brown complexion. They didn't say anything, but their scent changed as they tensed minutely. Thomas drew breath to say something, but Duncan smoothly beat him to it.

Duncan noticed her attention. "Ah. Ellery is very shy. I must ask you to respect their peace and only speak to them when they have approached you first. Come to me with any requests."

"Okay." Peeraphan had looked at Duncan when he spoke. By the time she glanced back to the sink, Ellery had gone.

Thomas only shrugged when Punch's questioning gaze fell on him. Very shy, yes. Duncan was fae and the fae didn't lie. He picked up a plate from the stack at the end of the counter and handed it to Punch, then took one for himself and began to serve himself portions of food. When Asamoah cooked, the dishes could come from anywhere around the world, and every one had a different origin of cuisine. It all tasted amazing together.

Once they were seated at the table, she didn't lift her spoon and fork until he did. He guessed she didn't want to eat alone and he was hungry, so he ate. Today, he tried a bite of the salad first. Flavors burst across his palate, sweet and salty, crisp and light. It was good, but he went for the jollof rice next. It was rich and meaty, savory with spices, and warming right to the core, definitely more satisfying for him. The seafood coconut curry was a close second today. It had salty heat balanced with a slight sweetness, finishing with a satisfying umami flavor lingering in his mouth. It had some of his favorite shellfish, but every bite left him wanting more and that wasn't wise for a werewolf around others.

Punch was finishing off her portion of jollof rice and her eyes rolled so hard, Thomas thought she might be able to see all the way to her memories of yesterday. "Mmm. This is all so good."

Asamoah grinned. "Do you have a favorite? Is this your first time tasting any of these?"

"I've never had jollof rice before," Punch admitted. "And I've had a lot of different kinds of curry, but this one is Caribbean style, isn't it? I'm more used to Thai style or South Asian."

Asamoah nodded, his grin only widening. "I'll have to introduce you to Nigerian jollof rice, too, to be fair. You're right about the curry. Is it spicy enough for you? Too spicy?"

They launched into a discussion about various curries and levels of spice. Thomas let the conversation flow around him, considering how worldly Punch had become for a human. She'd obviously grown to appreciate a broad range of foods from different cultures and cuisines. She held herself with confidence and her conversation style was engaging, personable. She made it easy to be around her. He wasn't surprised Asamoah was enjoying her company.

She was a bright contrast to either Thomas or Bennett. He could admit he and the vampire were dour most of the time. Even if they were in good moods, they preferred to snarl and snap at each other. Duncan was only slightly better, the fae tending to be aloof and enigmatic. Usually. Punch was drawing even the reserved Duncan out of his stiff shell.

"Will you join us?" Her question was posed sweetly, her eyes open wide and her expression earnest.

Asamoah began putting a plate together for himself. "Coming, sidhe?"

Duncan cleared his throat. "I generally fill the position of butler in this household."

Peeraphan nodded. Thomas watched as she obviously kept her thoughts to herself, whatever they were, and Duncan struggled between a wish to accept her invitation and the desire to maintain propriety.

But Asamaoh chuckled, breaking the awkward silence. "A butler. One of the Seelie High Court? You define the role you play in this household, sidhe, same as I do, and I think labels need not limit anyone here in what they wish to do. Besides, we are all considering her particular problem and searching for options to free her."

Thomas let his mouth quirk at the corner, knowing the sidhe would catch his amusement.

"Tch." Duncan's demeanor thawed a bit and there might have been a glint of blue flame in the glare he shot in Asamoah's direction. But when he turned to Peeraphan, his eyes were back to a cool silver. "I will join you, Miss Punch. It's easier to give guests a label for the most public-facing role I play in this household, but all of us are more than what may immediately seem obvious. Asamoah and I are both advisors for the Darke Consortium, as members of the household with greater depth of knowledge and experience. Bennett and Thomas prefer more direct roles in the acquisition of objects of power."

Asamoah broke in. "The back-and-forth between me and Duncan is a long-standing interplay. No worries, princess, the fae man was hungry and perhaps disgruntled that the only solution he had to offer was help cutting off the limbs trapped in those shoes. Your thoughtfulness is appreciated. The other members of the Consortium are not bad, of course, but they are a bit caught up in their own brooding existences."

Peeraphan almost spit water. She put the glass down carefully and pressed her napkin to her mouth before she looked up. For his part, Duncan had his neutral expression firmly in place. There might have been a quirk at the corner of his mouth. Maybe.

Thomas only scowled in Asamoah's direction. "The vampire, maybe. I'm just enjoying my relative solitude when I'm not called in to chase down dangerous items of power. Mine is not a brooding existence."

Asamaoh was laughing outright, a warm sound bubbling up from the belly, rolling over the entire room. "You two carry plenty of personal baggage, that's a fact. They also tend to get under each other's skin, even when Thomas is having a run on the furrier side of his personality."

"To be fair, they are driven by their respective natures." Duncan ate neatly, his posture upright and his movements elegant. "Historically, vampires and werewolves do not get along."

"I only know what I've picked up from watching movies and that's probably nowhere near accurate," Punch admitted. "For what it's worth, I've always generally been Team Werewolf."

Thomas grinned, inordinately pleased to hear that. Asamoah laughed again. Even Duncan stopped midsip and put his drink down.

Punch continued quickly, "Are the species at war, the way they're presented in movies or, you know, other games and stories?"

Duncan fielded that question. "Not more so than any other predators competing for resources. Among true animals, wolf packs compete with mountain lions and bears within similar territories, while lions and hyenas compete in other regions. At some points in the past, supernaturals such as vampires became more specific in their chosen prey and focused on hunting humans. As a result, they tended to consolidate their power in more heavily populated areas where they can feed in the relative anonymity of human crowds."

It was just as well to let an objective third party explain. Thomas had no desire to get into it.

Duncan focused in more on werewolves as part of his discussion and Thomas tuned in. "Werewolves have less control over their wilder forms, so they've stayed in more sparsely populated areas to reduce the amount of harm they might do and to avoid mobs of humans too frightened to learn to coexist. Vampires and werewolves each developed social structures, complete with biases and wariness. But when it comes to specific individuals, like Bennett and Thomas, the more immediate challenge for either of them is the strength of their individual personalities."

Hah. Well, it was all true. It was just something else to hear it said about him rather than living it.

"Thomas and Bennett." Asamoah shook his head. Thomas raised an eyebrow, but Asamoah kept his gaze on Punch as he continued, "Bennett was the first chosen for this consortium—or maybe he did the choosing. You'll have to ask him."

"Him or the dragon," Duncan interjected.

Asamoah grunted. "Not something I would bother the Lady with, really. It's more fun to prompt our Bennett. He was first and took on the position of steward once the contract was made with Lady Dragon."

Thomas had to agree it was more fun to poke Bennett.

"So Victoria Darke wasn't a part of the Consortium in an official capacity?" Punch asked.

Jealous? Thomas wondered, but thought that was out of character for Punch. There wasn't a sign of it in her expression, only curiosity still. He supposed it was natural to wonder about a person's past lovers. It was obvious there was something sparking between Bennett and Punch.

"No." Duncan shook his head slightly. "She helped research in some instances, early on, but she died before the Consortium was officially established."

Thomas didn't know much about Victoria Darke. He'd joined after the Darke Consortium had been up and running for at least a short while. Punch seemed to let the topic go in favor of asking about Bennett.

"So Bennett is the steward of what, exactly?" she asked. "This place? Or this Consortium?"

Duncan nodded. "The answer, simply, is both."

"I came from another consortium to help establish this one," Thomas offered. "They needed someone with experience to start fieldwork while the steward took care of administrative details."

He let his tone turn slightly mocking as he mentioned administrative details.

She gave him a faint smile. "You sound like you still reread your favorite 1959 science fiction novel. Still making a big deal out of officers working desk jobs and real soldiers going out into combat?"

He chuckled. It'd been one of the few rants Thomas would ever engage in when discussing best novels with another cousin, Stephen. "You didn't change much, Punch. Still have a wicked good memory."

Asamoah snorted.

Thomas glanced at Punch and thought she was cheering up some. "I spent time in actual military service. I've gained some nuance over the years. But vampires make administration and government an art form, and even if he refuses to be a major player in vampire society, Bennett definitely is better suited to organization and follow-up paperwork. He's had far more practice with words and numbers."

"Okay. Bennett is the steward—do you have an official title, Thomas?" She pulled her glass in front of her, holding on to it with both hands. "Are there a set number of roles or chairs or something?"

She wanted a seat at the table. That much was obvious. Well, it was worth discussing, later, after she was rid of the life-threatening curse currently making her feet tap against the stone floor of the kitchen.

Thomas shook his head. "No set number of chairs or other formal titles. We all take on duties around the grounds. I share oversight on security with Ashke when I'm on the property. Duncan acts as the main interface with all of us, so Ellery only has to communicate when they feel comfortable. Asamoah does amazing things with food and generally facilitates our research and brainstorming sessions. Our witch handles patching us back up when necessary and consults on any situations involving witchcraft, spells, and curses originated from humans. She also maintains the indoor and outdoor gardens, so don't pick anything without asking for permission. Even a weed isn't a weed if she put it there on purpose."

Punch laughed. "I think I'm going to like your witch."

Thomas grunted. He wouldn't be surprised if Marie got along well with Punch.

Soon, Punch's face took on a more determined expression. Uh oh. "What does a person have to do to apply for a position with the Consortium?"

He'd been waiting for it, so he answered, "There's no formal process of application. I stumbled into a situation where the sale of a mythic item was going down and I maybe had watched a few too many Indiana Jones movies. The Consortium based in the Northeastern United States had a representative on-site who jumped in before I made too much of a mess of the humans involved. I didn't want to be affiliated with any of the werewolf packs in the area, so working for the Consortium allowed me to keep my lone wolf status and still have the support of a team."

"My situation isn't very different." Excitement sparkled in her eyes.

Thomas popped a large piece of beef in his mouth and chewed, talking around it. "You got yourself trapped by a mythic item. You're sort of the definition of the victim in this situation."

"No." She came to her feet, pushing away from the table. Her rejection of the label was so strong, energy burst from her, and she was standing there with her wings spread.

Everyone froze.

It was a good thing she was still wearing the loose shirt and pants Duncan had given her the previous night. The pants had shifted down on her hips as her wings manifested and were staying up for the moment. She might lose them if she tried moving, though. Awkward.

Thomas did his best to keep in his laugh. It would ruin the assertiveness of the stance she was trying to maintain.

He lifted both hands, empty and open, his mouth curving in a slow smile. "All right. You're a protagonist with agency. Got it. Would've loved to see the kids' faces if you'd ever done this when we were younger and somebody tried to push you around."

"Teasing isn't a good look for you, especially when you're skating so close to patronizing." She glared at him. "You were never the type to make people upset when I was a kid."

"I reserve teasing for the people who can handle it. Picking on little kids doesn't qualify...and I apologize for patronizing you. Not my intention and definitely not called for." He held direct eye contact for a moment, until she felt her anger drain away at the quiet sadness in his gaze, then he looked away and continued his meal. "Speaking of qualifications, you also fill the prerequisite of having unique skills to counter paranormal forces. You can fly and apparently resist compulsion. Maybe need to develop those talents a bit, but the potential is there."

He thought she would continue to argue, but she seemed to let go of her anger between one long breath and the next.

She settled her wings to her sides, then scowled, possibly too worked up to make them disappear. "Still exploring the whole control thing, to be honest."

This time he barked out a laugh. "Aren't we all. No worries. Works in progress are a thing with members of any consortium."

Neither he nor Bennett were shining examples of control when it came to the more violent aspects of their natures. That was a topic for a later time.

"It might be nice to take a bit of a walk now," Asamoah suggested. "There is at least one more member of the Consortium you'll need to meet today and she likes to come in through the conservatory."

Thomas shot Asamoah a look but the muse only maintained a friendly, mild expression. Thomas didn't argue. If Asamoah wanted to change the direction of conversation, Thomas didn't want to insist on continuing.

"May I help with the dishes?" she asked.

Thomas cleared his throat. "I'll help with cleanup. You go ahead."

"I'll show you the way to the conservatory." Duncan lifted an arm, his hand outstretched to indicate the door through which they had entered.

She let the sidhe lead her away. "It was really nice sharing a meal with you all."

Thomas was glad she remembered not to thank anyone, not with fae around. He'd have to help her navigate how complicated it could be around supernaturals. And for him, being around family again brought its own set of complicated feelings.

He'd go for a run later in his wolf form. Things came clearer then.

One thing was for sure, with Punch awoken as a supernatural, he was determined not to leave her alone.

THIRTEEN

PEERAPHAN

This is the conservatory."

Peeraphan paused in the double doorway and took a moment to appreciate the sheer immensity of the space Duncan had just introduced her to. It was huge, massive, and while she hadn't seen it from the outside, she was absolutely sure that when she did, she would still believe it was much larger on the inside. It was not, however, enclosed within a blue box. Well, maybe she should withhold that assumption until she'd seen it from the outside. It was mostly glass, everywhere. Sure, the structure supporting the walls and curved ceiling was made of metal and concrete, but it had all been designed so the space was more about the gardens inside flowing almost seamlessly to the outside. It was breathtaking.

The stone tile path led from the doorway where she stood to a wide set of stairs and down just a few steps to a water feature of an elegant marble fountain and a deep koi pond. Trees and shrubs and flowers filled the spaces to either side as the paths split to encircle the water feature, branching into three different paths leading farther into the conservatory. The plantings were fully grown-in and lush, while still managed neatly. No plant was crowding or choking any other. Whoever was tending these gardens was really good at what they did. Peeraphan was betting the conservatory ambience changed with the light from dawn to dusk and well into night. No matter what time of day or night it might be, she was sure the experience would be equally magical.

In a particularly brightly lit spot was a cluster of dwarf banana trees and a specific tree Peeraphan never thought she would see growing in the Seattle area. Of course, this was indoors, and the tree could grow in California so it probably was fine indoors in this part of Washington state. Still, how was it getting enough light to flourish and even flower? She started to step over the border of petite flowers lining the bed to take a closer look.

"Don't step off the pathway," a voice snapped.

Peeraphan looked around and realized Duncan had disappeared. A woman strode up one of the pathways from deeper in the conservatory. She was dressed casually in hiking boots and close-fitting jeans streaked with dark dirt, as if she'd wiped her hands on her hips. She wore a soft flannel button-up shirt over a simple ribbed tank, and her dark brown hair was gathered into short pigtails just behind either ear. She had an angled jawline and high cheekbones complemented by softly curved cheeks and big brown eyes framed by subtly straight eyebrows above and slightly pronounced aegyo sal underneath. If she was wearing makeup, Peeraphan couldn't tell from a distance, but she had the Korean K-pop look down pat and she made it appear effortless. Her lips were even the peachy-pink-toned ombré Peeraphan liked to think looked like a girl had just finished eating a strawberry or cherry Popsicle. Heck, Peeraphan liked to do her makeup in a similar style sometimes.

As the woman approached, Peeraphan realized she was a couple inches taller. It was a new feeling. Peeraphan was already on the tall side when it came to other women of Asian descent. This woman had to be five foot six, maybe five foot eight. Not so tall by U.S. standards, but taller than average, for sure.

The woman came to a stop a few feet short of where Peeraphan waited and placed her hands on her hips. "I'm guessing Duncan or one of the others let you in, so I'm not going to insult you by asking what you're doing here. But I really wish they would give a few warnings to people they bring in here before leaving you to your own devices. Honestly, it would be better for everyone."

"You're right about the first part. It's possible Duncan didn't get to the latter because you arrived. I'm not sure." Peeraphan put on her best *unsure but please like me* smile and gave a little wave. "Hi. I'm Pccraphan, but you can just call me Punch. I arrived last night."

The other woman nodded and studied her for a moment. "Have you eaten yet?"

Pccraphan opened her mouth, closed it, then tried speaking again. "Just finished lunch actually. Do I look in need of a meal?"

Her parents and grandparents had always told her a guest should never go hungry, so maybe this woman was greeting her with the same belief in mind. But this question had been posed with a different inflection to it, and the woman was staring at her with brows drawn close in a worried expression.

"You look pale, and I don't mean Pacific Northwest-rarely-get-any-sun kind of pale." The woman tilted her head to one side, still studying her closely. "More like the color has drained from your face. And you said you just had lunch? Asamoah's lunch?"

Peeraphan nodded. "Come to think of it, I wouldn't say no to a nap. But it's probably more of a food coma kind of situation after an incredible lunch."

"Ashke filled me in on last night's dance across the moonlit stars." The woman smiled faintly. "Are you sure you got enough sleep?"

"Sure." Peeraphan was starting to get a little frustrated. Here she had introduced herself and this woman hadn't yet offered her name in return. Under normal circumstances, Peeraphan would've chalked it up to being distracted out of friendly concern. But in this place, names seemed to have a lot more behind them. It was possible this woman wasn't planning on trusting Peeraphan with it.

"Well, let's be careful with how far you wander anywhere today since we can't be sure what your current footwear is going to try as you get more tired." The woman was still scowling as she glared at Peeraphan's feet. She sighed. "It's a shame, because those are some gorgeous shoes."

Peeraphan giggled, the energy bubbling up from the loosening knot of tension in her gut. "I know, right? All mystical folklore aside, the style and color are timeless. And you'd think they would be torture to wear, considering what they're meant to do. They're not. They're freaking amazingly comfortable. It's obviously too good to be true, but sometimes I forget I'm wearing heels."

The other woman chuckled in response, an open and relaxed sound. "It'd be so much easier if items intended to kill a person looked as horrific as what they've been designed to do."

A few random images of particularly torturously designed shoes came to mind and Peeraphan lost it. She started laughing in earnest, gasping for air and then laughing even harder. It was infectious, because the other woman joined her and even reached out her hands to catch Peeraphan as she doubled over with the hilarity of it. The conversation wasn't even very funny—it was just a great release of anxious, nervous energy.

She might have started crying at the ridiculousness of it, but laughing felt better. Sure, she was feeling unhinged, but laughing was almost always her choice if she could manage it.

After a few moments, they both straightened. The woman looked down at Peeraphan's hands in hers. "You can call me Marie. I'm the witch who's going to help get your slippers off without having to drop a house on you."

Peeraphan gave Marie wide eyes and mock gasped, "Isn't dropping the house reserved for other witches?"

Marie shrugged. "Well, it's more my style to use a field of poppies to poison you, but lucky for everyone involved, I don't covet those shoes."

"Are poppy flowers poisonous?" Peeraphan was familiar with poppies in the context of seeds and bagels, and references to them in history classes. She hadn't thought a field of the flowers would really do harm in the real world. Then again, her understanding of the definition of the real world was evolving recently.

"It depends on the variety of poppy flower and whether you decide to ingest any parts of the plant as they are. I wouldn't recommend it." Marie sighed. "There are medicinal uses for the poppy seed and having a few sprinkled on a bagel is harmless. But let's not go farther down the rabbit hole on medicinal uses, because poppies aren't going to be the solution to you getting these shoes off and living to tell the tale."

Peeraphan wiped a tear from the corner of her eye. She was pretty sure it had been a happy tear from all the laughing, but she couldn't claim she wasn't teetering on the edge of hysterical no matter how many things she'd taken in stride over the course of the last twenty-four hours. Honestly, she was doing everything she could not to freak out, because it had been a lot—plus she really didn't want to die.

The dying part was especially messing with her mind, because she wanted to think there was a way out of this. Every time she did and she tried to get out of the shoes again, they just stayed on...and she thought about how much she wanted to dance.

Marie might have sensed Peeraphan needed a moment, because she fell silent and looked away toward the tree Peeraphan had been captivated by earlier. "I warned you not to step off the path for several reasons. Not all of the plants here in the conservatory are people friendly. And of that subset, not all of them are passive about the danger they represent to humans or other supernaturals. Since you are a supernatural I am not familiar with, it would be good for you not to touch anything in here until we know more about you. And at least one or two plants in here might try to eat you anyway. Maybe three."

Man-eating plants were not a common feature of most greenhouses. Somehow their presence made this conservatory even more epic in Peeraphan's estimation.

"I thought I recognized that one." Peeraphan rolled her shoulders back and shifted her stance to stand side by side with Marie as they both looked at the tree in question. "The English name would be plumeria, but the flower is called leelawadee in Thai. It's my mother's favorite."

"You're not wrong," Marie confirmed. "It's also called frangipani. Since you're referencing the Thai name, and you happen to be a legendary Thai bird person, can I assume you are at least partially Thai? I got Ashke's version of the situation. I might be a little short on details, especially regarding your conversation with Bennett and the dragon, but I figured it couldn't hurt to try a few things to get the shoes off with a bit of witchcraft."

"I'm willing to try almost anything." Peeraphan tried not to get too hopeful. "The dragon seemed pretty certain about a solution we could try."

Marie nodded. "And this dragon is wise. But she's also very old. The caveat with old things—especially as old as she is—is that the world changes and everything blurs together for such beings. As the

WINGS ONCE CURSED & BOUND

world evolves, the magic in the world also evolves. So there might be some things that work now that the dragon didn't think to try."

"That sounds fair." It made sense. But then again, magic and witchcraft and dragons were all new topics for her. Who was to say what was plausible?

"If it doesn't work, we can still make the journey in search of this cave of truth for you." Marie shrugged. "It can't hurt to try."

True.

Peeraphan followed Marie along one of the paths, curving through and around different parts of the indoor gardens. There were any number of cozy nooks and tempting spots intended for quiet introspection, or meditation maybe, or even to curl up and read in. Overall, the gardens probably didn't take up that much square footage. The various nooks had simply been skillfully arranged with plant life and seating and garden stones to create each private area. It was a really cool place.

Marie led Peeraphan to an area where the foliage opened up to the sky a little bit and several curving arches supported the dome-like glass ceiling. To one side of the clearing was a small table and set of chairs. A large pitcher and a satchel took up the majority of the table space. There was also a large bowl on the ground.

Marie walked over and tapped the back of one chair. "Have a seat."

Peeraphan did as she was asked.

Marie grabbed the pitcher. "Hang tight, I'll be right back."

She disappeared down one of the curving paths and returned a moment later. Kneeling, she edged the bowl closer to Peeraphan's feet and began pouring water from the pitcher. "So Bennett had an interesting idea with the seawater. He's not wrong about salt or running water, in general."

Mixed emotions swept through Peeraphan in a whirlwind.

Irritation was a tiny wisp compared to the exhilaration of flying, the butterfly-wing tickle of being pressed against Bennett, and the absolute joy of dancing through the air by moonlight...

"Whoa, those are some interesting shoes." Marie sat back on her heels, studying Peeraphan's feet.

Peeraphan realized she was sort of bouncing on the balls of her toes, despite remaining seated. With an effort, she stopped, pressing her feet flat on the ground. Or as flat as was possible wearing a cursed pair of heels.

Marie took the bowl in both hands. "Lift your feet for a second so I can slide this under, and then go ahead and put your feet in the bowl."

"There's nothing in there that's going to burn or hurt me, is there?" She didn't think so, but it also seemed foolish not to check.

"Just purified water for now," Marie responded. "I've got a few ideas to try, so we might be going through a number of footbaths."

And they did. Marie would add a few herbs, then hold her hands over the water. Peeraphan thought she detected something tickling the edge of her senses when Marie was concentrating. Nothing definite. Just a stirring of air and water, like vibrations or energy, but not so...tangible as either one.

"So, I'm trying a couple of different approaches," Marie explained between water changes. "I tried breaking the curse on the shoes themselves. But that generally requires knowing who cursed you."

"The shoes were given to me by a person I know." Peeraphan was hesitant to call Sirin a friend. "She said they were donated by a patron."

"Yeah, but this curse is old. Very old. Not likely to have been set by the person you knew, so figuring out their intentions doesn't help directly in this effort. It would be good for us to follow up on after you're safely out of these shoes, though." Marie set the bowl next to Peeraphan's feet again.

"There's also the origin of the shoes." Marie tossed in more herbs and a few drops of an herby-smelling oil this time. "They found the original fairy tale in the library and the source is Scandinavian. So using herbs and materials from that region might work as I try to magically break the curse that way."

Marie held her hands over the water and Peeraphan's feet again. The moments drew out long and Peeraphan did her best to think good thoughts—positivity and all that. Mostly, she wanted to be free of the shoes. Simple.

After a long minute, Marie shook her head. "Next."

Another bowl of water, more herbs. These looked distinctively different, and were mostly dried. "Since the origin of the shoes is Western and the nature of the curse also is, I'm trying East Asian herbs to support my magic this time."

Peeraphan tipped her head to one side. "Figuring the curse might not hold against a different kind of spell?"

Marie nodded. "Essentially, yes. Witchcraft isn't an exact practice. It's very personal. I'm half American, a quarter Korean, and a quarter Chinese. I know I draw my power from the natural world around me, and gain insight from working with growing things. Sometimes, herbs native to a particular region amplify my ability to work my will. It's how my witchcraft operates, anyway. I'm not formally trained."

Not confidence-inspiring, but Peeraphan studied Marie. There was an aura of competence about the woman. While she had to have known her words might foster doubt, she showed no outward signs of worrying what Peeraphan thought. Marie didn't seem to have anything to prove, at least not to Peeraphan. That built confidence, as far as Peeraphan was concerned. So she waited.

After another try, Marie sat back again and studied the shoes. "Good news and bad news."

"Is there any worse news than the fact that the shoes are still stuck on me?" Peeraphan asked.

"No."

Whew. Peeraphan let out the breath she'd been holding. "Okay. I could really use some good news."

"I can tell you the shoes were meant for you, specifically." Marie motioned for Peeraphan to lift her feet and took the bowl away. "I can also tell you that the woman who gave them to you wasn't the one who sent them."

"The patron was a vampire," Peeraphan confirmed, "and Bennett seemed to at least know who he was."

Marie nodded. "I haven't met Francesco directly, and I'd prefer not to. But I got the impression he has interacted with the shoes more than once."

"How does that even make sense?" Peeraphan clutched the sides of her chair.

Marie's lips twisted in a frown. "There are other individuals and organizations out there looking for mythic items. They use them for gain, or to sow chaos, or just to collect power. I'm thinking Francesco may have been using these to cause calamity, if you don't mind the phrasing. I don't know why, only get impressions from the shoes of those who've recently held them."

"Great." Peeraphan kicked her feet, letting them swing in an alternating rhythm. Then she realized she was moving her feet again and deliberately stilled them. "Why me specifically?"

"Also a good question." Marie rose and took the bowl to empty. When she returned, she sat in the chair opposite Peeraphan. "That, I don't know. Maybe you caught his attention someplace else, and so he started hunting you."

"That's reassuring." Peeraphan tried to keep her tone light, but her words sounded brittle even to her own ears. "I honestly don't do anything to catch attention, as far as I know. I just go to work, come home, go to rehearsal if I'm doing a show."

"You live alone?" Marie asked. "If you don't mind my asking."

Peeraphan nodded. "Ever since I left for college. I didn't want to rely on my parents' income anymore."

She'd wanted to be self-reliant and show her parents she wasn't a burden. Not that they'd ever implied she was. She'd just wanted to.

"Do you go out a lot at night?" Marie pulled a microfiber towel out of her satchel and handed it to Peeraphan. "For your feet."

Peeraphan bent to wipe down her ankles and the shoes. The satin was a few shades darker due to the wetting, but otherwise, still gorgeous. "I hardly ever go out at night. Too tired. I used to go dancing, but I haven't dated anyone who likes to dance in a while, so I haven't been for months now."

Seattle had a great dance scene, too. She could have gone alone, but she hadn't been ready for the whole socializing and maybe trying dating thing again yet.

She just wanted to dance.

Peeraphan realized she was staring at the shoes and made herself look up to meet Marie's gaze. "I'm not formally trained, either. I don't think there is training to be what I am. I'm mostly finding my way on my own and I haven't really made all that much progress. But a lot of it is instinct, and my gut generally tells me to stay in well-lit, populated places and to avoid standing out in a crowd."

Marie nodded. "I believe in trusting our instincts. Sometimes, we don't have access to training or resources or even generational knowledge. We have to teach ourselves."

"Yeah." It felt good to talk to someone who resonated with those sentiments. Who could say things Peeraphan might've said herself.

There was something soothing about this place, despite their current conversation, and she drank it all in. She felt a kindred spirit with Marie, and also with Duncan and Asamoah, these people she'd never experienced before. For once, she wasn't at a social gathering feeling surrounded by people, yet alone.

Every one of these people had a very private air about them, but they didn't make her feel like an outsider. Each of them simply included her in the shared group space while maintaining individual personal space. She wasn't sure how these people managed the balance of privacy and social relations, but it was so much better than how she'd struggled with community interactions in the past.

"This might not have worked, but we'll keep trying," Marie said, after a bit. "We won't leave you to deal with this alone."

Warmth bloomed in Peeraphan's chest. "I appreciate that."

FOURTEEN

BENNETT

ennett could have sought out Duncan or Ellery to find Peeraphan. He hadn't. Instead, he'd come to the guest room where he'd left her and discovered it empty. Even her small sugar glider companions were gone from the closet.

He turned slowly, surveying the room as irritation built rapidly into anger. It wasn't that she was gone, nor that she had even taken her tiny friends with her. It was that he'd come directly here with anticipation. He'd looked forward to finding her, and now he was disappointed. There was no reason to be.

Thus the irritation born of frustration.

He was behaving completely out of character, and was self-aware enough to recognize it, but not quite able to recover the professional detachment he preferred to maintain when it came to… anyone outside the Darke Consortium.

The longer he struggled with it and thought about the situation, the more irritated he became, because he was wasting time and energy. He shouldn't care.

But he did.

It had begun at the theater. He never should have looked into her eyes. But even then, he could have pulled back, maintained the detachment. But then he'd tasted her blood, her magic with its life-giving effervescence, and the boundaries he'd built within himself had cracked and crumbled.

He couldn't hold back, perhaps didn't want to, and he struggled to deal with feelings that activated more quickly and sank deeper into his consciousness whenever they related to her.

None of which would help him locate Peeraphan. Finding her was likely to amplify all of this, really, but he felt her presence would at least soothe the prickling need to be near her.

Leaving the room, he paused in the hallway only long enough to take in a deliberate breath through his nose and another through parted lips.

He didn't need to breathe to survive, but he did need to draw in breath to smell and taste the air. It was how he hunted.

He'd risen with Peeraphan at the forefront of his thoughts. He hadn't wanted to be near anyone in so many years, he'd stopped counting. He didn't have to. There had been a point when he'd known the number of years, months, weeks, right down to the days it had been since he'd lost the person he'd wanted to be with the most. The wanting had been an ache so fierce he couldn't stand the company of anyone who might have feelings for him. It hadn't ever disappeared completely, but it had thankfully faded, and the passing years had blurred as they'd gone by.

Now, after decades and more, he wanted to be in someone's company again. Guilt and defiance warred inside him. The memory of his beloved would have yelled at him, if it could, for being stubborn. He wanted to argue back, debate, plead, whisper, any exchange of words at all with her. She was dead, hopefully resting in peace. And his feelings for another, however new and undefined, shouldn't be ignored or he would be dismissing everything his previous love wanted for him as she had passed away.

He lifted his fingertips to his lips, lightly brushing against memories of the night before.

He was glad it was Peeraphan. Grateful it was someone who had respected his memory of his beloved so carefully. Angry that his choice was so simple, yet his feelings were such a complicated… mess.

It was a risk to allow himself to hunt her down, rather than calmly letting someone else find her and lead him to her. He couldn't, wouldn't go the safe route. Couldn't manage to disengage.

He wanted to experience the moment again when he found her, when she would glance up at him with her dark eyes, her kind heart looking out from them wary but unafraid.

Peeraphan was a completely new experience to him. Her quick decisions and impulsive actions, the way she took accountability for the outcomes of her choices—good or bad—were all personality traits he'd encountered in other people through the centuries, of course. But her particular spark, the timbre of her voice as she spoke, the way she moved through the world, and the effervescent flavor of her blood were uniquely hers.

Peeraphan was so very mortal in the way she thought and took action. Somehow, her impulsiveness was balanced with a maturity and yes, wisdom that Bennett had encountered in few people. She moved through this existence like a mortal, but she had the consideration and respect for others which came with the calm of a much older soul.

She had been in the hallway hours prior and he followed her scent trail downstairs and into the conservatory in the space between one second and the next. It took another moment to find her among the twisting paths that were deliberately designed to give the impression of more distance traveled.

He found her in a nook enclosed by varieties of eucalyptus,

potted to keep the trees from growing too tall for even the spacious conservatory. She was looking up into the branches of the fragrant shrubs and trees as her small companions scampered through the foliage.

He came to a full stop, struggling to control his drive. He could see her, reach out and touch her even. Approaching her caught up as he was in a hunt might frighten her, and definitely would frighten her sugar gliders. Neither would make her happy to see him. And he wanted her to be happy to see him.

As it was, a few inquisitive chirps and barks came from the foliage and he located both of them through the leaves.

Like their lady, the two tiny marsupials did not fear him. Though they might be compared to flying squirrels, these were not the prey animals running through the trees and across the forest floors of the Pacific Northwest. These were predators, in their own way, and though they might be wary of him as a bigger, badder, far more dangerous hunter than they were, it was not the same instinctive fear prey would experience.

Perhaps Peeraphan had a similar instinct buried in her lineage. There were many beings in legend who were described as part bird.

"How did you know to call yourself kinnaree?" he asked her, reining in his hunting drive and feasting on the sight of her, the scent of her.

It was enough. Barely.

"Hello to you, too." She smiled, giving the words a soft, welcoming feel. She held up one hand toward the foliage where her furry friends were hiding. "My mother taught me several traditional Thai dances when I was in college. One of them was Manora Buchayun. It's a portion of the folktale about the kinnaree Manora. As I was learning the dance, my mother told me the whole story so I'd have context and also because I've always loved folktales and mythology."

She smiled, her eyes taking on a faraway look. She must have been remembering. He did not want to interrupt what seemed to be a pleasant memory. Instead, he studied her face.

Her lips were curved in a soft, small smile, and her cheeks were ever so slightly flushed. Her arm was still raised above her head and she almost looked posed. There was a rustling in the leaves and one of the sugar gliders leapt, little paws outstretched and the loose fur-covered skin between wrist and ankle on each side stretched wide. It managed a somewhat controlled glide down to land on Peeraphan's palm, its momentum carrying it a bit farther until it ran down her arm to her shoulder. The second sugar glider followed, but stayed in her palm, having managed to stick its landing.

She gathered the one in her palm to her chest with a laugh. "In fact, I knew a version of the red shoe folktale because I also studied classical ballet. But there are different interpretations and definitely other red shoes in myth and even pop culture. The ruby slippers that took Dorothy home, for example. Myths change with the retelling. They morph from storyteller to storyteller, and sometimes they become something completely different from region to region. The story of Manora, the bird princess, holds some of its structure over time because the dances are taught. But other than knowing the bare minimum of what a kinnaree is—that they have wings and tails that at least the royal princesses like Manora can cast off to be mistaken for human form—the folktale doesn't tell me how to *be* a kinnaree."

There was a moment of silence and he waited, giving her space to fill it or not. Whichever she wanted to do. Now that he was near her, giving her what she needed mattered more than any fading feelings that had prompted him to search her out in the first place.

"Even when my parents finally recognized I was different, their first impulse was to ignore it. They had come a long way to build a new life, to give me more opportunities in my own life. They wanted me to grow up American, to look forward and become a part of this new place. Looking back into the past might be a fruitless endeavor and they wanted me to be happy and thrive."

He could understand that. Even if he had never had a child, never chosen to make an alliance with another vampire bloodline to procreate, he understood the desire to want the best for those in his life. He had wanted his Victoria to be happy and thrive for as long as she could. And she did.

Still lost in thought, Peeraphan continued, "My parents were a little disappointed when I switched from biology to the study of mythology and folklore. Honestly, I wasn't thinking about what I wanted to do with my life, only that studying to be a doctor and being in anatomy and physiology classes made me afraid that some-day, it'd be me on the dissection table. I didn't want to be discov-ered and studied to determine what made me what I am. Instead, I wanted to learn about myself, figure out if there were others like me, or at least others who weren't quite human."

She shrugged. "Not everyone has parents or aunties or uncles or grandparents to mentor them. Some first- and second- and even third-generation kids like me go in search of their cultural roots, relearn the language of their parents or grandparents or great-grandparents, learn to cook traditional dishes, study traditional music or dance. I'm trying to teach myself how to fly, among other things."

"Ah." He nodded and took a step closer. Her little friends didn't sound their alarm growls, so he took a second step to close the dis-tance between them. "I was born a vampire. Raised by vampires. Educated to survive and be successful as one of my kind."

To come into existence without guidance would have been diffi-cult. Frightening. He imagined it, and his desire to protect her from those feelings in the future amplified.

She tilted her head, just slightly, but it was still enough for him to see the pulse in her neck. "I thought vampires were made with a bite."

He should teach her awareness, so she could be cautious around other vampires. Not him. He would do everything in his power to ensure she need never be in fear for her life around him again.

"Some vampires are changed, and the process is begun with a bite. There is more to it." He shrugged. Best if he did not go into further detail unless she pressed further. "Others are born, like me, and we grow to adulthood like humans do. When we die, we rise. Because I was raised by vampires, I knew what I was and what I would become when my human life ended. Our society even had something of a ceremony around when those of us born as vampires decided to make the transition from our human lives to our vampire lives—a coming of age of sorts. I was able to make an informed decision. It's not the way for all born vampires. And for those who are made, the situations vary even more widely."

He had never doubted his desire to be a vampire. Never wished for a different fate, even centuries later, when his past love made a different choice and left him alone.

"So in vampire society, is there a major difference between being born and being made?" she asked. "I'm thinking of a bunch of movies I've watched over the years, and a TV show or two. Born vampires and made vampires were different classes in society."

"There are some vampire societies in the world where it matters. It does not for any vampiric province ruler on this continent." He lifted his hand and flicked his fingers, aware he might sound tired or perhaps even patronizing. He cleared his throat and attempted what he hoped was a better tone. "I don't care for those beliefs, personally, and I've lived long enough to have known plenty of my kind well enough to respect the individuals who deserve it. In truth, whether a vampire is born or made does not seem to decide how much potential power they have. I am not certain any correlation has been drawn or proven scientifically. Power does increase with age and success in the hunt. Some of our power is tied to how much we have fed, and for how long we have fed consistently."

"And do all vampires fly? Turn into bats?" Her questions were full of wonder, not horror. She was even leaning forward on the balls of her feet as her curiosity led her farther.

He smiled, amused. Delighted, even. "No. I fly. There may be one or two others in the world who do. It is a rarer talent and I am a reasonably seasoned vampire."

He was young enough in centuries to have the vanity not to want to be considered very old.

"Bats?" Her eyes sparkled with mischief.

He laughed. "I'm sorry to disappoint you, but no. There are many who can. I would not advise attempting to meet any of them without my escort."

"Wow." Not a whiff of caution from her, only wonder.

Perhaps he was doing her a disservice in not properly communicating why and how any other vampire could be a danger to her, and those she might hold dear.

"An adventure for another time." He shook his head, not because of her, but because he was already promising her another adventure after this night. Once she was free of the red shoes, he still intended to seek her out and be in her company, if she desired it.

He wasn't sure he recognized himself in his own actions. He and Thomas and everyone in the Consortium, including Asamoah and Ellery and Duncan and Ashke and Marie, were loners. They were apart from their own kind. Some of them could have found a community to join, to find companionship with others more like themselves. But all of the members of the Consortium, whether by choice or happenstance, had decided to live and work and spend their leisure time away from their supernatural communities. He, in particular, had lived for decades with no intention of breaking his solitude. He hadn't cared to.

And here he was, considering how to court possibly the only kinnaree currently alive.

He was almost appalled at the contradictions his current thoughts and feelings were creating within him. "For now, we both should proceed to the kitchen and have a quick bite to eat, then head out with the others. Marie left me a note saying we should be ready to leave at full dark."

"You think tonight will save me?" There was the tremor. Now her fear had surfaced. He thought it likely to have been there through the entire day, simmering just below surface thoughts. Anxieties grew in the dark when one wouldn't confront them in the light.

Instinctively, he focused on her primal emotion and he ruthlessly buried his sharpened hunger response. Fear was an incredible spice to any hunt and he had better control than to allow it to tempt him into breaking his chosen feeding restriction again. She would never again be put in a position of danger to save him, not if he could help it. She might not think of herself as an innocent, but the fresh perspective with which she experienced the world was a joy. He settled her firmly in the innocents category in his consciousness.

"I do not know if we will save you this night." He refused to lie to her, because he believed optimism with no certainty could be painfully cruel, but omitting the full truth was also a kind of lie. "But I hope so."

Her lips curved in a sad smile, her dark eyes almost liquid with unshed tears. "Thank you for your honesty. I couldn't bear false hope right now."

"Facing false hope requires strength better spent focused on your survival. I would be doing you a disservice to offer it to you."

His words did not feel sufficient, not in the face of the weight she had to bear on her own. She was too independent and too stubborn to lean on others. He admired her for it, but he also wished he had something else with which to offer her comfort. It had been so long since he even cared, and now he wondered if he even remembered how. He was rusty with this contempt for humanity. He paused, then opened his arms. "Will you accept comfort instead?"

She rushed into his arms with a speed almost superhuman. Her arms wrapped around his waist and she buried her face in the fabric of his shirt.

Carefully, because he wasn't absolutely certain where her sugar gliders were on her and he did not wish to do them harm, he closed his arms around her and held her close.

She was warm against his chest and within the circle of his embrace. He took in a breath to get the scent of her: bright citrus notes of lemongrass and fresh fruit blossoms, the richer whispers of frangipani and coconut, all tied together with the earthy element of sandalwood. Only when he was close like this could he smell and taste the complexity of her scent and remember the almost effervescent impact of her blood pulsing through her arteries. He thought perhaps her unique magics were manifesting through her scent and her blood, carried on air and water. If he tasted her tears, would they give him the same effects as her blood? Or like mermaid tears, would the emotion behind them influence the magic?

Regardless, she was filled with vitality, alive in a way he recognized as only coming with fleeting mortality.

Without thinking, he nuzzled her hair, so soft and silken against his lips. She stirred in his arms and he loosened his hold so she could step back, but she did not. She kept her hold around his waist and leaned back only enough to turn her face up to him.

"Kissing you last night was nice," she whispered.

If he had never thought of himself as damned in all his existence as a vampire, he thought he would be now, to resist such an invitation. He bent his head and she met him partway, her soft lips warm and pliant. She opened for him almost immediately, even teasing him with a flick of the tip of her tongue. He chuckled into her mouth and deepened their kiss until it was beyond teasing fun and more hunger, a giving and taking.

Desire burned through him and he could scent and taste her matching arousal. Her hands had tightened, gripping his waist and pulling him close as she melded her body to the length of him. He wanted nothing more than to bend her backward until her chin tipped up, exposing her throat...

He broke their kiss with a gasp, aware his fangs had extended. Her eyes opened, dilated and dark with her own passion, but she blinked as she took in the sight of his fangs. He straightened then, would have released her, but she didn't loosen her hold on his waist.

"Do you feed as part of sex?" Her voice was steady as she posed her question.

He pressed his lips together, willing his fangs to retract. "I have in the past. A vampire's facial structure changes in a true feeding— the lengthening of fangs is only the first stage. The upper and lower jaws come forward more to allow for a better bite on prey. As my face changes, I can be precise about my bite and feeding, or I can rend and tear, doing terrible damage."

He didn't breathe, didn't want to scent her fear. Not then. Really, he was hard-pressed to think of circumstances where he would ever want her to be afraid of him.

She kissed his lower jaw, her lips feather light against his skin. "But do you always feed?"

"No." The word came out harsh, dark, as his feelings churned in a mess inside him. "I have a dietary preference. I do not feed on innocent humans."

"In a lot of cultural and religious beliefs, sex and innocence don't go together. If you're having sex, does your partner still count as innocent?" Her voice was still calm but there was a thread of tension there.

Ah. He struggled to think her question through, remembering the night he'd had no choice but to feed on her or perish. She'd challenged him to define "innocent." Perhaps there was history there, for her. "The two are not mutually exclusive."

"Mmm." Her tone lightened and the corners of her mouth turned up slightly. "I agree. So?"

He wanted to kiss her again, but he sensed there was more than light curiosity to her question. A thorough answer was needed, so she could make an informed decision as to what would happen next between them. "I have fed during sex, when my partner found the sensations enhanced our intimacy. The moment when I break skin and begin to drink can bring a euphoria, sometimes immediate orgasm."

He had not been aware enough to lessen the shock of the experience for her, when he had fed on her. Had not been able to offer her the euphoria. Even before he had come to know more about her, he would have wanted to offer a kindness to her if he had to give in to necessity. Now that he knew her, and desired her, he wanted to give her pleasure, as he had with any partner. Simple.

But more than that, it was becoming important to him to contribute to Peeraphan's joy as she continued to explore life the way she did. He wanted to be a part of it. To give and also receive and experience the unique dance between the two of them—in the skies or between sheets. He looked forward to it.

Studying her, he grinned. "I can also refrain from feeding. I am more than skilled enough to bring us both to orgasm multiple times, regardless."

She laughed, the sound unfettered and genuinely joyous without breaking the intimacy between them. "Thank you for answering my question. I figured I should know before things got much hotter."

"To give you a better understanding of my feeding habits in general"—he kissed each corner of her mouth and noticed her sugar gliders had scampered down to the ground, heading back to the nearest tree trunk—"I have declared a feeding preference. It's easier to say I do not feed on innocent humans, and more reassuring to those who might hear it. In reality, I actively seek out and hunt human predators, those who would do others harm and take pleasure in their power over their victims."

She blinked, thick lashes sweeping down and back up to reveal her old soul again. "Is there a difference in taste?"

He nodded, lifting a hand to brush a few strands of her hair clear of her cheek. "It's an acquired taste, to be certain. Their blood is full-bodied, with a deep bitterness that leaves a dry mouthfeel. Still, it's very satisfying."

Her eyes were wide as she listened.

"Before you ask, I do not have to kill my targets and I usually do not." He paused. "But I have."

"Every circumstance is different, and I'm not in a position to judge everything you've ever done, but are you someone who's ever killed for cruel fun?" she asked, not pulling away from him but remaining still and patient, waiting to hear what he had to say.

"Never for fun," he said seriously. "I have fed more often than necessary for my own survival, to maintain my strength and ensure I had the power to protect those within my care. There are those who would hate me for what I've done. I will never stand completely in the light and wear white as they did in movies, once upon a time."

"I can accept that," she whispered. She rose up on her tiptoes and kissed him.

He let her, savoring the sensation of her lips brushing against his. Heat swept through him, chasing the sensation of touch.

He chuckled as she nipped his lower lip playfully. "Is it fair for you to bite, when I dare not?"

"You can bite," she whispered against his lips, "just a little, not enough to break skin. I don't think I want you to feed, at least not our first time."

His cock jerked, already erect in his dress slacks. He groaned. Pressed against him as she was, she had to be aware.

Her giggle—delighted, with no hint of cruelty—confirmed this.

He took her mouth, then. No more teasing. This kiss was carnal and eager, edging toward chaotic in the most delicious way. She met his energy with her own enthusiasm, bringing an element of saucy play he enjoyed. Her hips pressed into his and her hands drew him close. He let his own wander, coasting over the small of her back and gripping her behind, lifting until she barely had contact with the ground.

A low sound of what he thought was approval came from her throat and he set her back down, keeping one arm around her waist to steady her. He explored with his other hand, sliding up her side to grasp one of her breasts. He found her erect nipple with his thumb, gently rubbing over it through the fabric.

She gasped, and elation washed through him. Her reactions were wonderful.

A sharp bark came from somewhere above them, followed by a second. She jerked slightly and turned her head. "Someone is coming."

He growled, and paused to listen. She was right—Duncan had just entered the conservatory and was making his way along one of the paths. "Are your small friends purposely trained as lookouts?"

The sugar gliders had excellent senses. Not better than his, but he had been more distracted.

She smiled as she stepped back from him. It took effort to let her go. She ran her hands over her clothes to straighten them. "I've learned to pay attention to their natural behaviors."

He nodded.

She gave him a rueful smile. "If this night goes well, would you be interested in continuing where we just stopped?"

He darted in and gave her a vampire-quick kiss. "Yes."

She gave him a bright smile. "Okay."

FIFTEEN

PEERAPHAN

Peeraphan followed Marie through the dark, keeping her flashlight and headlamp trained downward on the trail in front of her. They'd all piled into an SUV and driven for about thirty minutes, give or take, before turning off the highway and onto a couple of smaller residential roads. The trailhead had been tucked between two private properties, with only minimal signage to indicate the trail was there at all.

"Are you certain you won't accept my offer to carry you?" Bennett asked quietly.

His lips brushed the shell of her ear, sending shivers of warmth through her and down her spine.

She shook her head, resisting the urge to look at him because she didn't want to blind him with her headlamp. "I'm okay so far."

"The offer remains, whenever the trail gets too rough."

Sure. Really, she should take him up on his kind offer. He had superhuman strength as a vampire and it wasn't like he hadn't already carried her in the recent past. In multiple situations.

It was just that she'd started out on this trail telling everyone the story of how her friend from Boston had walked two miles over gravel in stilettos without a single stumble, so she knew it was possible—if the shoes weren't cursed. Now here she was and it was the principle of the thing, for as long as her stubbornness could hold out.

Not her most shining moment. True. But it was happening.

If Peeraphan had been wearing any kind of sensible footwear for light hiking, she would have been fine. Wearing heels on the trail was arduous at best, not even taking into consideration the fact that her actually cursed shoes were literally trying to kill her at this point. Bennett had a hand cupped under her right elbow to help steady her every time she stumbled. He and Thomas, following behind a short distance, could both see in the dark and thus could see the trail ahead. It was Marie and Peeraphan who were equipped with headlamps and powerful utility flashlights. They were handy for self-defense, come to think of it: compact, fitting into the palm of the hand, and would add a little weight behind a punch.

Cory and Tobi were tucked safely in their carry pouch in the guest room closet back at the manor. She'd been confident in their bond with her to allow them to run loose in the conservatory. But out here, when she didn't know where they were going or what magic Marie was going to make happen, she didn't want to risk leaving her two furry friends behind someplace far away.

"This place will work," Marie said as she stepped off the trail and over a fallen moss-covered tree.

Peeraphan threw her leg over the trunk and sat on it, making sure she was steady before she brought her other leg over. She made sure of her footing before she stood again and continued to follow Marie past a few more silent shadows in the dark. The forests of the Pacific Northwest were lush and verdant, and Peeraphan had gone on her share of day hikes in them. But the feel of these woods was different, more mysterious, at night. Giant ferns and shrubs made it harder to discern where there was a clear path and whether you were going to walk into a huge tree. It was more necessary for them to be able to find their way than to go undetected, so they'd opted for the lights despite the sacrifice of stealth.

Marie didn't continue for long, stopping at the edge of a small clearing with a tiny trickling stream. The moon shone through breaks in the tree canopy, just a few streaks of pale light here and there.

"This is the place?" Thomas asked, stepping to Peeraphan's left.

Bennett didn't tug her, but he shifted his hand from her elbow to the small of her back. Thomas wasn't any kind of competition, but she wasn't sure if she should make a point of telling Bennett so or if it wouldn't change his reaction anyway. Now didn't seem to be the time and it wasn't over the top, even if it was a sign of jealousy. Besides, she liked the feel of Bennett's hand there.

"No, this isn't our destination." Marie shut off her headlamp and removed it, then turned to face them. "The place isn't anywhere in this world, but this will do to get us there."

Peeraphan followed Marie's actions, turning off her lights and tucking them away in the pockets of the trench coat Bennett had loaned her. It was ridiculously too big for her and made to end just above his knees. It engulfed her and extended well below her own. But it was warm, and she had pockets!

"We're using magic in a sympathetic spell to allow us to travel from one place to another." Marie was still expanding on her response to Thomas. "The place we're going to is unreachable by normal means. But it is located in deep forest, at the foot of mountains. It's not here in the Cascades, but those who looked for it where it was said to be located, once upon a time, didn't find it, either, because humans didn't know the way."

"How did you find it?" Bennett asked.

Marie held out a bundle of dried herb roots. "By accident, the first time. I ran out of my supply of jatamansi and my usual supplier didn't have any more. It's rare and even harder to find from a supplier who has good harvest management practices. So I brought the little I had left to this area, since my supplier said the plant liked to grow on moist, rocky slopes. I cast a finding spell, hoping I could find more of the plant or something similar but native to the Pacific Northwest. Instead, I traveled and found a place that isn't on any map in the human world."

She shrugged. "I go once a month, when I can, and I'm still finding herbs I never encountered anywhere else. When we go, we can approach the cave, but we can't venture too deep into the woods around the clearing."

"Who says?" both Bennett and Thomas asked at the same time.

Marie was silent for a moment, then answered in the darkness. "A hermit. I don't know his name. I think he was human, once. Now I don't know. Either way, the beings in those forests would pose a danger to someone like me and I'm not interested in pitting any of us against their strength, either. Keeping the neutrality of this clearing is important, so it's best to take the hermit's advice."

Okay, then.

"He's not a threat to us," Marie added. "Even when I go alone, he doesn't always show himself. His sense of self-preservation is the main reason he's survived alone where he is. He's like a forest mouse, not dangerous and mostly harmless, just very good at going undetected."

Bennett considered for a moment. "If he leaves us in peace, I will not hunt him."

"Agreed," Thomas joined in. "He's not on the menu for you anyway."

Bennett growled.

Peeraphan wondered at the surety in these two predators. Seriously, their confidence was off the scales, and from what she'd seen of Bennett's fight with the other vampire, vampires and were-wolves were every bit as deadly as old lore made them out to be. Probably more. People had a tendency to downplay the real danger anything besides themselves represented, always creating a human savior capable of winning against the things that struck fear into the hearts of humankind.

She was gaining new perspectives and realizing humans were not the apex predators in any part of the world. A new question to add to her growing library of questions to ask someday, when there was actually time to find out: What kinds of hunters were in the place they were going to?

It said something that no one bothered asking in advance, because she had to take this chance at surviving. She'd have gone regardless of whether she knew what else could be waiting there. Funny how a chance at not dying took priority over a chance of something else being able to kill you.

"Let's get going, then." Marie pressed on, her tone fairly cheerful. "When I cast my spell, focus on wanting to follow me wherever I go. That's it. Your intent matters. Don't get distracted or you'll remain here, or worse, get lost somewhere else."

And not knowing where could be very scary.

The number of ways she could die tonight were adding up, and Peeraphan wondered if she was actually coping with the layers of fear or if she was going to curl up in a ball somewhere and deal with the aftermath for months, maybe years, after. She could accept those consequences, if she had a lifetime to continue to look forward to.

Marie lifted her hands with a bundle of dried herbs nestled in her palms. She whispered words for only the wind to hear.

Peeraphan's power reveled in air and wind—more and more as she'd been purposely using it since the previous night—so she heard, too, but she didn't understand them. The witch's words were in a language Peeraphan didn't know, but the words had a familiar shape to them, like a sister language. Magic gathered around them, coming from the clearing. Marie's power was summoned from the plant life of the forest and she wasn't asking for more than the plants could give, as far as Peeraphan could tell. If anything, the plants were perking up, swaying with the night breezes. The air was fresh with the scents of evergreens and dew, moss and ferns.

The magic around them swirled with the wind, questing, searching. It coalesced into a circle of light on the forest floor at Marie's feet, no more than three feet in diameter. She turned to them, her eyes bright with power, her smile stunning. "Follow me."

The witch turned to face the circle, took a step, and fell through. Peeraphan stepped forward, but Bennett slipped his arms around her waist, holding her close from behind.

"We go together," he said, his voice loud enough for Marie and Thomas to hear his intentions as well. "Let me take our landing. Agreed?"

She had a chance to refuse, to argue. But what he said made sense. This way, she wouldn't go alone and he'd be immediately able to protect both her and Marie while Thomas brought up the rear. She nodded.

When she felt his arms tighten around her, lifting her slightly, she tucked her feet up and shut her eyes. She pictured Marie as she had just seen her, imagined following her. Guided imagery suited Peeraphan, visual cues being the easiest way she remembered things, and when she was sure she had a mental picture of Marie clear in her mind, she opened her eyes.

Mist. The mist was everywhere and they were still falling. There was no visibility, which was probably for the best. Easier to keep Marie in her thoughts and concentrate on following her to where she was going. Bennett's arms were a comforting security around her waist, his chest and abs a solid presence against her back. She was glad he'd come with her.

It wasn't as if she couldn't have taken the step herself—she'd spent all of her adult life first establishing and then maintaining her independence. She'd created a distance from her family for her own freedom but also with their safety and well-being in mind. Everything that had happened since the theater would mean changes to her life she hadn't even begun to consider, but she felt certain there would be more distance from her family because of it. Not once had she even thought to call them, ask them for help or support or comfort. It wasn't as if they wouldn't have tried. It was because she was afraid of the trouble and hurt it could bring them, because these problems were beyond anything her family could fix or even understand. And maybe going forward, she'd still have to manage alone, but since she had Bennett's company, she could appreciate his support in this moment.

They fell for what might have been forever, or only a half a moment. Then Bennett landed, taking the brunt of their combined weight with slightly bent knees. He took a few steps forward immediately, then set Peeraphan on her feet and let go, giving her back her personal space. As mist cleared around them, more mist poured up and out of a hole in the grass just behind them. Thomas popped up through the portal and landed in a crouch, like a superhero ready for combat.

The portal closed, leaving them in a moonlit clearing surrounded by rapidly dissipating mist. Marie stood a little farther to one side, smiling, her cheeks flushed pinky peach and her lips parted slightly. Her chest rose and fell noticeably as she breathed in her nose and out her mouth, catching her breath.

Magic, Peeraphan decided, exacted a different kind of price from user to user. Peeraphan's magic was something she'd been born with and she had a reservoir to draw from, in a way. She thought of it like stamina or cardiovascular fitness. She didn't experience much fatigue until she was getting low on her own resources. But it seemed as if Marie drew her magic from outside of herself and it took a physical toll on her body to do so. There were a lot of possibilities for different kinds of magic out there, depending on the person and, honestly, what kind of supernatural they were.

Marie gestured for them to follow her. "This way. This clearing is pretty large, curving around the edge of the foot of the mountain here. There's even some cliffs above us. Your cave is tucked below one of the sheerer drops."

The clearing was both similar to and different from the flora of the Pacific Northwest, and more closely resembled a meadow out of the old East Asian historical fantasies Peeraphan's father liked to watch. The flowers around them were an explosion of color and texture, overwhelming and unfamiliar in a way that made Peeraphan feel as if she was in an Impressionist painting, until she leaned closer to examine each plant individually.

Some glowed in the moonlight and others released a steady stream of softly glowing pollen into the air. Some turned their flowered faces to her as she bent over them for a closer look and others tipped away from her. Once even quietly trilled an alarm when she stepped too close. She was fascinated by the perfect shape of every petal, the velvet surface and perfect ombré where colors transitioned, and the fragrant perfume of each plant. She could have explored this place forever.

"Yeah, this place has that effect, the first few times you visit." Marie's voice next to her ear snapped Peeraphan back to the present goal ahead of them.

Peeraphan jerked up to stand straight, without any idea of how long she'd spent transfixed.

Marie gave her a wry smile full of sympathy. "I spent hours wandering, my first time, until the hermit warned me it was a part of this meadow's charm and a protection for the medicinal plants to be found here. You have to have mental discipline to forage here, and it's advisable to only take what you absolutely need and plan to use, personally, not distribute any of it for personal gain."

"Wow." Peeraphan glanced up at Bennett, then back at Thomas. The both of them were scanning the tree line not so far away.

They didn't seem to be experiencing the same problem with getting caught up in the magic of this place. Was it only her?

Marie lifted one shoulder and dropped it. "I told them it was best for me to bring your attention back, having experienced it. Let's go."

Peeraphan nodded, stuffing her embarrassment deep inside to deal with some other time. She was going to replay that whole experience, oh, only a few thousand times to imagine how she could have managed to avoid falling into that trap or be broken out of it. No need to start all that now. That was what sleepless nights were for. She firmly told herself to forgive, because these were new experiences and all the caution in the world wasn't going to save anyone from at least a few stumbles.

Bennett came close to her side as they were walking.

"The attraction has multiple components," he said quietly, mostly for her. Thomas could probably hear him, but Bennett continued with an almost academic tone. "The sheer saturation of color is one. Fragrance is another. I imagine several of the plants around us have a tactile defense as well. I may not have been drawn in because I only minimally sampled the air when we arrived, to detect any other presences. My senses weren't swamped the way yours were."

Fair. Her chest blossomed with warmth as he offered her those thoughts. He hadn't assumed he'd avoided the situation just because—he'd considered why and offered the reasons to her. It did make her feel better.

Still, she had been the only one, and there was at least one other person who needed to breathe who hadn't been caught up. She glanced back at Thomas.

He growled. "You weren't the only one. I broke out of it because Bennett's presence irritated the hell out of me."

"A lycanthrope's sense of smell is not always an advantage," Bennett stated.

"At least I don't give an entirely new definition to the term 'picky eater,'" Thomas fired back.

They were both scowling, but neither of them was particularly tense. Their words lacked the sharp edges of a real fight. It was more like the comfortable bickering of close family.

She smiled and turned to keep walking.

"I'm reasonably sure this is the place you're looking for." Marie crouched next to a spot against a cliff face. "I was looking for certain types of fungus, and the hermit showed me a cave nearby, but warned me that going into this one would result in me having to face everything I didn't want to know about myself in order to come back out."

"That's one way to look at the truth." Peerphan kneeled down to peer into the cave entrance. It would've been easy to miss. Long grass and bushes hid the spot and made it blend into the cliff. The opening itself was only a few feet tall. She would have to crouch to get inside, not quite on her hands and knees, but almost.

Bennett leaned in, a hand on her shoulder, but Marie reached out with an arm to bar the vampire's way. "This is not a place where you go."

Bennett stiffened, his hand on Peeraphan's shoulder tightening a fraction. "Careful, witch."

Peeraphan eased back from the opening. "What happens in there?"

Marie looked from Bennett to Peeraphan, nibbling her lower lip.

Peeraphan smiled. "If it were me, hearing what the hermit told you, I'd have gone in to find out what his warning was about, and I'm not even well practiced in my abilities. I'm guessing you, good enough to be the witch for the Consortium and to have gotten here in the first place, went exploring."

A brief smile was Marie's initial response, but she narrowed her eyes and addressed Bennett. "The dragon might have told you, but she rarely ever makes sure we actually listened to her. This cave, it made me examine truths about myself. Not every tiny little thing, but definitely the big truths. Truths so big they're lying deep beneath the surface where it's easy to pretend they're not there, like the bottoms of icebergs or like sea monsters. For humans, that can be traumatic."

"We are not human." Bennett didn't sound concerned.

"That's the point." Marie huffed in frustration. "For supernaturals, living among humans? For vampires? What if you have to face being dead? What if facing the absolute truth of being a walking dead person affects the magic that makes you a vampire? What if it changes the magic and you really do die, completely and irrevocably? Worse, what if you're still a walking dead person, but your intellect and heart and soul are gone and we end up with a revenant or some kind of ghoul or zombie? We have no idea what the outcome will be when the magic of the cave compels the magic that defines who and what you are to acknowledge it."

Bennett stilled. Peeraphan could still feel his hand on her shoulder, but he was the kind of absolutely still that humans couldn't be.

Marie pressed on. "What if Thomas goes in there and he has to face the truth of his dual nature? What if his truth is more about the wolf than the human, and the truth of it affects the magic that allows him to shift between one form and the other? What if his truth makes him only a human or a wolf, forever? We don't know. It depends. And every time you go in there, it's a different journey, based on where you are in life and what balance your mind and heart and soul have when you go in."

"Wow." Peeraphan stared at the cave entrance.

"I want to say I wouldn't go in there, now that I know, but I'd be lying." Marie laughed, a kind of broken sound, full of regret. "I've gone in more than once, hoping my truth had changed. And it did. A little closer to what I wanted and never anything I'll be comfortable with, ever. It's who I am."

"And I have to go in, because this is the only way we know of to save my life." Peeraphan rolled her shoulders back and looked down at the red shoes. "Let's hope knowing is at least half the battle."

Marie cracked up with genuine laughter. Thomas cleared his throat suspiciously but Bennett raised an eyebrow in a quizzical expression.

Peeraphan wondered if Bennett had ever spent time watching cartoons. It was hard to imagine.

"I'll be here," Bennett promised suddenly, his words holding an intensity Peeraphan wanted to explore more. "If you do not come out on your own, I will come after you. I will not leave you here alone."

Peeraphan twisted around to face him, horrified. "You heard what she said!"

Bennett met her incredulity with a completely calm expression. "Yes."

"Did you listen?" She searched his face. Not even a muscle twitch. She was actually pretty sure he wasn't breathing on purpose.

"Truth is powerful." He nodded. "But I have lived a very long time and I have never not been a vampire. I think the truths I must face lie in different aspects of my existence. It would be worth it to face those to bring you out again."

She blew out a puff of air in frustration. "I will come back out on my own two feet, sans shoes—I will even crawl out on my hands and knees if I have to. You keep yourself outside of this cave, Mister Tall, Dark, and Definitely Not Going to Turn Into a Revenant or Ghoul. Got it?"

He remained silent. She glared at him. After a long moment, she glanced past him to Thomas. Her childhood friend and favorite cousin was watching them both with brows drawn close and lips pressed together in a serious, brooding expression. He gave her a short nod.

"I got this. You wait and see." She stressed the word "wait," then stepped into the cave before she could hesitate any further.

The first step was a doozy, the ground sloping more steeply than she had anticipated, and she fell forward. The shoes definitely had something to do with it, but still, she cursed at herself for not having anticipated it enough to prevent it. Instead of putting her hands out to catch herself, she tucked and rolled with the fall, hoping to avoid damaging her hands or breaking her neck. Before she could do more than be frightened, she had come to a stop in a heap at the bottom of the slope, well inside the cave.

She took a minute to orient herself and do a mental inventory of her body, deciding she hadn't done more than add to her collection of bruises. She turned her head and called back up to the cave entrance, the moonlight shining down from it. "I'm okay!"

SIXTEEN

PEERAPHAN

Shouting had probably been just a fraction less cautious than Peeraphan's cursed misstep and crashing tumble into this place.

She quickly scanned the darkness around her, unsure of whether some danger was going to burst out of the deep shadows to attack her where she sat in light that pooled in from the entrance. Her heart beat out a staccato cadence as she listened, even breathed in through her nose for whatever information scent could give her. Then, she did what she probably should practice making an immediate habit of: she extended her magic senses outward. Air and water could tell her more, over a longer distance. It was harder to do when she was this tense, this anxious, this afraid.

But what monster could live in perpetual truth of what it was?

Her magic senses told her Bennett and Thomas and Marie were up at the cave mouth, crowding the entrance and listening. Thomas was testing the air with his own sense of smell, and she almost felt his sniffs like a gentle inquiry brushing her shoulder. But leaning in to comfort wasn't what she needed right now, however tempting. She needed to know what she might be facing in here.

She found nothing alive in her immediate vicinity. Nothing

stirred the air or the water in her space. No heart beat in here, no lungs drew breath save her own.

No danger about to pounce on her the minute she moved. Okay. There was something good, then.

Check complete. And she would live another day to work on this as a habit. Her world was more dangerous than she'd ever imagined and she wanted to live in it longer.

She brushed off her hands before pressing her palms to her cheeks, trying to cool down the flaming embarrassment. They all had to know she'd taken a fall if they were gathered at the entrance. And all she'd done was call up to them with her inane reassurance that wouldn't have reassured her if she'd been up there waiting for one of them. The entire group had come here to help her and she hadn't exactly proven she'd be an asset to their Consortium yet.

"Honestly," she whispered into the hollow emptiness of the cave, "I might've just added a major point in the Too Stupid to Live column."

A sound cut the silence, like a drop of water falling into a pool: loud and with a musical quality to it. But it didn't echo in the space.

Peeraphan pushed herself up to her feet, thankful for the thin layer of dark silt on the rocky cave floor. If she had to walk deeper into the cave, it was a little better footing for her to manage than bare rock. With the shoes tripping her up at every opportunity, she might even do better crawling. She'd try walking first, though, because it was harder to react defensively from her knees to whatever might happen.

"Hello?" She pitched the greeting like a question and waited.

Nothing.

If anything, the space around her began to dim and she realized it had lightened just a bit when she'd heard the first sound. The droplet.

She extended her senses again, this time trying to get a better feel for the space around her. She smelled moisture and dampness—not stagnant or rotting, but more like the cool scent of lush vegetation where there was no breeze to give an impression of openness. Air moved across her skin, coming in from the entrance up the slope behind her. Air flowed like water, so if it wasn't exiting past her, there must be an opening for the cave someplace else where the air was going out. Her magic followed the air, but a short distance into the cave it slowed and swirled, heading straight up and splitting into a myriad of smaller paths. There wasn't a path to follow, really, only a space here in the side of the mountain, and cracks too small for a human to traverse heading up to the surface of the mountainside. Nothing drew air and exhaled, no living thing was in the cave with her.

"Well, I'm reasonably sure I'm alone here." She decided that speaking out loud wouldn't hurt.

Another drop of water chimed through the silence. This time she caught the slight brightening of the space around her.

"Is that how the magic here works?" she asked the cave. Maybe it was sentient in some way.

No response. If anything, the space around her darkened again.

Okay. Just talking to the cave wasn't going to guarantee progress. But seriously, what was she expecting? She took a careful step forward, then another, and tried to make her way as far into the cave as she dared. Which wasn't far, because the light coming from the entrance really didn't extend very far. If her magic could generate light somehow, she hadn't figured out the trick yet.

"There are no hand-me-down notes for the self-taught diaspora, especially when one is a supernatural no one realized actually existed," she muttered. Not because she expected something to happen, but more to counter the rising anxiety she felt there alone in the dark with no idea what to do next. "Me, that would be me."

This time, the sound of the water droplet was louder and the ambient light brightened more. She scowled, considering the difference between each of the things she had said out loud so far. Actually, she needed to consider everything she had done since she'd entered the cave. There hadn't been any apparent reaction to her moving around. There also hadn't been any change that she noticed as she moved slightly deeper into the cave. "If I step forward or try to go any farther it will be too dark for me to see. It'll be too easy to hurt myself." It was a simple fact. "I wouldn't like the idea of stumbling around in the dark of the strange cave even if I had proper gear and footwear, much less the current situation with no gear and a drop-dead-gorgeous pair of murder shoes."

With the droplet chime this time, the ambient light brightened enough for her to see dim shapes suspended in the space in front of her. Four spheres hung in the air, all on their own. Other than them, there was nothing in the cavern.

"I'm still not sure where the light is coming from, but gods, I feel better when there's at least a little light." She said the last part of that almost reverently because wow, she had been freaked out by the idea of being in absolute darkness.

Another chime, and this time it was just a bit lighter, light enough for her to watch mist coalesce into a fifth sphere.

It was definitely happening in response to the things she was saying. And this was a cave of truth.

"Quirky thing about my memory," she said into the silence, "I'm mostly a visual person when it comes to remembering. My memories are like pictures and movie clips inside my head and when I want to remember details, I have to concentrate and sort of zoom in on those visuals. But I also remember conversations and things that are said really well, too. I almost see the words when I think back to them. I remember every statement I've made so far, coming in here."

Three chimes. Three new spheres formed to join the others. They weren't all the same size, but each of them hovered there in front of her. One of the new ones was also the biggest. She thought there might be something inside that one, and before she could let caution win over curiosity, she stepped forward to examine it more closely.

It was very much like water: colorless. The biggest one seemed to have a filament of something floating in it, almost insubstantial and maybe faintly glowing. The other spheres, as she looked closer, careful not to touch, had particulates in them—fine specks or motes—too small to tell if they were anything but silt in water.

There wasn't a sphere for each statement she'd made, no. But there was a sphere for each truth she had uttered out loud. She could almost check off the things she'd said and so far, it was the most plausible theory she had: tell a truth and it would materialize and at least bring light into the darkness.

"Okay," she said. "Let's do this."

And so she stood there, giving truths.

"I wanted these shoes, from the moment I saw them." A chime sounded and a small sphere formed.

Seemed right, to start with the damned shoes. They had brought her to this.

Or had they?

"I was donating my time for that performance and I wanted something, at least one thing, to be the best of the best, for me." Another chime, fainter, and an even smaller sphere.

Oh, this was like death by a thousand paper cuts. She paused. No. Wrong form of torture. But she felt like she was bleeding a little, just the same. It was awkward, and terrible, thinking about the truth of things randomly.

"I was wrong, being selfish." She waited.

No chime. No sphere. The cavern waited, the spheres hanging in the air.

She thought about what she'd said and amended it. "I wanted the shoes for myself."

A chime sounded. Faint. And another tiny sphere formed to acknowledge her small truth.

What was the difference? Frustration twisted inside her and she scowled, rubbing her forehead before combing her fingers through her hair. The temptation to beat her head against a wall was becoming a literal impulse.

But she shouldn't have to beat herself up for the truth. She'd spent years telling herself that, working on changing that for herself.

The statement that had gotten no reaction had been what she might have said to her mother or father, if they'd asked her if she understood what she had done. A thing she'd learn to admit over and over again as a child, as she learned to share and be a good little Thai girl. It was a thing she'd come to recognize as the expected truth, but she didn't believe it.

And wasn't the world full of truths told by other people? But right and wrong, those were relative to perspective. Remembered anger welled up and fused with the simmering anger she'd been keeping shut tight in some back compartment of her mind over the last couple of days, from even before the shoes happened. She was doing things because someone else told her it was right—and it'd been easy to believe because they'd had the best of intentions—so she'd been wrestling with her feelings her entire life. Even as an adult, she'd been struggling to keep her temper while having to be around Sirin, a childhood friend—no, a nemesis.

Having to face a person who was doing great in the eyes of her mother and her parents' friends. Having to be around someone who made their own parents proud when Punch was still just trying to avoid adding any more disappointment in her parents' gaze.

She didn't have to work with Sirin. She'd done it anyway, because it wasn't anyone else who was the problem.

"I don't hate Sirin, but I hate how I feel when she's in the spotlight."

A chime sounded. The sphere that formed this time was larger than the others.

"I'm years out of college and I haven't gotten anywhere. I still need to figure out what I want for my life and I'm already tired. Absolutely exhausted."

Another chime. Another sphere, about the same size.

Well, she'd thought there were multiple statements of fact there. Facts had to be true, right? She thought if she'd avoided right and wrong or beating herself up over whether she was a good person, those would be truths.

"Damn it." Tears welled up, burning and making her blink rapidly. She breathed slow through her nose to force air through her constricting throat and into her tight chest. "I'm nothing. Nobody."

Silence. The existing spheres only hovered. The cavern remained waiting.

The tightness around her chest eased. Relief seeped through her body. It wasn't true. It wasn't. And she had been afraid it might be, but she hadn't wanted it to be. A tiny voice inside her cried and cried, because it wasn't so. She wasn't nobody.

"I'm Punch," she whispered, and the words sounded agonized. "Peeraphan."

Two chimes. Two larger spheres formed.

"And I want people to see me," she continued, fighting against growing tightness in her throat and chest.

Another chime. Another sphere, bigger this time.

"I want people to listen to me."

Chime. Sphere.

"I went through college, came this far, doing as much as I could on my own to prove I could. So people would finally respect me. So no one would think it was because my parents, or anyone else, gave my achievements to me."

Three chimes. Three spheres. And it was getting both harder and easier at the same time, because while these felt like confessions, they also felt like shouting into a storm. She put her anger and frustration behind her words. Her heartache and hurt.

"I've been good enough at everything."

Chime. True. As the sphere formed, she glared at it. *Good enough* wasn't enough for her. It was she who wanted more. And she said so, creating another sphere.

"Every job was like a step down a path I was supposed to take to prove myself and I kept searching for my path, my thing, the thing I loved to do."

Another chime. Another sphere.

"I'm an adult, but the part of me chasing after Sirin is still a child hoping someone will notice how well I'm doing." She drew in a shaking breath and added with a sob, "I still haven't accomplished anything I feel proud of."

Another chime, louder now. The sphere that formed was bigger.

"If I'm not proud and I'm not happy, then what the hell am I doing?"

Silence. No answers. This wasn't a place where answers were hidden. Everything here was coming from her.

The spheres didn't form for facts about the world or about someone else, but they did form when they were about her or her perceptions of the world and people around her.

Fine. But if she kept on this way, she'd tear herself to pieces and maybe even do herself damage. Not okay. Not even to save her life. Because what would there be to save if she destroyed herself?

So she thought about what she'd learned in therapy. So worth the time, and she was going to need to thank her therapist when she got out of this. She was definitely getting out of this.

Each truth she was tempted to speak, she stopped and thought about it, framed it in a more objective light without the temptation to judge herself. She wanted to stop beating herself up and it wasn't easy, but she could try in this moment, when every thought mattered.

"I keep focusing on what I am because I don't feel like I fit in anywhere. I keep blaming it on what I am because I don't want to look at who I am."

Two more chimes. Two more spheres.

And thank goodness these didn't hit her like physical blows. It didn't tickle, either, but this was a better cleansing than what she'd been doing to herself before. She could do this.

So she did. Giving the cave more truths. More confessions of what she wanted and who she wanted to be. And none of them were specific. It wasn't about particular career goals or accolades, not limited to accomplishments or even failures. It was about anything and everything related to her identity.

As more spheres formed, she was able to glimpse more of the cave and realized it extended farther back than she had initially imagined. She walked forward, through the liquid gallery of honesty she was creating, and reached the edge of a pool. She couldn't tell how shallow or deep it was. It was absolutely dark, the surface reflecting back a cavern speckled with bioluminescent moss of some kind. Which shouldn't be, because moss didn't grow without sunlight, and none could've reached this far into the cave. But here it was and it was beautiful in a way that made her almost forget to breathe.

Stepping stones led to the center of the pool, and maybe some creature might rise up out of the hidden depths to snatch her, but she didn't think so. She gave the caverns more truths, and more spheres formed around her, a few leading out over the stepping stones.

More truth. More spheres. Some big and some small. Some she'd never clearly thought about until this moment. She was enchanted and exhausted at the same time. It was getting harder to think of truths to offer that she hadn't spoken out loud previously. The larger spheres had come from the deeper truths, the ones that'd taken a stretch to give and even hurt a little. This portion of the cavern had opened up to a larger space over the pool and she felt the need to fill it. She wasn't sure she had enough little truths to make that happen.

"I know I need to dig deeper and speak bigger truths," she admitted to the cave, "but I thought I could make do with all these littler things and maybe if there were enough, I wouldn't have to touch the ones that are really going to hurt."

A single shining sphere coalesced around her, the filament inside twisting in a dance within the water like seaweed in the ocean lit by the sun's rays.

She'd been trying not to beat herself up, not to judge herself. But this was different. This was like lancing a festering wound she'd neglected for too long. She'd been avoiding it and it had kept her from growing.

Pain sucked. Anger and frustration and fear tasted bitter and she didn't like herself when she held on to those feelings for too long. That was the problem, wasn't it? She'd been struggling to like herself. Dreaming of being something else.

"I always wanted to be special, different," she confessed. "I dreamed of being a mermaid when I was little. Imagined I was being called into the ocean. Not because I actually recognized the call of magic, but because I wanted to be magical."

Truth took form and floated just in front and above her, the biggest sphere yet.

"I was wrong to want to be better than others." She choked back a sob, because it slipped out even when she'd been trying not to let it and that statement cut deep. Self-hatred came easy for her. Because it was an echo of what people had said to her growing up. She should excel and do her best and contribute to her community, yes, but she should have been humble. Doing better didn't equal being better than others.

Nothing. No chime. No sphere. Not truth.

She sobbed. It had to be enough by now. What was this going to take?

The shoes were stuck on her feet, still. They'd been made to punish a person for their sins. It didn't matter what faith the folktale had been written for, the curse of the shoes was straightforward. They only came off when a person had faced their sins. This cave was a cathedral and she needed to fill it with confessions, and only the real ones would set her free. So why hadn't another sphere formed?

Because it wasn't true and she knew it.

"It's easier for me to say what I think others are thinking about me, give them their truth," she muttered.

Truth. A sphere formed and she stared at it like it had the ability to mock her. But there was nothing on its surface, no features to form any kind of expression. It was just there, and everything she felt from looking at it was what came from her.

Tears welled up and there was no one to hide them from, so she let them fall. Frustration ate at her insides. Resentment rose and left the burning, sour taste of bile in her throat. Sins were awful things. Not just because it was awful to commit them. That was what society had taught her. But the people who'd given her love? Support?

Accepted her? They'd never once uttered the word "sin" to her. Not once. Her mother, her father, her grandparents. So what were the actual sins she had to face about herself? What was the truth?

What was hers?

"Celebrating what I've accomplished has never been wrong." It had never been a sin. "I've been convinced I have to be more and more humble the more I do well, and that's not okay. Society beats humility into us until we don't dare say we're beautiful. When I look at how hard I've worked, what I've done, and how I did those things, I'm beautiful."

Three chimes sounded. Three glowing spheres formed, the biggest yet.

Pressure eased in her chest.

She laughed, and sure, it sounded a little watery, but it was laughter. She uttered her truths, then. The things she wanted to say, but no one would have listened. Or if they had, maybe her thoughts and theirs would have fed off each other and the shared frustration would have turned their good intentions ugly. Here, she could safely speak her truths and witness them take form in the space around her. More and more drops of water gathered and hung in the cavern. She kept going until she felt hollow, empty.

Looking down, she wiggled her feet in the shoes. They'd lost some of their intense jewel tone, but they hadn't loosened their grip on her feet. She still couldn't get them off. But she was sure she was right. This wasn't about lust or gluttony. It wasn't about greed or sloth. It wasn't about wrath, envy, or pride. She was sure her life was full of moments that could have been, and were, labeled one or more of those descriptors. And nope, it wasn't about the "sins" she had committed that others might perceive as wrong.

It was about truths inside herself that she wasn't willing to face.

If she was hiding from them, she was regarding them as sins, by her own definition. Whatever a truth was, she was holding it so close, the truth was going to hurt to pull it loose and examine it.

Bennett's face floated in her mind's eye and she said the first thing that came to mind. "He is beautiful to me."

A chime sounded. A sphere of water formed.

Rushing, before she buried the next thought, she spit the words out. "But I never wanted to be a vampire."

Another chime. Another truth floated in its own sphere.

Oh. She closed her eyes. Thought about things she'd said since she'd come face-to-face with Bennett, her first supernatural. "I've known I was different since my body started to change and magic started to be a part of who I was."

Another chime. She didn't open her eyes, didn't look. If she did, she wouldn't keep going, and there was more.

"I saw him. I was delighted, but I didn't want to be him. I didn't want to be any of them. I just didn't want to be alone." Didn't want to be the only person who was different. Didn't want to be the odd one out.

Another chime. Or had it been two? She wasn't counting anymore. There'd been too many to count.

"He isn't sure I can accept everything he is." She explored that, poked at her own heart. "I wanted to show him I could, but that's not the right reason. I need to think about whether I do accept him. It hasn't been long since I met him. Do I feel this way about him because this thing between us is right and real? Or because I'm lonely and I want this?"

There might've been a chime there, another note of music among the tones in the cavern. They'd started reacting to each other.

"Right now, I don't need to think about him." She struggled to slow herself down, stop looking outward. Stop projecting. Think hard about why Bennett had doubts about whether she could accept him for who and what he was.

He'd asked the same thing of his past love.

A human love.

She was exposed. Vulnerable. Staring into herself and admitting it for the first time.

He'd treated her as human.

But she wasn't. Not a human with kinnaree powers. Not a human at all.

He'd responded to her and treated her as human not because he thought she was, but because she had been acting human. She'd presented herself that way to him. And she had to own it. Say it out loud. "I still think of myself as human. Even while I want to be something else, someone different, I'm holding on to being human. Human, but more."

Another chime, louder than any of the others. Some of the answering tones in the cavern resonated in major chords, but others created minors. The results were aching and uncomfortable. Her heels were loose inside the shoes.

She was figuring out what she was. Magic powers were a part of it. But there was more. Her blood did things to Bennett. It meant others might want her for those effects. It meant danger. She'd instinctively hid because being alone was dangerous. It meant a life outside of what she'd known before or ever thought possible. It meant learning. Exploring. Sure, it was scary, but it was exciting, too. And it wouldn't be easy, but it was possible. Bennett and Thomas and Marie and the others were living it. It was possible. She needed to let go of who she thought she'd had to be before.

She swallowed against the ache in her throat. "I'm not human. Not at all."

Another tone sounded in the space around her, answered by

minor chords and major. Mostly minor. The sadness in the music her truths made washed through her. Her soles were sweaty inside the shoes, slipping.

"I am kinnaree." It came out as an exhausted whisper, but she had said it. She heard it. Excitement fluttered in her chest.

Pure and clear, a tone rang out. She opened her eyes and drank in the sight of the largest sphere yet. Her truth floated in the center, woven of threads of gold and sapphire.

She stepped out of the shoes and reveled in the cool stone beneath her bare feet.

Never had she felt this peace. This relief. She was wrung out, exhausted. So tired, she struggled to expand her lungs. But she was free.

She turned toward the entrance, looking back the way she'd come. Spheres hung suspended to either side, at varying heights. Some floated high, near the ceiling, and others were just out of reach. Still more were at eye level and chest height. A few hung so low, they hovered just above the waters of the pool. The reflection on the still surface gave the impression of an extension in space, making her feel like she was in the center of a globe, surrounded. She stood there, facing them all, her truths and their light. It was overwhelming in that moment, looking and listening to them all. She wanted to go back now, to her friends. To her life.

She took a step back the way she'd come.

The spheres hanging around her, with their light and their musical notes, began moving. They spun around her, picking up speed. Fear sparked and she bent to grab the shoes, starting across the stepping stones back to the edge of the pool. A few tiny bubbles of water hit her in the shoulder in wet splashes. She gasped and kept going. One the size of a baseball smacked into her hip and another the size of a volleyball caught her in the side of the head, the impact knocking her to the ground at the edge of the pool.

She cried out as her truths came back to her, slamming into her back and her sides. She covered her head with her arms as best she could, struggling to keep her sanity as everything she'd given out to the cave returned in a fraction of the time. She swallowed it all, too fast to process. They were all hers.

After forever and a split second, it finally stopped. She let her arms fall and shuddered, feeling too full inside her mind and her heart. She pulled herself up, standing on wobbly knees. Hanging in the air in front of her was the last and largest sphere. Her final truth.

She could see herself in its surface. Her golden-tan skin, her dark brown eyes filled with centuries she hadn't yet lived. Snow-white wings at her hips and tail feathers, long, curved, and exquisite, rising up behind her.

For this one, she wouldn't brace herself. She held out her arms, welcoming, and met it halfway.

SEVENTEEN

BENNETT

Bennett stood at the entrance, watchful and waiting. One would think having lived for centuries, a successful hunter and survivor through the changes of the world, he would have developed a certain amount of patience. In fact, he had been known for his ability to maintain his composure and keep a cool head even when anticipation had become a form of torture over the course of days and weeks, even months.

It had only been a few hours and he was ready to rip apart the mountain to get a glimpse of Peeraphan.

"If I leave to scout the perimeter, can you hold your shit together?" Thomas asked.

Bennett did not dignify the hound with a verbal response, only bared fangs.

Thomas growled in response. "Diving in there and potentially ending your existence will not benefit anyone."

Marie sighed. "How do the two of you manage to work together under one roof?"

At least the witch had a constructive task to keep her occupied while they all waited. She had selected a tree branch and trimmed it into a reasonably straight stick and sharpened the end with a boot knife. Then she'd gathered a few fronds from one of the tropical fruit trees at the edge of the clearing and woven the edges into a flimsy, but serviceable, basket. Both of those had taken up a good chunk of time and given him something to watch in between scanning the forest edge and sky for potential dangers. Now she was poking at the base of various clumps of plants, carefully pulling up a few at a time with the roots intact and leaving behind others to give them room to grow—or so she had told him. He had lost interest, and as each second passed was growing more and more agitated.

He detected movement at the far edge of the clearing, a flash of moonlight on fur. Thomas dropped to a crouch, silent and ready to move to defend, if necessary. Marie froze and turned, slowly. The witch was not as obviously intimidating as a vampire and a werewolf, but any attacker would regret targeting her. Together, they searched the shadows of the surrounding forest, and Bennett caught a better look at the being that had allowed them to see it. A flash of fur and feline eyes caught the light of the moon and reflected it out to them.

The lion, the likes of which Bennett had never encountered before, must have decided not to stalk them. Instead it stepped out of the shadows, remaining just within the shelter of the trees. It stood proud, with a grace the modern world's lions had lost in the captivity of zoos and enclosed habitats. It was the color of moonlight, silvery white, with a mane as red as fresh blood from the artery. The red streaks swirled through the fur of its body, deepening to a darker red over each of its paws. It lashed its tail, tufted with the same blood red at the end. This big cat was built larger than its counterparts around the rest of the human-inhabited world. It had a large, broad head and a wide chest. Its hindquarters were heavily muscled to help it spring forward and take down large prey. Bennett couldn't be sure, but he'd spent a long time walking the world, and he had a hunch this was a solo hunter.

It studied them as Bennett took his time assessing it. Then red lips pulled back and it opened its jaws, letting out a roar with enough resonance to shake the forest around it. None of them flinched. As power displays went, it was a simple enough message: it knew they were here, and now they knew it was here, too. It looked at them, blinking slowly, almost sleepily. Bennett thought he might use the same look when he had decided a being was neither threat nor worth the effort to hunt down. It shook its head, the red mane framing its face a glorious cloud, then it turned and melted back into the darkness of the forest.

"That was new," Marie whispered.

"You've never seen it before?" Bennett asked, intrigued.

"No." Marie started poking at the dirt again. "I've seen a white elephant or two—true white elephants, not the pale gray ones they call white—and there's at least one black elephant with wings."

"We're not talking about big ears on a pachyderm, are we?" Thomas asked.

"Wings. Scarlet wings you'd see on a bird. They were huge. Would have to be, to lift an animal so big. The wingspan was maybe twice as large as its body. It had tail feathers, too, and a ridiculously intimidating set of tusks for defense." Marie's voice held more than a little awe. "The hermit called it a karin puksa and said it was rare."

Thomas barked out a laugh. Bennett was inclined to share the implied sentiment. Rare indeed.

"All relatively peaceful creatures. This is the first time a predator made itself known."

Marie paused, then resumed pulling up plants by the root. "I think the forest is full of creatures, and a lot of them have been aware of when I've come and gone. They're curious, but me by myself poses no major threat. The two of you, though..."

Bennett nodded. "Each of us is a formidable hunter, and the two of us here together is not a thing to be ignored."

"Will this make it too dangerous for you to come alone in the future?" Thomas asked quietly.

Bennett tightened his jaw. He refused to regret taking this chance. Though he would make an effort, if needed, to offer Marie escort, rather than have her take increased risk as a consequence of bringing them all to this place.

"The witch will be safe, this night and in nights to come." The statement came from the far end of the clearing. A human approached slowly over a gentle rise, leaning heavily on a gnarled walking stick. His wiry body was wrapped in what looked to be tiger skins. He was old, as humans went, his dark skin leathery and wrinkled, knuckles swollen. Bennett could almost hear the man's tendons and joints creaking as he moved. The man was almost bald but for a few white strands, but his beard was prodigious. His face was deeply etched with age, the kind of creases made from strong emotions like rage or generous laughter. Maybe both. There was sharp intelligence in the man's eyes, though. "She has done no harm, and so she is welcome to return so long as she stays within the protections of this clearing."

"Bhante." Marie inclined her head in greeting.

Bennett and Thomas remained silent, watchful. Bennett did not offer the man any kind of challenge and neither did Thomas, but they were more certain now that this place was no simple forest in the world they knew. They could not be certain how their strengths would match up against what lived here.

The old man grinned then, his lips peeling back to reveal strong and uneven teeth stained a dark color. "Either of you is a challenge, just standing there. I do not think it would be so easy to believe you will do no harm."

There was no value in getting angry at a simple fact. He had long since accepted there were things he was not entitled to by default, and trust was at the top of the list. Bennett felt the corners of his mouth tug upward in wry acknowledgment.

"The kraisorn rajasri wouldn't have made itself known for anything less." The old man cackled. "There's been more excitement this night than I've had since the last time one of the gandharva came to try to harvest fruit from the makkaliphon tree. That was a night of chaos, oh my."

Bennett made note of the unfamiliar terms. Perhaps if the night went well, Peeraphan would have research to do when they returned to the manor. At the thought of her, Bennett glanced back at the cave entrance. It had been too long.

"Don't." The hermit's tone was kind, but had power behind it, nonetheless. "Few believe in the old gods, anymore, especially creatures of night and the hunt such as you. But you believe in those you choose as your peers, I think, colleagues and companions. Do not break a promise for lack of faith in the one you have in your heart."

Bennett bared his fangs at the hermit, but he did not move toward the cave entrance.

"Truth is a powerful thing." The hermit approached until he was just outside arm's reach, still close enough for either Bennett or Thomas to end him, if they chose. "It can set a person free or trap them in a cage of their own making. It can do both at the same time. Your companion is on her way back. But when she returns to you, what will you do when you both leave this place?"

Bennett tore his gaze from the cave entrance and glared at the hermit. "What do you know?"

The hermit opened his eyes wide and held his hands up to the starry night. "Me? Many things. Especially about these forests and the creatures who make this their home. I know many of us who reside here are long-lived. Others have the chance to see the full moon only three times before they pass. I know none who come from these forests are born immortal—not like you. The things I know, none of them will make you feel better, vampire. I've lived a full life watching the creatures of the world come and go, making their choices. You are the first of your kind to visit this place, and still, you are not different. You have a choice ahead of you, and there is too much history clouding your path forward."

Bennett heard her before anything else, the sound of her heart beating hard as she made whatever climb she needed to reach the cave entrance again. He rushed forward and reached out to help Peeraphan as she emerged on her hands and knees, carrying the red shoes in one hand.

"Hey," she panted. She waved the shoes. Her wings had manifested and opened as she cleared the entrance, balancing her as she rose unsteadily to stand on bare feet.

He took the shoes and passed them back to Thomas without taking his gaze from her. Her face was drawn, tired, streaked with mud and tears. Her clothes were soaked through, the trench coat he had loaned her gone. He stripped off his sport coat and wrapped it around her shoulders, then curved one arm around her back and hooked the other behind her knees to scoop her up and hold her against his chest. Rather than struggle, she sagged against him.

"You're exhausted." His statement came out in a harsher tone than he intended.

"Truth." She nodded, and a sound escaped her that was something between a laugh and a sigh.

Anger roared through him. She was hurt. She was hurt. And he had done nothing to prevent it. He'd only stood by, waiting. Rational thought burned away as emotions boiled up. He gathered her closer to him, wanting to punish whatever had done this to her, but there was nothing to fight, no being from which to extract any kind of vengeance. It was a cave.

Maybe he could bring down the mountainside after all.

But destroying the place wouldn't spare her whatever she had just survived.

Marie approached and Bennett had to bite back a snarl. Marie kept her focus on a point just below his eyes, not meeting his gaze directly but still warily keeping watch until he gave her a sharp nod. She rushed forward and looked Peeraphan over as best she could while Bennett kept Peeraphan gathered close against his chest.

"She's bleeding," he ground out. It was a struggle to control the desire to feed when he was this angry. He could taste her blood on the air, smell it when he drew in breath.

"All I see are superficial scrapes and the beginnings of a bunch of bruises." Marie sifted through her makeshift basket of herbs and twisted a few into a tiny bunch, bruising the leaves before dabbing them against Peeraphan's abrasions. "Do you have any sharp pains anywhere?"

Peeraphan shook her head. "Just bruised and battered."

"What hit you?" Thomas didn't exactly have his temper under control, either, if the gravelly garble of words was anything to go by.

"Nothing alive, strictly speaking." Peeraphan leaned her head into the curve of Bennett's shoulder. He pressed his lips to her hair, hiding his fangs. She swallowed. "It's hard to describe, but you could say the truth hit me from all sides."

Marie snorted. Bennett glared at her.

Marie didn't meet his gaze, but she shrugged. "It's a singular experience every time." Then she laid a gentle hand on Peeraphan's shoulder. "Let's get you back to the manor."

They headed back to the spot where they had first arrived and Bennett was glad Thomas was there to take point. He'd never admit it out loud, but the werewolf had some useful skills to protect the group with. The hermit was following at a distance, but if the man was a danger, he would have done something when they'd all been focused on Peeraphan.

"Bennett," Peeraphan whispered. Her words caressed his jaw with warm air.

"Hmm." He was still too angry over her being hurt to trust himself to speak.

"This truth thing. I want to tell you the last truth it took to get the shoes to release me." She sounded so tired.

He wanted to get her back to the manor with enough time to tuck her safely into bed before he had to give her over to Duncan and Ellery's care with the dawn. "You can tell me once you've rested."

"It seems obvious," she continued anyway. "I don't want to wait because I might convince myself it was a little thing. But it was the biggest truth I had. I've been talking a big game all this time, about how I'm not quite human."

"You're kinnaree." Bennett planned to do more research into the lore around her kind and the history.

"Yes, but we've both been hung up on me being of kinnaree descent, a human born with kinnaree powers." She wiggled a little in his arms so she could look up at him more directly. "Or maybe you weren't, but I was. Wings, tail, I was still holding on to this idea that I was human, or part human."

"And you have a clearer perspective now?" He wasn't certain where she was going with her line of thought, but he tried to listen, tried to follow. It was important to her, so it would be important to him to understand.

"I'm not human at all." She made the statement a fact with a firm tone of finality. "I have to let go of this need to be at least mostly human, because I'm not. I'm kinnaree, a true throwback."

He nodded. He was happy for her. There was possibly more to

consider, later. "I will do everything in my power to help you as you learn more about what that means."

She smiled up at him, and he paused midstride to give her a quick kiss.

"I never thought I'd live to witness the genesis of Bennett the lovestruck vampire," Thomas muttered.

Marie choked back a laugh.

Bennett snarled as Peeraphan turned her face into his shoulder to muffle her own giggles. It was a half-hearted effort, at best, because all of the anger twisting inside him had evaporated. He had his partner and she wasn't as frail or fleeting as his past love. He could put that memory to rest and live for the present.

They gathered as Marie prepared to cast the return spell. No movement along the tree line bordering the clearing. No more creatures putting in a cameo appearance this night.

Bennett glanced back at the hermit. The hermit grinned, showing gaps between his stained teeth.

"Witch, you are welcome back to this clearing, so long as you continue to do no harm while you are here." The hermit sounded as if he was reciting a well-used phrase. Marie looked unsurprised, only nodding in response. But the hermit didn't stop there. "Hunters, you may come again, but know that you must abide by the laws of these forests if you ever choose violence here."

Bennett thought it was fair. Thomas must have, too, because the werewolf said nothing.

The hermit didn't wait for an answer from either of them, though, instead resting his gaze on Peeraphan. The man's expression softened around the mouth and eyes, though his stare was no less intense. If anything, Bennett might have thought the man looked sad. "Kinnaree, your kind still reside in these forests. You are welcome to return."

Thomas stiffened. Marie paused in her spell. Bennett's hands convulsed around Peeraphan. In his arms, she was the only one who hadn't been present for what the hermit had told Bennett earlier.

None of the beings of this place were immortal.

Before he could open his mouth to further interrogate the hermit, the hermit lifted his walking stick. Mist billowed up around their feet, surrounding them until it was barely possible to see anything.

"No one move!" Marie's voice called out.

Bennett let his fangs and jaws pull forward, but he remained still, otherwise. If something attacked, he would be as ready as possible, even with his arms full.

The mist cleared as quickly as it had gathered, and they were standing in a different clearing. The night sounds and humid air of the Pacific Northwest surrounded them.

"I think he threw us out." Marie spat out a frustrated curse. "If he could do that all this time, he could have saved me a whole lot of effort on return trips in the past."

Bennett said nothing, clutching Peeraphan close to his chest. They were out in the open and the hermit had made him absolutely certain the woman he held so dearly to him was utterly fragile.

Terribly mortal after all.

EIGHTEEN

PEERAPHAN

Peeraphan wriggled in Bennett's arms, concerned. Something about the last invitation from the hermit had bothered everyone, especially Bennett. Or maybe she was projecting because she wasn't absolutely ready to face the implications of what the hermit had said. Her kind still resided in those forests, somewhere far away, inaccessible to human travel. But they were there. Someone could teach her about herself. Possibilities were popping up like popcorn inside her head and she didn't know how to examine any one of them in the middle of the chaos.

"Bennett?" she craned her neck to get a better look at his face.

His face had changed, his upper and lower jaws pulling forward and his fangs emerging. His eyes were an intense red, almost glowing in the night. He wouldn't look at her as they all stood there.

"Taking point." Thomas was abrupt, too. "Bennett, you good?"

"Just go," Bennett snapped.

Something was definitely wrong. There was real temper behind his curt statement and Thomas growled low in response. The two stared at each other for a long moment, the time stretching out until Peeraphan was sure they could hear her escalating heart rate.

It was Thomas who turned away and moved ahead toward the trail, tossing the red shoes back toward Bennett, who caught them and allowed Peeraphan to hold them against her chest.

Marie sighed, having remained motionless through the tense moment. She made eye contact with Peeraphan and opened her mouth to say something, then hesitated, as if she thought better of it, and just gave Peeraphan a small smile instead. "I'll follow the two of you and make sure we don't leave any signs of being here."

Peeraphan made a mental note to ask about that. Ashke oversaw security back at the manor for the whole island. They all worked as a group to ensure safety and security when they left the island together. She imagined it was even easier for Bennett and Thomas to move undetected when they were traveling solo. But aside from remaining unknown to humans, why go to such great lengths?

"Maybe I should walk. Just holding the shoes shouldn't be a problem," she whispered, keeping her voice low enough for only Bennett to hear. As far as she knew, Marie didn't have the kind of supernatural hearing Bennett and Thomas had.

"No need." Bennett's words came out clipped.

This was the exact opposite of what she'd thought would happen once she'd shared her truth with him. Maybe she'd misunderstood his misgivings around them trying to be together. She'd thought he'd be happy to think of her as kinnaree and not a human with kinnaree blood. But even cradled close in his arms as she was, there was a distance between them. He'd shut down.

Maybe her expectations were too storybook-like, too idyllic. All her romantic experience had been the sum of fleeting dates through college and the first decade afterward. Even she had felt caught in a transition stage, definitely adult but always sort of waiting for something more out of life, wanting to level up in some way to a deeper sense of *yes, life is good*. It was possible she wasn't seeing some perspective out of sheer inexperience. Hell, he had several centuries on her—maybe she was being immature.

She tapped his chest. "Seriously, I should walk. Free up your arms...,"

In case of what? An attack. It sort of made sense. She thought she'd read in some novel or other that a bodyguard couldn't be as effective if his arms were full of stuff—in this case, her.

"You have no foot protection." Again with the terse statements.

Irritation sparked and her face heated with temper. "Look, I'm not sure what your problem is, but I'm regretting sharing my deepest truth with you. Hell, I'm angrier hearing myself say that out loud because 'deepest truth' sounds corny and cheesy to my own ears now. I got vulnerable and you're throwing up walls. Maybe now isn't the right time to talk it out, but I'd do a lot better on my own two feet, walking off a little bit of what I'm feeling so I don't just keep running at the mouth like this."

His jaw tightened, and she buried the desire to reach up and run her fingertips along his jawline, soothe those tense and bunching muscles. She didn't think her touch would be welcome at this moment, and didn't that just suck?

"I apologize." His fingers tightened on her shoulder and thigh, just above the knee. "I am considering information we discovered while you were inside the cave."

She thought back to the strange hermit. The man had seemed a little unhinged, but there had been a kindness about him, at least toward her. "What did you learn?"

"A fact about the nature of the forests we just left, that perhaps made me face a truth of my own," Bennett said in a low voice, almost as if he was speaking to himself. "The reason I have reservations about giving my heart to a human again is the agony of living on after my companion has passed away. It is more than difficult with colleagues, painful with real friends, but love? Incapacitating."

Understanding hit her and it was like running straight into a brick wall. This wasn't about humanity versus supernatural—it was about kinds of supernaturals, about the distance Bennett maintained between himself and the world. "What did you learn about kinnaree?"

"None of the beings who live in those forests, or come from them, are immortal." He uttered the fact as if it pained him.

And the hermit had welcomed her back, let her know how to find more like herself.

"That's...we don't know enough. Werewolves aren't immortal, but Thomas has lived a really long time. I'm in my thirties and people mistake me for a decade younger all the time. I could be like Thomas. Just because I won't live forever doesn't mean I'm going to leave you as soon as..." She trailed off, unwilling to hurt him more.

As soon as your past love did.

It was unfair to be jealous of a woman, a relationship, that was long ended. She wouldn't give herself to those feelings. Instead, she said, "We still have a lot to learn about me."

About us.

But Bennett's face had gone cold and blank. He had his mask in place and he was shutting her out.

Irritation and fear crashed together and anger ignited inside her.

"Let me down." She didn't make it a request this time. "I need space to think."

He didn't. Instead, he burst into speed, hurtling down the trail and past Thomas. The air around them blurred as he used his vampiric speed to take them to the trailhead faster than the others could keep up. He stopped at the SUV they'd left parked in the little cul de sac next to the trailhead and settled her on the hood, her feet dangling over the side.

"You can walk when we get shoes on your feet." He didn't linger or make eye contact with her.

If anything, he seemed defensive, like he was being harassed. More than ever, she wanted to know what was going on inside his mind.

But he moved away, heading to the driver's side door. They'd brought sneakers for her, hoping for the best. It'd made sense to leave them in the back of the SUV.

Silence.

She looked over. He was standing there, glaring at the side of the car.

"What's wrong now?" Maybe he'd tell her. Now that she asked, fear whispered to her. Maybe she didn't want to know.

He scowled, still studying the car door. "Thomas has the keys."

Something popped inside her, like a bubble, and she laughed. Couldn't help it. The level of ridiculousness undid her and the escalating anxiousness from his attitude unwound as she let go of the nervous energy.

"I'm betting he'll be here in just a second and the two of you can do your thing," she said.

Ah. She felt better. She was still anxious, but she could wait until they got back to the manor to talk through whatever was causing this distance between them.

She lifted her chin, catching Bennett's gaze. "I'm not going straight home when we get back. I care about the people I've met here and I'm invested in us. It's worth it to me to talk this out."

The hard lines around Bennett's eyes and mouth softened. His lips parted. "This. Between us. I had hoped…"

He trailed off, shaking his head. He was at a loss for words for the first time since she'd met him and her heart ached. He was tearing a hole in her chest and he wasn't even trying. That was the problem.

"You're scaring me, Bennett."

He met her gaze then and the look in his eyes was bleak. "I can't—"

Something hurtled out of the shadows and slammed into Bennett, taking them both into the side of the car with a force that crumpled the whole door and thrusting the SUV up, the driver's side wheels lifting off the pavement. Alarmed, Peeraphan manifested her wings and tail, leaping clear of the vehicle and taking flight.

Francesco was tangled with Bennett, the two of them grappling in the twisted remains of the SUV. Adrenaline shot through her and her first thought was to get clear so Bennett wouldn't have to worry about her getting caught up as collateral damage. She summoned an updraft and beat her wings downward to get altitude.

Something else streaked toward her from behind. A loop of some kind of rope passed over her head and wrapped around her torso, pinning her arms to her sides and her wings to her hips. She squeezed out a wordless cry as she fell toward the earth, suddenly bound and trying to angle her body to roll with the impact. Someone caught her just before she hit the rough asphalt. This wasn't Bennett or Thomas, or even Marie. This was a man in a leather jacket, smelling of smoky chili peppers and nutty toasted sesame. He tossed her unceremoniously over his shoulder, his hands holding the strange rope binding her instead of gripping her directly.

"No time for introductions," a cheerful tenor voice stated.

"It'd be good for you to go to sleep now," a second, deeper voice added.

"No!" She tried to struggle.

Her bindings tightened, entangling her even more somehow. More than rope, the length of it had coiled around her and the coils rolled as they contracted. Visions of a snake constricting around its prey flashed through her mind.

Then the world went black.

BENNETT

Bennett glared at the indigo sky, stained faint orange at the horizon. There'd been times when he'd lingered as long as possible to glimpse the first moments of dawn, so he could dream of a sight he had never seen in real life. Now he hated the coming of the sun.

"Find her." He was on the edge of a rampage, his anger edged with desperation.

"We need a war room for times like this," Duncan observed, the calm of his tone providing counterpoint to the tension drawn tight in the room. "The library has the space and information at one's fingertips, but it does not accommodate...this."

Duncan swept a hand in an arching motion to indicate Bennett standing in the center of the room, balanced on his toes and ready to destroy everything around him. Thomas was pacing at the edges of the library like it was a cage, restless and probably just as eager to go on the hunt. Marie was cursing and searching spell books, not even bothering with turning the pages by hand. Instead, she stood over a tattered old tome, her hand high over the open book, and the pages turned themselves at speed.

Bennett snarled.

"It would make organizing the group much more effective to do exactly what you're all trying to do." Duncan remained undeterred. Contrary to his practical commentary, he had dropped his glamour and was laying out a series of fae swords and knives on a table in front of him, checking each blade and the accompanying harness.

Thomas pivoted and came near, his eyes having changed to a vivid gold. His wolf aspect was dangerously close to the surface. "We arrived just as they were leaving. I checked the area around the car. Found their hiding places. It was a planned ambush for sure. There was nothing we could use to track them to wherever they came from or wherever they're going."

Francesco had disengaged as soon as his partners had carried off Peeraphan, leaving Bennett tangled in the remains of the SUV. Shame and guilt flashed through Bennett. He had made too many assumptions, allowed himself to disregard Francesco because the other vampire had been beaten back once before. He had not thought more carefully about Francesco's presence at the theater despite knowing Francesco had probably joined one of the groups looking to collect mythical items for their own gain.

The attackers had succeeded in surprising him because he had allowed himself to be distracted. He had been too caught up in his past history and paying attention to Peeraphan's reactions to his words. He had left their teammates behind. He had allowed himself to be ambushed.

Peeraphan had been taken.

"Time is key and I cannot fight the dawn." Bennett swallowed the bitterness of what he was admitting. "You all need to go after her."

"We need a way to track her or any of her kidnappers," countered Marie. "And Duncan's right. You standing in the middle of the library, ready to destroy everything around you, is ineffective. Thomas pacing around about to throw bookcases through the windows isn't better. I need something with a connection to the people we're looking for and none of the kidnappers left anything behind that we could find, much less use. Not a hair or a piece of gum— nobody even seems to be a smoker anymore—*nothing*. We can't go find her without a trail to follow."

"And they had enough magic to hide their scent trail," Thomas added.

"Hey!" Ashke came rushing into the room, the light emanating from his small body glowing red. The small winged fae clutched the straps of the pouch carrying Peeraphan's sugar gliders. "Look!"

Bennett held out his hand imperiously.

Marie cleared her throat. "You and Thomas are generally not the first candidates I would choose to handle cute, fuzzy creatures. You could hurt them without meaning to."

Bennett did not drop his hand. "These are not rodents who feed on seeds and fruit, herbs and grains. These hunt prey for their meals, protect their space. They recognize another predator when they are faced with one." He glanced around the room. "And more."

Ashke deposited the pouch in the palm of Bennett's hand and unzipped it. Cory and Tobi immediately burst out, rushing up Bennett's sleeve and disappearing into his jacket. He felt the prick of their tiny claws through the thinner material of his shirt as they climbed around his torso like a tree trunk. He walked slowly over to Marie, presenting himself and them for her scrutiny.

Marie leaned close and the tiny pencil-sharpener growls started up in response. Clearly, Cory and Tobi did not consider all of the Consortium members to be friends yet. Normally, Marie would have been the first to gain the trust of animals and people. But these sugar gliders were Peeraphan's and Bennett had been in closest contact.

Marie shook her head. "They could probably fine-tune a locator spell closer to their person, but we can't use the bond they have with her to locate her long distance."

"Ellery and I were too efficient, I'm afraid." Duncan sighed. "We destroy any hairs we find when we clean guest rooms, for the protection of our guests."

"They took the red shoes along with her." Thomas was barely intelligible, his words garbled through a constant low growl. "Even if we could use those, it's not an option."

Dawn was coming and Bennett was risking falling to the ground as a corpse if he remained in the library much longer. He had not fed yet, either.

Wait.

"How long does a donor's blood remain in a vampire's system?" Asamoah's voice came from the door.

They all turned and stared at Bennett. His mind raced. He had fed on Peeraphan—not even one of his normal feedings, but a desperate one. He'd almost drained her. Honestly, if he had known she doubted whether she was kinnaree versus human, he could have told her a human should not have survived that night. He hadn't admitted it to himself or thought it important at the time, because the outcome had been positive. She had survived, and saved his life, too.

Rather than say anything out loud, he offered his hand to Marie. "Be quick."

Marie picked up a small paring knife with a two-and-a-half-inch curved blade, pulled off the protective sheath, and nicked the pad of his fingertip. Then she pressed a small bottle to the tiny wound, catching the drops of blood as they welled up, before his vampiric magic healed the cut.

She stared at the small bottle for a moment and nodded. "This'll do. It'll take me some time, but I can work with this."

"Go rest, Bennett." Thomas moved into his peripheral line of sight.

The werewolf didn't come within touching distance and had never gotten behind Bennett, even when they were both raging. In this, Thomas was aligned with Bennett, not a threat or a competitor. An ally.

Thomas continued, "I'll take over here and you can join the hunt when you rise, if we haven't brought her back already."

Bennett looked first to Marie, then to Thomas, and met the gazes of Duncan and Asamoah and Ashke. These were his colleagues, his teammates, his…friends. He could put his trust in them.

And when they found Peeraphan, he hoped he would have the chance to repair the damage he had caused in her.

He left, streaking through the manor, barely making it to the dark safety of his suite in time to stumble to a halt in his rooms. He had not yet made it to his resting place when his dead body dropped to the floor.

NINETEEN

PEERAPHAN

eeraphan snapped awake and immediately froze, unable to
see anything. There was fabric tied over the upper half of her
face, more like a hood than a blindfold. It still kept her from
knowing where she was. She tried to move, but the binding kept her
arms trapped against her sides. Whatever it was must have relaxed
while she'd been unconscious, because it tightened around her again
as she tried to get free.

"Easy there, can't have you hurting yourself now, can we?" She
cringed at the familiar voice. Francesco.

She had no idea what he meant, but it definitely couldn't be
good. The last thing she remembered before losing consciousness
had been the voices of two other people, while Bennett had fought
Francesco. Her stomach twisted and fear constricted her chest as the
absolute worst-case scenario immediately came to the forefront of
her mind. Bennett wouldn't have let anyone take her while he was
conscious and able to do anything about it.

He couldn't be dead. She wouldn't even think it.

The car door opened and she realized she must've been lying
on a car seat, probably across the back seat. Fresh air flooded in at
her feet. She smelled evergreens and lush forest vegetation plus the

salty brine of the sea, a combination she associated with the Pacific Northwest. Hope bloomed in her chest. If her captors hadn't taken her far and she hadn't been out of it for long, then maybe help was coming soon.

Air pressure changed as a body started to lean in at the car door. She kicked with both feet. Her bare feet connected with a hard body, and whoever it was let out a curse in a language she didn't know. She pressed her lips together in a grim smile as hands wrapped around her ankles and tugged her out. Bound as she was, it wasn't the moment to try to get away, but she also wasn't going to offer no resistance at all.

"Don't be too satisfied," Francesco hissed in her ear. "Our client appreciates a certain kind of spice. You are only demonstrating your value."

"I don't like this." She knew that surly voice, but only barely. She'd heard it when they'd been attacked, when she'd been taken. It was one of her kidnappers.

"Our objectives were the wings and tail of a Thai bird princess, like in the folktale," another voice said, the tone sharp—her third kidnapper. "Not an actual bird princess."

"This is better." Francesco sounded unconcerned. "You checked for yourselves. The wings and tail manifest. They cannot be removed. So we deliver what we promised in the form of an entire, living myth. I've notified our client of the change and he is delighted."

"This isn't right." Gravel crunched as someone took a step.

Francesco snarled. "You both signed a contract with Babel. You are bound by oath. Are you going back on your word?"

Silence.

"I thought not. If you can't stomach finishing the job, go. I will complete delivery."

Peeraphan strained to hear more, belatedly remembered to

extend her magic. Her senses stretched out, but only to find the dis-placed air of two people who had just left. Damn it, she needed to practice using her magic more. If she'd been using her sense of air while they were back in the forest, knowing everyone was taking precautions against any dangers, she'd have sensed the ambush.

Too late now, but if she got out of this she was definitely going to work on her survival skills.

"Don't strain yourself trying to break your binding." Francesco was back, leaning close to speak into her ear. "My client likes to be assured the specimens we bring him are in good health and filled with a certain vitality. We are assured a higher finder's fee if he observes you alive and kicking right from the beginning. Why else would I remove the sleep talisman from your clothing?"

Nausea turned her stomach even more. The implications of Francesco's statements stacked the odds against her, by a lot. What was worse, she had played directly in his favor, too. She considered her options, uncertain what the best next step would be. But there were always options. There had to be. She just needed more infor-mation and an opening.

He set her on her feet and she felt the slight prick of short-cropped grass in a well-manicured lawn under her soles. His hands gripped her upper arms as he propelled her in front of him, so she was walking forward blind. She could hear water against the rocky shore and the calls of sea birds. Reaching out with her magic, her sense of water gave her the taste of salt and kelp and cold tempera-tures. If she knew more about the feel of bodies of water, she'd be able to tell more, but the sense of water currents and curved shore-lines made her hope she was still in the Puget Sound area. She also kind of wondered if he was about to push her off a cliff.

Nah. She couldn't be so lucky.

Besides, there was a client somewhere. Francesco had said so.

She thought back to times when her uncles had sometimes tried to dicker with sellers in the booths at Pike Place Market. If there was one thing sure to irritate people in the middle of bargaining, it was a chatterbox of a young person spilling random commentary and potentially oversharing.

"You have the red shoes. I hear collectors want a lot for them. Are you making a separate deal for those?" She pitched her voice to carry, uncertain how far away this potential client was. Maybe if the client found out about the red shoes, there'd be some tension to inject into their business talk.

Francesco only tightened his grip on her upper arms.

She whimpered. "You're hurting me."

"I was assured your team would be able to deliver a specimen in good condition," a new voice called out. "Is it even the specimen we discussed? To my understanding, a Thai *bird* princess would have wings."

The speaker had an attitude and pattern of diction indicating he was well educated and accustomed to being answered when he asked a question.

She reached out with her air sense and felt the way he drew air into his lungs and breathed it out again, with sour notes of chemicals and a hint of rot. He was a smoker, maybe. Air also carried sound to her—maybe not as effectively as Bennett or Thomas might hear, but she thought she heard a heartbeat in this moment. A heartbeat besides her own tense rhythm. So the speaker had a pulse and drew air to breathe; she was going to guess human for the moment, because she didn't smell the same kind of musk she detected around Thomas, a sort of mix of earthiness and sun-warmed trees.

The person could be a witch, or whatever other types of human magic users there might be. She was going to need to study up in the future. Regardless, she couldn't think of any kind of human who would be wise to talk that way to a vampire. She also wondered what kind of motivation a vampire as old as Francesco would have to be doing work for a human. What kind of advantage or calamity could Francesco cause by handing her over to his…client? The world had gotten a lot more complicated once she'd become aware of supernaturals.

To get away from either of them, she needed whatever was wrapped around her torso removed. She considered launching herself into the air and trying to ditch the hood as she went. She hadn't tried a straight jump from the ground into flight, though. She wasn't sure she could do that, then summon her wings, then get a good enough downbeat to gain any kind of altitude. She would need the chance to summon her wings first. Or she could go back to hoping Francesco would push her off a cliff.

Bad vampire jerked her to a halt.

She whimpered again.

He hissed.

"This is what you call ensuring 'good condition'?" The person she assumed was the client sounded angry now, not just arrogant. "If she has bruises, I think I'm justified in assuming she's damaged in other ways."

Francesco snarled. Oh wow, this human really had no concept of his own mortality.

She bit her lip and let loose some of the fears she had been keeping under tight rein.

"I hurt everywhere," she said, her voice tight with the sound of apprehension. "Please don't knock me out again. I only just woke up."

"The deal was that she'd be unharmed." Every word escalated in volume and pitch.

"She is alive and able to walk toward you on her own two feet," Francesco said smoothly, cold anger chilling his words. "She is obviously capable of communicating, and arguably intelligent, considering the way she is manipulating you."

"Fascinating." Temper had evaporated from the client's voice, replaced by delighted curiosity. "Is that an undocumented ability for her kind? Is it a magical effect, perhaps similar to a mermaid or siren? I may have to consider fitting her with preventive measures."

Fresh anticipation skittered through her. Who was this man? Some kind of collector, apparently. And if he was collecting specimens, she wondered if he really did have a mermaid or siren already. What kind of preventive measures did he have to keep them from influencing him with their voices? Her fear grew sharp edges. She couldn't wait too long to find the perfect opening. She needed to take the first opportunity she could get.

Or make one for herself.

"Unknown," Francesco said in a way that implied he didn't particularly care. "You can study her at your leisure."

Ew. That gave her impressions ranging from dissection to perversions, and her creative imagination was definitely not an advantage here.

Peeraphan's magic helped her sense the air shifting around her, so the client didn't surprise her when he touched her face. She jerked back anyway, repulsed. Tactile contact was its own form of communication and the way his smooth fingertips crept over her cheek tripped every alarm and raised every red flag she had.

"Where are the wings?" the client asked.

"They were gone when she lost consciousness. She can summon them at will," Francesco responded, unconcerned.

"I require a demonstration."

Well, she wasn't going to be accommodating. Or actually, it could depend on what kind of demonstration. "No problem. I'll show you I can fly."

"Silence." The one word lashed out in a quiet threat. Seemed like the client didn't like people who spoke before they were spoken to.

Francesco chuckled. "Payment is due on delivery. Our agreement does not include a demonstration. I would think the integrity of our organization would speak for itself. After all, we've brought you several items of interest in the past and invested significant time and resources into acquiring this representative of a lost myth for you. If not for our seer, this one would still be hiding in plain sight in the middle of downtown Seattle."

"I've no issues with our prior transactions," the client grumbled, his tone slightly less antagonistic but still adamant. "This one seemed too good to be true, even with the accuracy of your seer. Past business experience only goes so far."

Francesco sighed. "In the interest of nurturing client relationships, if you pay now and payment is confirmed, I will remain to ensure your new specimen provides you a demonstration before you take her into your facility."

It was unclear to Peeraphan as to whether there was a question of her actually being a kinnaree or whether there was suspicion of her being a plant inside this client's property. Too many undercurrents, not enough words.

The client cleared his throat. "Fine. Payment sent. As for a demonstration, I have something in mind. How do you get that... thing...off her?"

Oh well, she was glad she wasn't the only one unfamiliar with whatever it was keeping her tied up. It was something of a toss-up as to whether she would want to avoid these bindings or that client's touch more. Assuming she got herself out of this situation. There was hope, if Francesco gave in to the overdose of confidence he'd already been demonstrating the few times they had interacted.

"The noose with its coils is a mythic artifact, a gift from the king of the phayanak of the Mekong River to a human hunter generations ago. It was used to capture the youngest of the kinnaree princesses when they came down from the mountains to bathe under the light of the full moon." Francesco was in full-on mansplaining mode. "To make it release, you treat it as you would a snake constricting its prey—grasp the tail and unwrap."

Oversimplified. She had a friend who worked with animal control who had shared with her a fair number of incidents involving constrictors and feeding errors. There were some considerations when it came to getting a constrictor to uncoil from caught prey. She sort of hoped the client would find himself suffering one or more of those complications.

The fabric was yanked from her head and she blinked rapidly to clear her vision. It was night. She should have guessed—she was being held by a vampire, after all. She wondered if he'd driven all the way here in a vehicle with tinted windows—no, not possible. Bennett had said vampires became literal corpses during the day. So he and his conspirators must have hidden somewhere until he had risen again with the setting of the sun. There was no sign of whoever they were. Probably didn't matter for the immediate situation.

She was on a lawn overlooking a very impressive view of water with islands in the distance. She'd seen a similar view, if not exactly the same, once when she'd brought her mom up to Friday Harbor to go whale watching. The air here tasted the same. It made sense. The San Juan Islands were full of very private, elite properties, and it was also easy to live comfortably while still maintaining a low profile.

The very contemporary, very large custom-built home behind the client wasn't exactly what she would consider low profile, but these things were relative. The client himself was a tall man with long limbs. His skin was fair, and if he'd ever spent a day unprotected from the sun, he'd probably have had freckles. His red hair was somewhat long on top and slicked back, trimmed neatly on the sides. His face would be aristocratic if this were another time and place, with its prominent brow and nose. His wide mouth and thin lips were pulled in a smirk. He reached out with slender fingers and grasped something below her peripheral vision. She wasn't going to look down. She wouldn't drop her gaze for him.

"I am Jonathan Saghier, your new master."

Like hell. She kept her thoughts to herself, though. He didn't deserve them.

He continued, assured of his status in the current company. "Kinnaree are legendary for their musical talent and their dancing skills. You will perform for me now, and whenever I want in the future. You'll find I treat my specimens well when they are obedient. I have a number of ways to discipline you if you're not."

Of course he did. She didn't intend to be around to find out.

She'd been busy looking around, taking in every detail she could. "Light the firepit."

He raised a hand, ostensibly to strike her. It took everything she had not to flinch.

"The bird princess Manora danced for a king and queen of humans before such a fire," she said quickly. The client held his hand, the impending punishment suspended, waiting. She continued, "The Manora Buchayan is a dance I learned as part of my Thai classical dance studies. Even if you've seen it performed, you've never seen it performed by an actual kinnaree."

This. This was her opportunity. But she needed the fire.

The client lowered his hand. "Fine. We'll light the firepit, and you will perform for me. If you try to flee, Francesco here will bring you to me and I will punish you sufficiently that you will never try again."

She nodded, finally casting her gaze to the ground. Let him believe he'd intimidated her. She didn't think Francesco appreciated being used as the means to carry out a threat, either. The client made a lot of assumptions and it was to her benefit to let him keep going.

Minutes later, the firepit had been lit. It was ridiculously impressive, she had to admit. Big enough to park a car in, which was fine with her: the bigger the fire, the greater the heat. The highest risk to her plan at the moment was Francesco. She didn't know the full scope of what the vampire could do. He'd almost killed Bennett permanently the first time she'd encountered the vampires, and she had been avoiding thinking about what might have happened the second time. She didn't have bandwidth to be distracted about thoughts of Bennett or Marie or Thomas yet. Didn't want to think about whatever it was Bennett had been about to say when the attack had happened. If all of them were alive, and she hoped they were, they were looking for her and she would do her best to go to them.

Even if Bennett didn't want her.

"That's all the preparations we're going to do. No more delays." The client reached for the tail end of the bindings and yanked. It loosened and dropped in coils around her feet. He turned on his heel, as if he was sure she wouldn't just try to flee right there, and took a seat in an armchair, facing the fire like he was sitting in a throne. "Show me this dance."

She stepped out of the coils, watching for a moment in alarmed fascination as it continued to slide and slither over itself like a live snake might. It was hard to make herself stoop and touch it, but she gathered the heavy loops in her arms. It was dry to the touch and smooth, the way a snake would be. Not unpleasant except for the knowledge that it had been used to bind her just a short while ago, that it had the power to hold her despite her magic.

She brought it to the client and placed it at his feet. He didn't know how to use it. Better for it to be with him than in Francesco's hands, where it could be used against her in the next few minutes.

A few steps and she was in front of the fire, close enough to feel the heat of it seeping into her back. There was no music, but that was okay. She knew it, could imagine she heard the delicate *ching* and firm *chup* of the instruments used to set the rhythm. She started on her knees, sitting on her heels, back straight with hands pressed together in front of her. She began with small movements of her upper body and arms, transitioning to a standing position and summoning her wings and tail as she did. With each movement, each step, she stretched her arms and legs and wings, using the gestures of the dance to encourage her blood to circulate and bring strength back to every part of her. Dancing helped her shake off any stiffness or soreness from being tied up and stationary through the day.

The client was sitting forward in his chair, mouth dropped open, mesmerized. And he should be. She was an excellent dancer. She tilted her head just so, her movements mimicking a bird's as her wings extended and folded. The dance alternated between slow, graceful tests of balance and strength and faster steps of fun playfulness, helping her flit to and fro before the bonfire. She held poses for just the right amount of time, poised to seem as if she could fall into the fire at any moment, the way Manora was meant to have sacrificed herself in flames. She let the steps of the dance carry her around the firepit once, then again, aware of Francesco's watchful tension. She summoned her magic carefully, subtly, using her wings to waft air across the flames and encourage them to burn higher and hotter. The vampire was poised to grab her if she tried to make a break for the edge of the lawn and the drop to the sea below, and she allowed herself to glance in that direction once, twice. Let him prepare to counter an action she didn't plan to take.

It would better her chances of succeeding in what she did intend to do.

The dance was drawing to a close, and here were the greatest shows of elegance and vitality. Her wings swept through the flames in the firepit, her air magic drawing motes of fire in trails behind her wing tips as she turned. She spun and stepped forward, then pulled back and turned the other way, calling her magic…and leapt directly into the firepit.

The fire roared up around her, the hot updraft providing a boost as her spread wings swept down and propelled her skyward. Luckily, the fire had burned long and hot enough to give her enough lift to get well out of arm's reach before the client even had the chance to shout.

She had no idea if Francesco could fly, but she thought maybe not if he wasn't already in the air coming after her. She flew as fast as she could, risking one look back over her shoulder. Francesco stood below, having lost precious fractions of a second in trying to retrieve the binding from under the client's feet. More shouts were rising up around the property. She didn't waste any more time. It would suck to get shot out of the sky.

She beat her wings, climbing through the skies in a bid for more altitude and reveling in the feel of the winds carrying her.

Elation sang through her. She'd done it. She'd escaped!

TWENTY

MARIE

"No!"

"Wait!" Marie tightened her grip on Bennett's arm, grateful she had already had a hand on his sleeve in the dark. Otherwise, the vampire would've been too fast for her. "I can help her."

She extended her free hand outward toward the fire and Punch, whispering the words of her spell as she pulled magic from the trees and plant life around her. The bonfire flared up higher, far higher, the heat lifting Punch up and out of reach even faster.

"She's clear." Bennett slipped his arm from her grasp. Then he rose out of their hiding place inside the trees bordering the property and launched into the sky himself.

"Are there any more security, besides what we see out there?" Marie asked. "We don't want anyone to shoot her down."

She remained crouched in the shadows with Punch's sugar gliders safely in their carry pouch slung over her shoulder and across her torso. The tracker spell had worked, but now she wasn't absolutely sure how best to proceed. Bennett and Thomas were more suited to direct confrontations.

She preferred to let them take the lead while she hung back and provided support. But they had barely arrived in time to witness the end of Punch's dance. No time to form a more thorough plan of action.

"So far, I've only scented human patrols," Thomas rumbled. He was still in human form, but his eyes caught any and all light in the night and reflected it back at her. "I'll take care of any perimeter security, remove any threats, then I'll lead Dunacan and Ashke in to deal with the building itself. You look for a chance to retrieve the shoes, if you can."

She nodded in agreement and he melted into the darkness.

The client was screaming and Francesco was ignoring him. Instead, the vampire streaked back to an SUV just a few yards away from her. He opened the side door and tossed the looped coils of a mythic item in, giving her a glimpse at a satchel laying open on the seat. Sultry red satin and a tempting sparkle peeked out.

The red shoes.

The vampire didn't even bother to close the car door. He turned and rushed back to where the client was ranting at a few private security henchmen, pointing at the sky.

Funny thing about mythic items like the red shoes: they had a passive ability to catch the eye. The satchel might have even been closed before, but probably slid open with a touch of magic to help a new victim stumble across them.

Marie bit her lip. She had cast a spell on herself, a sort of you-can't-see-me effect. It didn't make her invisible, but it allowed a passing glance to overlook her and even dampened any sounds or scent from her. Problem was, it worked best when she was holding still. The more she moved, the more likely a vigilant person might detect her, especially a supernatural. The vampire, client, and henchmen had moved to the cliff edge and seemed to be in deep discussion as to what to do next though. The only place they could go farther away would have been into the client's ridiculously large home. This might be her best chance.

She broke cover, heading straight for the car. Shoving the coils of the noose Francesco had left in the back seat into the satchel with the shoes, she closed the bag and hooked the strap over her shoulder. She took extra seconds to close the car door as quietly as possible, relying on her spell's influence to muffle the sound. Then she turned and ran straight back to the tree line. As soon as she reached the trees, she ducked down and crawled through a patch of thick underbrush to another hiding spot in the shelter of a thicket. Peering out, she was pretty sure no one had seen her.

It would be a bad idea to stay in this location, though. Francesco would return and could track her by scent—maybe not as well as Thomas could, but vampires did have heightened senses. By the same reasoning, Thomas would be able to find her when he returned, so she didn't need to stay and wait for him. Checking the satchel to be sure it still contained her loot and adjusting the strap so she was sure she wasn't crushing the sugar gliders, she turned and crept through the thicket to a large game trail where she could move a little faster.

She made it a few hundred yards away, then froze as the sounds of boots crushing twigs came from up ahead. It couldn't be Thomas—he was quieter and had also gone in practically the other direction. Maybe a security patrol? The beam of a high-powered flashlight swung through the darkness. Yup. They must have come up from the water side. It was a big property. Looking around her, she tried to decide the best place to hide.

Hands came out of the darkness and grabbed her. Before she could scream, one hand clapped over her mouth as the other grasped her shoulder. Then an arm wrapped around her waist and yet another hooked under her legs, behind her knees. Just like that, she was high up on a large tree branch, tucked between two very warm, very solid bodies.

"Shh." The warning tickled her ear.

She nodded and the hand over her mouth released her. Marie turned to look at the speaker. She couldn't see a whole lot in the shadows, but there was some moonlight here. He had dark hair and dark eyes, features that spoke of Asian descent, and...tails. He had fox tails as long as his body waving gently around him, each one orange fading into white with a touch of black at the very tip.

"We mean you no harm, witch." She turned to face the second speaker. His voice was deeper, almost sullen. Another fox, also with nine tails—though this one's tails were a deep, burnished red fading to charcoal at the tips. He had rougher-hewn features and a burning intensity. He also had the "I could tell you more, but then I'd have to kill you" vibe going, and if he dropped that line, she would believe him.

Lips brushed the upper shell of her ear again. "In fact, we're happy to invite you to play hide-and-seek. They're it."

Fox Number One made it sound like fun and games, but his tone teased with more decadent possibilities.

Footsteps. The guards came up the trail and passed right under them. Both men positioned their tails to shelter them and maybe to break up the silhouettes of their forms, she thought. Just more shadows in the darkness, no people shapes up here.

The heat of her two helpers enclosed her, their faces very close to hers. Their arms were still interlocked, cradling her between them. Each of them had a thigh pressing against her. It was like they were comfortably holding each other and had included her in the embrace. They waited in silence as the security team passed under them.

Fox number one chuckled, finally. "I never get tired of wondering when a human is actually going to look up."

"Why are you helping me?" She squirmed and their arms moved with her, allowing her to shift her position a little but not letting her go.

There had been multiple attackers in the ambush earlier tonight. Someone had been helping Francesco. They'd taken Punch and brought her here, to a collector. Marie wondered what they might do with her.

"Ah. Well. About that." Fox Number One ducked his head.

Fox Number Two rumbled, "We owe your friend."

"We thought she had certain items of interest."

"She did."

"But she wasn't even wearing the red shoes anymore."

"It was more expedient to take her with us to determine how to acquire the items we wanted." Fox number two sighed.

"Not the shoes, though we did snag those as a bonus," Fox Number One clarified. "The shoes were a way to confirm she was a supernatural. A means to an end. We thought her wings and tail were removable."

"Our background information identified her as human." Fox Number Two had an edge of defense to his tone. "We thought her resistance to the red shoes indicated she had another mythic item in her possessions—wings and a tail of a kinnaree."

"She is the bird princess and the wings manifest as a part of her." Marie snapped her mouth shut. No need to give them any more information about Punch than they had already revealed they knew.

Fox Number One made a clicking noise with his tongue. "Folktales and legends can change a bit, depending on the story-teller. The version of the bird princess myth we were going by indicated the wings and tail were items worn by the daughters of the king of the bird people."

Ah. Well, Marie figured she had a grasp on the situation. "So you grabbed her, intending to take the items you thought she had and let her go?"

Both nodded and Fox Number One continued enthusiastically. "It wasn't until we had her and searched her that we realized the wings and tails are a part of her as a kinnaree and not items worn by a human."

Uh huh. Still not okay. "She still ended up here, with some guy screaming about getting his specimen back as she flew away."

Fox Number Two didn't respond, but his brows drew together in a scowl. It was Fox Number One who shook his head. "It didn't sit right with us to hand her over to the client as a specimen of his private supernatural creature collection. We wouldn't have taken this contract if we'd known about this from the beginning."

She glared at each of them in turn.

"It's starting to become a thing in certain elite circles." Fox Number Two dropped the words like stones, his distaste evident.

His companion nodded. "Item collection, that is. There's always been private collections of art and literature. It's not surprising that collectors would want the actual objects featured in those tales."

"You said you wouldn't have taken this contract." She had a growing sense of foreboding.

There were always collectors and adventurers competing to get their hands on items of myth and magic. She and others in consortiums around the world had experience dealing with those. This seemed to be a bigger kind of competition.

"The organization we do freelance work for gets a lot of interesting engagements from such clients." Fox Number One gave her a boyish grin. Harmless. Right?

No. She wasn't falling for it. "And what organization is that?"

Fox Number Two leaned close enough to rumble in her other ear. "Babel."

The name didn't ring a bell, but the richness of his voice sent delicious shivers through her.

Fox Number One's grin widened. He was incredibly attractive with his upbeat energy. "Members of the organization have a lot of fun with chaos. The idea of acquiring items of myth and magic and tossing them into the hands of humanity is entertaining. It's interesting to see what humans will do."

"That's awful." She was aghast. "Like giving a child a hand grenade to play with in a playground."

"Oh, now, there's a complicated perspective." Fox Number One tugged a lock of her hair gently. "Who gets to be the parents of humanity? Should anyone be? Sometimes humans are very creative about doing good with a thing that's only ever been used to do evil. You might be surprised."

"Either way, we never get bored of watching," Fox Number Two added.

Anger boiled up inside her. "My friend Punch isn't a thing."

They both sobered.

"True," Fox Number Two agreed.

"Which is why we noped out as soon as we realized what Francesco had really promised the client." Fox Number One shrugged. "And here we are, doing a little bit of good to make amends. We do have morals."

"To a certain extent," Fox Number Two said.

"The point is that the collecting of living beings is a complicated topic." Fox Number One turned his face up to the moon. "Arguing the rationale is a slippery slope and there's potentially no actual line to draw between right or wrong. But keeping a sentient person as a specimen in a supernatural zoo lands definitively in the wrong category."

"So if you all hadn't shown up, we would have intervened," Fox Number Two added decisively.

If the first young man was all bright and charming, the second had a dangerous, steely edge to him. The combination was doing some interesting things to her heart rate. And this was not the time. Shouldn't ever be the time.

"Well, we might have intervened anyway, just on principle." Fox Number One laughed quietly. "There's no way we could let a lovely lady like you be taken by a pack of anonymous sentries."

"Nice support, by the way," Fox Number Two added. "For a witch who doesn't use blood magic, you are exceptionally powerful. That was a nice bit of power to cast at a distance."

She shook her head, feeling like she'd lost a battle inside herself trying to stay angry at these two. It was clear they had no ill intentions toward Punch and they'd done their best to fix their mistakes. It didn't mean she wasn't suspicious of them. Their intentions were nowhere near pure. "Fine. I appreciate your help. Is it safe to let me go now?"

"Safe? Yes." Fox Number Two was staring at her, his gaze intense.

"Do we want to?" Fox Number One nipped her ear.

She sucked in a breath, but before she could react, they were gone and she had to clutch at the tree branch to keep from falling. The night air was chill against her skin in their absence.

TWENTY-ONE

BENNETT

ennett flew after Peeraphan, watching for any signs of attack, hoping the collector had no means readily available to bring her out of the sky.

"Bennett!" Ashke joined him. "Want me with you, or should I go help Thomas?"

A good question. Rational thought had left him momentarily as he had followed to make sure Peeraphan made it out of immediate danger. But now, watching her wings take her higher and higher, he was certain she was out of range of the sort of firearms human security might be carrying. The tightness in his chest eased a fraction and he looked back down toward the island and the collector's property.

He couldn't leave yet. And perhaps Peeraphan should be given the chance to witness what they were about to do to the property. It might spare her a measure of fear and anxiety later.

"Wait," Bennett instructed Ashke as he gathered his power and shot forward in a burst of speed.

He caught up with Peeraphan in moments, staying just below her until he could get ahead and into her line of sight. Then he turned to face her with his hands up and open.

She cried out, a strangled sound that seemed part frustration and part relief. Then she plowed into him, her arms wrapping around his waist. Her body trembled against him and he wondered at the courage she'd had to fly through the fear of her ordeal. There were many who would have been frozen, paralyzed, overwhelmed. But here she was and she had broken free on her own.

She was amazing.

He lowered his arms, holding her to him gently, adjusting his flight to steady them both. "You're safe. You escaped. You're safe."

He murmured the assurances over and over until her grip on him eased. She lifted her face from his chest finally and looked up at him, her gaze searching. "You're here."

Uncertainty hit him like a brick. Had she thought him dead? Worse, had she thought he wouldn't come? But there wasn't time to ask her yet. There was more to do. Instead, he nodded. "The others are here, too."

He lifted his chin and she looked over her shoulder without releasing him. He felt smug about that, at least. Ashke had been keeping pace with them, the winged fae waving when Peeraphan turned. Bennett allowed their flight speed to slow a bit more and Ashke caught up to them.

"You're safe! We worried!" Ashke said, zipping around them in a full loop. "Your escape was epic! Now we can deal with that collector without worrying about a hostage situation. This is great!"

"Deal with...?" Peeraphan turned her gaze back to Bennett.

"You don't have to stay for this." Bennett wanted her to know she had a choice. But he also thought he had come to understand her enough to anticipate what she would choose. "But it might give you some satisfaction to be a part of what we're doing next."

"Thomas has already started!" Ashke exclaimed. "You won't be able to see from here. Nobody will see. Not yet. But he's dealing with perimeter guards a few at a time. The forest around the property is good for privacy, but also good for us."

"If you want, you can go with Ashke and provide support from the air," Bennett offered. "I should go back and deal with Francesco. Duncan will enter the building and neutralize any security inside, then remove any items the collector has that could be dangerous."

"Specimens." Peeraphan bit out the word. "If that man has any specimens, we should set them free."

Bennett nodded. "It would be good if you were there to help. There may be more than Duncan can carry out on his own."

There might be frightened beings who would be comforted by her presence. They might trust her where they wouldn't the sidhe, not to mention a werewolf or a vampire. It would allow them all to move quickly, before human authorities arrived on site.

"What can I do?" Her face was still pale but her voice was steady.

"I'll be headed to the roof to call out to Thomas and Bennett any danger we might be able to sense. You can come with me," Ashke offered. "We'll be out of reach but important to the operation until Duncan needs us inside."

Bennett nodded in agreement, searching her expressions for any sign of fear. He did not want to push her too hard, but he also couldn't just take her away back to the manor without dealing with her attacker. Francesco would continue to be a danger if not neutralized.

"You'll be able to see with your own eyes that they will not be a threat to you anymore," Bennett whispered, for her only.

There was another moment of hesitation, then the muscles along her jaw tightened with what he had come to recognize as resolve. Her arms loosened from around his waist and her wings lifted, catching the winds and pulling her from him. "I'll go with Ashke."

"I'll be nearby, ensuring the exterior is made safe," he promised her. "Call and I will come for you. No matter the distance."

Her hands opened and closed into fists. He could hear her heartbeat despite the wind rushing around them. Accelerated, maybe, but strong and steady. There was a maelstrom of emotion churning in her dark eyes.

"We have some talking to do," she whispered, the wind carrying her words to his ears. "But this... You're right. I want to be a part of this first. Just don't get yourself killed. I'll do everything I can to keep myself free, and we'll have our conversation after. Promise?"

Ah, he'd be damned if making a promise like this wasn't tempting fate. He couldn't promise, not until he dealt with Francesco. And he'd already underestimated Francesco a time too many. "I promise to do everything in my power not to get myself killed and to present myself in a timely manner for this conversation."

"You've been around us fae folk too long," Ashke chortled. "You're starting to give your word the way we do."

He shot a dark glance at the fae, scowling.

But laughter bubbled up from Peeraphan. He couldn't hold on to any petty ire when the sound of it lit the dark corners of his soul the way it did.

Finally, she nodded at Ashke. "Let's do this."

THOMAS

There hadn't been time to track and neutralize every roving pair of security guards. If Thomas had tried, the perimeter of the property was large enough and there were enough separate teams that someone would have tried to check in with someone else and realized something was wrong. The longer they could avoid having any alarms going up, the better. So Thomas took out two sets of guards and hid their unconscious bodies from immediate discovery, figuring it was a sufficient window in the live perimeter defenses for Duncan to slip through.

Not that Duncan had needed his help to pass through the woods undetected. He was fae. No human would have been aware of him if he hadn't wanted to make himself known.

"What do you think?" Duncan was standing next to Thomas, as if thinking of the sidhe summoned him.

"Seems like surveillance around the property is limited to fairly standard cameras on the house, facing out toward the tree line and main approaches."

There were plenty of areas of dead space—places where it was possible for an intruder to move or wait unseen—both at the tree line and near the main building. Thomas chuckled. "I could make it to the house even if I was human."

"Ah, well then." Duncan grinned. There was an edge to the sidhe's smile, and anticipation glinted in his eyes.

Not for the first time, Thomas wondered what Duncan's place had been in the sidhe courts before he had decided to live away from Under Hill. The choice to serve the manor and the Darke Consortium as a butler was also an interesting one. Some people had a passion for the vocation, but Thomas wondered what path Duncan had taken in choosing it.

A flicker of movement caught Thomas's attention and as he looked up, Ashke and Peeraphan were landing on the flat roof of the main building. Moonlight had shone on the white swan feathers of Peeraphan's wings, or he might not have seen them at all. Relief washed through him to see her safe. Pride swelled his chest, realizing she'd returned with Ashke rather than fleeing. He wouldn't have blamed her if she had. She had been kidnapped, probably been ter-rified. She'd gotten herself free on her own and that was already a lot. That she would return meant she definitely had the makings of a member of the Darke Consortium.

"Well, it seems we have cover from above." Duncan sounded pleased. "A good start for a potential new member."

Maybe the sidhe had thoughts along the same lines as Thomas. Maybe he didn't. It was hard to tell how fae minds worked. For now, Thomas would adjust to accommodate this change in the resources available to their team.

"We focus on the exterior and interior, then," Thomas pressed on. This wasn't the first time they'd had to enter a place uninvited to remove one or possibly more objects of myth and magic. There hadn't been time to acquire sufficient intel on this specific property to develop a plan, but each of them was clever enough to improvise as they went. They thrived on the element of uncertainty, really. When one lived as long as any one of them did, it was in everyone's best interest if they didn't let themselves get too bored. "I'll keep the attention of any human security personnel out here on the lawns while I clear the area around the house. If there's an external hub for the security system, I'll take it out."

"If it is inside, I will disable it," Duncan stated.

Thomas nodded. Really, if the house was only staffed with humans, the group of them were overpowered for this particular mission. But they couldn't be sure the human collector didn't have some kind of paranormal support. Besides, if Francesco hadn't left, the vampire was potentially still somewhere on the grounds.

Thomas bared his teeth as his gaze swept through the shadows around them. He wouldn't mind getting a piece of the bloodsucking bastard who'd taken Peeraphan. She was more than a distant cousin he'd known years ago—she was family.

"We'll leave you to it, then," Duncan said quietly, drawing a sword from nowhere. It flashed silver in the moonlight, brighter than one might have thought it could.

Thomas nodded, tightening his control on the temper churning below his skin. It had been a long time since the moon could overcome self-control and call his wolf forward against his will, but tonight, he wasn't particularly inclined to keep his wolf in check. The sidhe grinned back at him and Thomas snorted. Duncan knew exactly what was happening.

Mischief, especially where Duncan and Ashke were concerned, was far from harmless.

Thomas glanced up again, searching for Ashke and Peeraphan. The two of them had crouched low, minimizing their silhouettes, probably blending into what looked like shadows to the human eye. It took a supernatural with night vision to find them. As he watched them, Ashke glowed with a soft, gentle light that illuminated Peeraphan holding up two fingers of her left hand, then tilting the same fingers to point at her eyes. Then she turned her hand to point down to Thomas's left.

Thomas nodded sharply in acknowledgment. Ashke's light went out and the two were lost in shadow again. Not bad. He'd have to find out if Ashke had told her what to do or if she'd thought of it herself. For the moment, though, he had security guards to hunt.

TWENTY-TWO

PEERAPHAN

Peeraphan scanned the area as best she could. She didn't have particularly acute sight at night, but the security teams seemed to be using flashlights and it hadn't been hard to spot those from this vantage point. Ashke had suggested the hand signs to communicate to Thomas when they'd realized he was looking up at them.

"Best not to make noises to draw attention to us," Ashke had whispered. "I can make my light only visible to supernaturals. Humans won't see. Well, not unless I let them, and that would take a few extra steps. We don't have to worry about it right now."

Peeraphan had only shaken her head and done as Ashke suggested. So many new things had hit her in such a short amount of time, she wasn't going to cope with it all unless she did her best to just be a sponge and soak up all the information about this new dimension to the world she lived in. She'd process all these tidbits later and when there was time to freak out about how humans just walked through their world unaware of the layers of magic around them, the supernaturals among them.

Duncan had left Thomas's side, heading toward the front of the building—honestly, it was basically a mansion, all modern architecture in ninety-degree angles and huge glass windows. Below them, Thomas melted back into the trees. She waited, holding her breath, until she saw a large shadow streak out behind the approaching guards. One went down without a sound, but the other managed to turn and the light from the flashlight revealed Thomas, his face grim as he lashed out faster than the other man could react, smashing the flashlight out of his hands. The two shadows grappled in the darkness and Thomas easily overwhelmed his opponent. The whole thing took seconds.

"He probably won't even have to change form," Ashke whispered. "If he's not going to kill them, it's better if they remember a man took them out. We'd have to bring in a fixer team if they start babbling about monsters."

Right. Of course. "Some of the guards saw my wings."

"But you were a kidnapping victim. They're not likely to volunteer that information," Ashke pointed out. "And you take a form pleasing to the eye, like a human only more so. People like them don't react well to werewolves and vampires in the dark. The risk is highest when one of us inspires fear, not wonder. The less humans see of anyone else, the better."

Thomas had dragged both his opponents to the tree line. He was prowling along the edge now, skirting the lawn as he circled the house.

"He's spotted two more," Ashke whispered. "But there's another set coming up from the water's edge on a different path. We should distract them."

"How?" She had no weapon on her. She should probably learn how to use something. If she was going to continue to be of help from above, maybe a self-defense weapon would be good, and also something that would allow her to provide cover from a distance. Whatever that might be.

"You can control air movement, right? You've been doing it to fly." The confidence in Ashke's voice was contagious.

She nodded. "I think so. I've mostly been going on instinct, but I feel the air, think of the wind."

He hovered in front of her, starting to sparkle and emanate glowing specks.

"Is that fairy dust?" She couldn't keep the incredulity out of her voice. She wondered if she should start picking out happy thoughts.

Ashke grinned. "Blow the dust at them. Just blow and think about how you want the wind to take it all the way to them."

She lifted an eyebrow askance, then decided he knew more about how to use magic than she did. She could believe in him, even if she wasn't sure of herself. Still, she turned her head to take in a deep breath—it didn't hurt to be cautious—and faced him to blow his fairy dust out, away from the roof and over the lawn. She felt for her magic and thought hard about how it should carry the dust farther, to the two approaching men. A breeze stirred her hair, caressing her cheek, and Ashke's fairy dust rode the gentle current in a swirling path through the night to the men. The dust swirled around their faces and they both breathed it in.

Elation filled her and she covered her mouth to smother her laugh. She'd done it!

Ashke did laugh, quietly, the sound of it mellow and deep like low-pitched bells. "They won't fly like in the story of the boy who didn't want to grow up. But the gift of fairy dust can allow humans to sense more than they normally can. Not as much as us, but enough for them to be aware of things they pretend won't haunt them. Like spirits."

"Ghosts?" She stared at the two men. They had been standing still, their flashlights hanging at their sides. It was like they were in a daze.

"More like figments created by strong emotion and intent, less like the souls of the departed." Ashke still sounded amused, but there was a coldness to his words that sent a chill across her skin. "People who work for men like the jerk who wanted to keep you, they don't tend to be good people. They don't ask questions as long as the pay is good enough, or maybe they've done bad things themselves. Maybe they enjoy doing bad things. Like is drawn to like, and even if they don't give an actual ghost a reason to haunt them, malignant spirits are drawn to them anyway. The spirits cling and whisper things, egg humans on, encourage them to do more and more bad things. And now, those men can *Hear* them. They can See them."

Peeraphan watched as the men stumbled away from each other. One started screaming. The other had lifted his hands in front of him, trying to ward something off. But she saw nothing. If anything, the shadows around them were thicker and deeper, as if the moon was blocked by a cloud over just them. But when she glanced up to the night sky, there were only wisps of clouds catching silver light. Nothing big enough was there to stop the moonlight from falling on those men.

"That was a gift?" Her voice cracked as she uttered the question.

"Beware gifts from the fae." Ashke shrugged. "But honestly, those men are only now aware of what their actions have gathered to them. If they hadn't lived the lives they had, made the choices they made, would they be confronting so many terrible spirits now? I don't think so."

Peeraphan nodded slowly. It made sense.

Ashke grinned at her, and his teeth were pointed and sharp in his wide smile. He was, she realized, not a simple person. But neither was she. "What next?"

Ashke laughed again, the mellow bell-like sound warmer this time. "Thomas can handle the others. As they come, I think. Duncan has had enough time to neutralize any dangers inside the house. Let's go help him."

"Wait." She cupped her hands under Ashke. "Can I have some of your fairy dust to keep in my pockets? If anyone catches us by surprise, I want to have something I can throw in their faces. Self-defense. You know?"

Ahske's smile dimmed for a moment. "You'll See, Punch. If the faery dust touches your skin, you'll See, too. You'll Hear. You'll feel any figments touching your skin. Smell their scent in your nose. I don't know enough about your history to know if you will be okay."

She looked into Ashke's eyes. "You go through this world experiencing it all. You can See what's around me."

He nodded, chewing his lower lip. "You don't have anything of the fae realm clinging directly to you, no spirits, either. Not really. Nothing bad, that's for sure. But we're about to go inside this house and we don't know what's in there."

"Okay." She dropped her hands, embarrassment heating her cheeks. He was right. Maybe she shouldn't have been so eager to ask for something of his to have as self-defense. She swallowed and steadied herself—she could work with what she had. "I'll just have to keep my magic at the ready so if you start to release your dust again, I'll send it where it needs to go."

Ashke's smile was back. "That'll do. We'll practice together in the future, too. Think of other ways. But this'll work for now."

She smiled, encouraged. She was going to need to do a lot of thinking and learning and practicing. She was going to need to develop skill sets that would be useful to these, her new friends. She was gaining a lot of experience on the fly, so to speak, and it felt good.

Really good.

"Let's go help Duncan take objects of myth and magic away

from a truly terrible human being." And free any other beings that asshole had collected as specimens.

For the first time in not just days, but years—maybe the majority of her life—she had something she wanted to do that was bigger than just herself and the expectations of her immediate family. This felt like a purpose.

BENNETT

Bennett had two immediate targets: Francesco and the human who fancied himself a collector of rare and mystical things. Rage simmered, cold and patient inside him. Peeraphan was safe and it was time to ensure these people would pose no further threat to her.

He'd been circumspect on his return flight, because the human had armed bodyguards. Normal bullets weren't likely to stop Bennett, but if the humans were dealing with Francesco, and knew Francesco was a vampire, they might have armed themselves with something with a better chance of taking out a supernatural.

And then there was Francesco himself.

The other vampire was a match for Bennett in strength, speed, and ferocity. While Francesco could not fly, he did have a talent for hiding in shadows from even those with supernatural senses. So Bennett was more cautious than he might have been if it had only been the humans to take into consideration.

The collector was easiest to find. The man stood at the edge of his property overlooking the ocean, wildly gesticulating at the sky. His ability to throw a tantrum was long, considering the time it had taken to ensure Peeraphan's escape and return. The man was still going and his pair of bodyguards stood to one side of him, their faces masks of neutrality. It was a good bet they were used to his tirades. Francesco had slipped away. It didn't mean the other vampire wasn't nearby, but it might be best if he dealt with this group now rather than attempt to confront them and Francesco at the same time. Bennett came at them from the tree line, moving in a low crouch, getting as close as he could before engaging.

"This is unacceptable!" the collector was shouting. "I don't care if you have to get a helicopter out here, I want you to go after that bird princess!"

They were all looking up at the sky in the direction Peeraphan had flown, their backs to the massive firepit. They were overconfident in their perimeter security and unaware Thomas was out there, wreaking silent havoc the way hunting werewolves could. The flames in the pit had calmed down without the aid of Marie's magic to stoke them higher. He didn't like putting flames at his back, but it would be his best approach. He had to be quick.

"Sir, by the time we're able to get a helicopter here—"

Bennett charged the remaining few yards, snatching the first guard from behind in a hold across the front of the man's chest. Bennett bared his teeth, his bone structure changing as his upper and lower jaws extended forward and his fangs lengthened.

The other guard started to shout, but Bennett reached out with his other arm and grabbed the man by his face, effectively muffling him and surprising him into dropping his weapon. He batted at Bennett's arm, scrabbling at Bennett's hand over his face.

Bennett struck the exposed side of his victim's neck, flicking his tongue over skin to taste the blood welling up from the wound he'd inflicted as the first guard struggled ineffectively in his hold. The taste of blood spread through his mouth, sparking impressions of sweet plum and tart raspberries with smooth undertones of vanilla and mocha. Ah, not a truly evil person, this guard, by any stretch, not one who had indulged in the darker sins the human race could visit upon each other. This man wasn't a murderer or rapist or the sort to have tortured others. Such acts left a stain on the soul and a taint in their blood.

It was an acquired taste, and Bennett's preferred prey. This man was fortunate. Bennett only took enough blood to force the human to faint and dropped the limp body to the ground.

The collector screamed, stumbling back and tripping over his own feet. He didn't even try to help his bodyguards, only scrambled backward in a crab crawl.

Bennett pulled the second bodyguard to him, simply taking hold of the man's shoulder with a free hand and forcing his head to tilt. This time, he struck at the base of the neck where it met his shoulder. This man's blood gave impressions of higher acidity, the fullness of ripe black cherries and the spice of pepper, with woody undertones of aged oak accompanied by an almost smoky note. This man had taken lives, tortured his victims, done unspeakable things. The man had enjoyed it.

Therefore, Bennett had no compunctions about enjoying him to the fullest. He drank the man dry and tossed his corpse into the firepit.

By the time human authorities came to investigate this place, their coroners would not be able to determine the cause of death. Not with any certainty.

Power coursed through Bennett. There were drawbacks to the kind of oath Bennett had taken, limiting his feeding options to specific preferences, but the magic that held him to his oath also provided positive incentive. With the blood of the right kind of prey, his strength, speed, and senses were enhanced. Energized and well fed, he turned toward the collector with a broad grin, aware that the blood from his kill was still being absorbed into his skin.

The collector had collapsed flat on his back, one arm held before him as if he could ward off Bennett in some way. The acrid scent of urine filled the air.

"Please..."

"Late is the hour to plead for mercy." Bennett spoke in low tones, allowing his aristocratic speech pattern to come to the fore. "You believed you were entitled to keep another person, one who thinks and feels, a beautiful soul."

"She got away." The man's upheld hand trembled as he pointed skyward. "I don't have her."

As if this despicable person wouldn't have kept Peeraphan if he could have. Anger burned hotter in Bennett's chest, singing through his veins with the fresh blood he'd consumed. He let loose a quiet snarl.

"I haven't kept anything like her, none. She would have been the first. I won't. I won't ever..." the man babbled.

"Blood will tell. Blood cannot lie." Bennett bent and grasped the man's upper arms, yanking him up and striking his neck.

Sour plum and cedar notes hit Bennett's tongue, tart cherry and hints of blackberries. The man might have lived his life outside the law, but he hadn't personally committed the unforgivable crimes that defined a human as legitimate quarry for Bennett.

Even so, it didn't preclude the potential for what the human might have done if he'd been able to successfully hold Peeraphan as part of his collection.

Bennett held the human up at eye level, the other man weakly scraping his toes at the ground. Bennett captured the man's attention, until he could see the deep, blazing red of his own eyes reflected in the man's frightened gaze.

"You live to meet another dawn," Bennett informed him, pushing at the man's mind with his vampiric power, ensuring his message was inscribed in the man's memory. He could break the man's sanity if he wanted, roll over his will until there was no ability left to advocate for the self. Yet in this moment, Bennett would only ensure the man remembered. "But the moment you take another person as property, as an object to own, I will know. It doesn't matter who. I will come for you, human. And your time will be ended."

The human's eyes rolled up and back into his head as he was overwhelmed with his own fear. His head lolled back and he hung limp in Bennett's grasp. Bennett let him drop in a heap on the ground, grimacing in disgust. He stepped over the unconscious human, pulling a handkerchief from an inside pocket of his suit jacket to wipe his hands.

A snarl cut across the night, answered be a deep werewolf's growl. Ah, it seemed Thomas had found Francesco. Bennett set off in the direction of the sounds, around the side of the mansion. They couldn't afford to prolong the confrontation much more. Even if no audible alarm had been triggered, they couldn't tempt fate.

It took moments to reach them. Thomas was fighting in human form, which put him at a disadvantage. Bennett cursed inwardly. Thomas was a formidable werewolf, but Francesco was powerful and had the experience of centuries to his advantage. Thomas would have had to change form to survive, much less win, against Francesco.

Bennett understood why Thomas hadn't shifted. It took time for a werewolf. It was harder to convince a human they hadn't seen a monster if someone were to witness Thomas in action. It had been the wiser choice to stay in human form, and Thomas was more than a match for any of the human guards on the property.

Bennett watched, timing his approach, and cut in with a solid shoulder check to Francesco that sent the other vampire skidding across the lawn. "Mind if I cut in? I have a prior claim for this dance."

Thomas stepped back, growling, but the werewolf had excellent control. "If you must."

Bennett grinned. "Appreciated."

Francesco bared his fangs and hissed.

Thomas gave them both space. "Yeah, yeah."

"I'll trust you to check on the others."

Thomas growled again. "Of course." But the werewolf backed toward the main entrance of the mansion.

Francesco shook his head. "Really, Bennett, what makes you care so much about your precious colleagues after such a long break from being directly involved in the lives of mortals?"

It didn't matter that some of the members of the Darke Consortium were mortal. Thomas was, though werewolves were long-lived. And many members of other consortiums were human. And Peeraphan... Well. Now wasn't the time to think of whether Peeraphan was or was not.

Bennett smiled, showing his teeth. "You've always been one to make sweeping generalizations. Terribly sloppy of you."

They circled one another, both assuming careless postures that belied their alertness. They had fought too recently for there to be any illusions. Without the element of surprise, they were too evenly matched. Their fight would either be a blink in time or a drawn-out brawl.

Francesco sneered. "I suppose caring for one mortal breaks the dam, lets all that pesky sentimentality flood through your mind, influencing every decision you make and action you take."

Bennett's lip curled and Francesco darted in to strike. Bennett caught Francesco's wrists as the other vampire reached for him, fingers curled like claws, nails lengthened to points that could have done slashing damage. They struggled to a standstill, Francesco unable to break Bennett's grip and Bennett not daring to release his hold. Not yet.

"Caring for mortals is not a weakness," Bennett said. "I've come to that realization recently. Rather, I learn from their courage in the face of their mortality, the way they make the most of every moment they have. Their creativity. Their ingenuity. I draw strength from their tenacity. From her. You made a mistake in taking her."

Bennett jerked Francesco forward, pulling him off balance as he twisted to one side and let Francesco's momentum take him past Bennett. As he went, Bennett released one arm and twisted the arm he still had behind Francesco's back. There was a sickening pop as Francesco's shoulder was dislocated, and Bennett took that opportunity to sink his fangs into Francesco's briefly exposed neck.

Francesco's snarl ended on a high-pitched note, but the vampire turned with the motion. He ripped free of Bennett's fangs and managed to yank his injured limb from Bennett's grasp. "Perhaps I did. But love is so fragile. A weakness. All it would take is her death, and you might not survive the loss this time."

Francesco crouched low, changing his elevation, and charged forward instead of backing away as Bennett had expected him to. Francesco's shoulder caught Bennett across the thighs in a takedown and Francesco turned his head to tear into the side of Bennett's thigh with his teeth.

Bennett roared, sprawling on top of Francesco, bearing the other vampire down to the ground and rolling free. Bennett got his feet back under him, his weight slightly to one side as he favored his injured leg.

Francesco spit out the chunk of fabric and flesh he'd taken from Bennett, ignoring the blood weeping from the side of his neck. "It makes you a little too close to mortal, old friend. You fight too much like one of them. You would be better to simply take their money and enable them as they destroy each other. Babel is much better suited to beings like us, Bennett. The consortiums are far too...humanitarian."

Somewhere closer to the house, human shouts rose up and Thomas growled. Ashke's bell-like laughter sounded out across the night as well. A breeze came around the corner of the house, carrying an elusive musical refrain. The trees along the edge of the lawn behind Francesco stirred and there was a groaning sound as the woods loomed close in a way they shouldn't have been able to. Magics were thick all around them, the magics of multiple supernaturals. Fae and witches and a single bird princess.

Bennett chuckled. "Feel that? I am not alone. We are here for each other, my colleagues and I, with ties more binding than human contracts. What will Babel, your human-run organization dabbling in chaos, give you to compare? Or are you more of a tool to them than they are to you?"

Francesco hissed.

Bennett straightened, riding the wave of his own power despite his injury. He'd fed very well this night. "You have no friends, no companions. You have no vampire allies to support you, no thralls to back you. Your insistence on being solitary, stroking your ego by acting as some kind of nefarious mastermind, has become a kind of weakness."

Doubt crossed Francesco's face, a fleeting shadow there and gone. But Bennett saw it.

"It isn't worth even telling you to take your toys and go. You are bleeding out as we speak. You've lost." Bennett curled his lip in disgust. "We will keep the items left here as our winnings for this game."

Francesco hissed one more time, then backed away, fading into shadows the farther his steps carried him, until Bennett was standing alone in the moonlight.

Twenty-Three

Bennett

B ennett flew behind and slightly below Peeraphan. If there was any kind of attack, however unlikely at this point, he wanted to be in a position to intercept.

She had launched into the sky beautifully, but she was still new to flying and might not have the stamina for long flights in strong air currents. She also didn't know to hide herself. Once they were over water, he approached, giving her plenty of time to acknowledge him.

She looked straight at him and then away, continuing her flight path without a second glance.

Ah. He guessed he deserved that. The danger had passed and they were all on their way home, but there was still a difficult conversation to be had and he had left their last one on a hurtful note. "Let me help you."

"Is there some added danger I need to know about at this point?" Her tone was flat.

"No," he admitted. Not one to be identified with any certainty. She had escaped on her own. There was no pursuit. They had all dealt with the people responsible. "Not immediately."

There would be precautions to take from here on out. Her life moving forward would never be without increased risk. He also had no doubt she was capable of grasping such considerations once she'd had a chance to get to a place of safety and process everything.

"May I escort you back to the manor?" He could not assume she would allow it, but he also could not leave her. Besides the fact that she might not have the stamina to fly so far after the ordeal she'd been through, he simply could not make himself leave her unprotected. "The manor is a good place to regroup and decide next steps. Take a warm bath. Eat. You need to collect your sugar glider friends."

She didn't answer for a long moment, though her flight slowed.

"Now that all of that is behind us, I'm angry," she said finally. "The last thing you said before I was taken was that you can't. Can't what? My mind keeps going through the possibilities and every one of them felt horrible."

"I am sorry."

"You don't get to be sorry about me being angry," she snapped. "You should be sorry for giving up on us, you and me, before we even got started. Coward."

He winced. She wasn't wrong. "Yes."

This was his fault, this distance between them. She had told him herself that she had made herself vulnerable and he had—how had she put it?—thrown up walls.

"I would like to defend myself in some way, dispute your point. But you are not wrong. I had been thinking out loud when I had been speaking to you, but I *had* been giving up, trying to rationalize abandoning this thing growing between us." He paused. He was still thinking as he spoke. There had been little room in his mind for anything but the blinding rage at those who had taken her from him, and at the root of his anger, deep fear of losing her. "I am not communicating well."

She did not speak, but she turned her head to look at him with those beautiful eyes of hers. In the moonlight, they were dark, and the sadness he saw in them was his fault.

"I am sorry. In the last twenty-four hours, I have experienced an entire gamut of emotions I had long since thought faded to ashes." If they had been on the ground instead of the air, he might have fallen to his knees before her. He was shattered. If he had been breathing, he would have struggled to draw breath. He did not want to risk never communicating to her how he felt, what she had come to mean to him in such a short period of time. "I have spent so long sustained on so little, I was not prepared to feel happiness again, or desire—not simply physical, but for your quick intelligence and gentle wit, your expansive consideration and caring. I was experiencing so much, all revolving around you. I allowed myself to think of our relationship as real if you were immortal, capable of spending eternity with me."

"You didn't even give us a chance in your head." There was hurt in her voice. A tear caught the moonlight as it fell down her cheek, and the air currents dashed it away as she turned her face away. "You just got it into your mind that mortal meant someday too soon, I was going to leave you alone. Well, news for you, I woke up not knowing if you survived the latest fight with Francesco. I had to live through the idea I had outlived you and if I got away, I'd have to face a life without you."

Ah. She did have an idea, then, of the gaping hole in one's being. He bowed his head. Her empathy was so much greater than his and he was a fool. She had always had a grasp, from the moment she had learned of his and Victoria's past love, of what losing a loved one had done to him. She had never professed to feel the same way or assumed she could intellectually understand without having experienced it. She had accepted and done her best to respect his feelings, even while he had done his best to leave his ability to feel locked away with Victoria's memory.

"It's not the same. I get it. You lost her and you had to live that loss every day. You still live it. But I got a taste of it and it gutted me," Peeraphan continued.

He flew next to her in silence. He didn't know what to say. Only knew that she was here and if she decided to fly on without him, it would leave him shattered.

"But you know what? I didn't regret meeting you." Her voice steadied. Her wings arched up and beat downward, taking her higher. "And sure, it might be instantaneous infatuation under duress, but I'm pretty sure I'm in love with you, and I don't want to waste a day, not even a minute, denying myself the joy of it for fear of how much it will hurt to lose you. It doesn't matter what lifespan either of us have."

Fireworks burst inside his chest and sizzled through every part of his being. He shot forward and upward, catching her in his arms. "You're right."

He bent his head toward hers, not caring as her wings flipped up and back in surprise, letting them both go into free fall. He pressed his lips to hers, crushing her softness against him, until she opened for him. He darted his tongue, tasting her sweetness and drinking her in, barely aware of their descent. She softened in his hold, melting against him as they fell, until she gasped against his lips.

He didn't release her, but he did use his power to stop their downward momentum.

Her hands were caught between them and she spread her fingers, palms flattening against his chest. "I want to spend that life with you. So. You need to decide what you want to do. Either way, I'm headed back to the manor. Because Thomas is family, and Marie and Duncan and Ashke are friends. New friends. And then...then I want a place in a consortium, somewhere, if not this one. I want to take the next steps to build a new future for myself."

She would do it without him if she had to, it was clear. He had no doubt she could. But he wanted to be a part of it if she would let him. He couldn't think of the right words to say with all the feelings welling up inside him, so he only agreed. "All right."

Then he kissed her again. Holding her close, he reveled in her warmth and sweetness. He was fortunate, so very lucky she was willing to give him the chance to make it up to her. He didn't intend to waste a single moment of it.

She broke their kiss with a gasp. "What if we run into something?"

He grinned, wildly happy. "I'm reasonably certain I could survive the damage."

She laughed. "We."

Still, he called his power to him, leveling them out and taking over their flight. She tucked her wings in close and wrapped her arms around his waist.

He pressed a kiss to her temple. "We could survive the damage, but I couldn't survive a life knowing you were out there and I gave up the chance to experience the world with you."

She turned her face up to him, lips parted, and he did not refuse her invitation. Their kiss was slower this time, and he savored the taste of her. She was so alive, vibrant, and his. He ran his hands over her shoulders and down the curve of her back, grasping her behind and squeezing until she groaned deep in her throat.

"We're going to crash into a plane or something," she whispered against his lips.

He chuckled. "This is an interesting time to explore your particular magic. Can you sense the air currents? Feel when an object might be in your path?"

A pause. He took advantage of her distraction to kiss his way across her jaw and down her neck until the flutter of her pulse teased his lips. He licked the spot.

"Yes." Wonder was in her answer.

He lifted his gaze to her face. Her head was tilted back, her lips slightly parted, her eyes closed. Desire crashed through him, and he ground his hips into hers so she could not miss how much he wanted her.

When he managed words, his voice was coarse with need. "Then you do what you can to warn us and guide us past any obstacles, and I will fly us to my bedroom as quickly as possible."

Her eyes snapped open, laughter sparkling in her gaze. "Deal."

He kissed her again, wild abandon filling his heart. It would be a challenge for them both, requiring their respective magic, and it was absolutely silly. He intended to make it very hard for either of them to concentrate.

PEERAPHAN

They'd barely avoided a seaplane and at least a half dozen tall evergreens that Peeraphan had done her best to warn Bennett about in the midst of their very distracted flight. Finally, he'd brought them to a hover outside a pair of French doors. He barely broke their kiss long enough to open the doors, float them inside, close the doors, and bring them past the blackout curtains enclosing the tiny alcove within his larger suite.

His hands had been wandering all over her in flight, lighting up her senses, and she barely had the mental capacity to look around the huge suite before he brought them to a massive four-poster bed.

His bed.

Her chest tightened with warmth and the kind of hope that she barely dared admit to. This was his space, not a guest room, not somewhere neutral that belonged to no one. He'd brought her into the space he kept for his own privacy. And that was a level of intimacy she hadn't asked him for, but she was going to embrace all the same.

He leaned back from her, both of them still several inches above the floor. His eyes glowed ruby red. "I want to be with you."

"Yes." It came out as a whisper, so she nipped his lower lip to make sure he knew she was coming to this with no trepidation. Excitement and curiosity coursed through her, and she was really happy to be alive. Even better, living in this moment with him.

He smiled and it was pure wickedness. Her breath left her in a whoosh. "Ever the energetic bunny, are you not?"

She blinked. "Did you just crack a pop culture joke?"

"An old one, I admit." He pulled her clothes off, pressing a string of kisses along her skin as he did.

Joy bubbled up and she laughed. She didn't resist, didn't want to. But she spared some portion of her mind to keep herself suspended in air. It would save them both a little bit of awkward struggling with clothes. She just hoped she could manage it.

"Well done," he commented as he reached her feet and looked up her body at her. "You are beautiful."

She blushed, the heat of it burning her cheeks as she resisted the urge to wrap her arms around herself and cover up. She had never stood in front of a lover completely exposed like this. She gathered as much moxie as she could and lifted her chin, doing her best regal princess impression.

His eyes smoldered red and his expression was one she'd never seen before. It made her feel beautiful, like there was nothing else in this world. Only him looking at her.

His smile widened. "Shall we test your abilities further with more...distraction?"

"What did you have in mind?" Butterflies flitted through her stomach. Daring. She wanted to be daring in this moment and so she would be. "I like a challenge."

He cupped her feet in both hands before running his hands up the backs of her calves. The barest touch of his fingertips sent electric sparks along her skin. As he reached the backs of her knees, he exerted quick pressure, pulling and lifting.

She let out a surprised squeal and her wings shot outward to catch her as she fell backward. He steadied her, lying back on air over the bed. "Try to hold yourself here."

Her magic, her concentration, to hover above his bed while he...

His hands exerted gentle pressure again, until she opened her legs for him, spread for his pleasure.

Oh wow, if she'd thought she had felt exposed before, this was a whole different level.

"I want to kiss every part of you." He followed words with action, pressing a soft kiss on the inside of each thigh. There was just a hint of fang against her skin, but he didn't bite.

Her breath hitched and her heart rate jumped. She wanted this, trusted him with this.

"If at any moment it becomes too much, tell me to stop, and I will. I promise." His voice had gone hoarse, primal. His lips brushed over her most delicate area, his words carried on a hot puff of air.

Delicious sensations ran through her from those barest of touches, amping up her already sensitized skin. Certainty coalesced as she surrendered to him. She hadn't had any doubts, but his promise melted away even the shadow of doubt.

"Okay." She hardly got the agreement out. She aching for him and there was no room in her mind for embarrassment as she shivered in anticipation, barely keeping a corner of her mind to control her magic.

His hands pressed on her inner thighs, spreading her legs even farther apart. His tongue, hot and wet, pulled a cry of pleasure from her. "You taste exquisite, love."

She shuddered as he followed through, kissing and nibbling at her. He was teasing her, working her up to a frenzy, and even as she wriggled her hips, aching for him to touch her just there, he wouldn't. He tasted her, darting his tongue into her, then exploring her again.

"Bennett." She wasn't sure if she was encouraging him or cursing him or begging him.

He chuckled and shifted his grip, cupping her bottom in one hand. She reached out, barely able to keep herself aloft, grasping for anything. Just as he slid a finger inside her, she caught hold of heavy fabric. There were drapes to enclose the bed. Oh.

His mouth closed over her and he sucked, his finger pumping, and her thoughts scattered as waves of pleasure took her. She lifted her hips, moaning, and he changed to two fingers, his other hand steadying her midair, gripping her buttocks. Pleasure crested higher and higher, tightening until she broke apart with a cry and lost control of everything.

She fell on the bed, caught in the throes of her orgasm as he stroked her gently through it. She shuddered, barely aware of the soft fabric of the sheets against her limbs and the rustle of her wings at her sides. When she could see clearly again, he was stripping off his own clothes. His eyes burned red and fangs glinted behind his parted lips. His body was gorgeous, defined, as if he had been the inspiration for the marble sculptures of the most beautiful heroes of legend.

Only he was fully erect and beyond epic.

"Oh." Wow.

She watched him as he climbed the bed, covering her with his body. She wanted him, wanted to touch every part of him; the closer they could be, the better. He kissed her, long and deep.

When he withdrew, his voice was unsteady as he locked gazes with her. "I can wear a condom, if you wish. My seed will not take without a specific ceremony and I do not carry any disease of the living. But if you will be more at ease, I can wear one for you."

Well, there was obviously a whole lot to talk about when it came to those details. But he had the pertinent points addressed. No pregnancy until she understood the ramifications, and no STDs. Okay.

They could enjoy this. If anything could build her confidence in him, it was the way he was anticipating questions she hadn't even thought to ask. Maybe she should have, but she was grateful she hadn't had to. Not in this moment. With him, she could take her time and find her way to discovering what she didn't know.

"Thank you." She kissed one corner of his mouth, then the other. "I trust you. No need."

He nodded. He reached between them with one hand, positioning himself until she could feel the tip of him at her entrance. A wash of emotions crossed his face and he caught her gaze again. "May I?"

Her heart might explode. "Yes."

He slid into her slowly, stretching and filling her until she groaned. Her eyes rolled back. She couldn't help it—he felt so good inside her. She clutched at his shoulders, holding on as he buried his face between her breasts. When he lifted his head to look at her again, he was pure ferocity.

He drew back and thrust into her and she couldn't look away even as the pleasure drove upward again. He set a fast rhythm, filling her completely and grinding his hips just before pulling back. Her nails dug into his shoulders as she held on, biting her lip.

A sweet metallic taste spread over the tip of her tongue and he froze. She must have drawn blood when she bit her lip and he must have realized at the same time. She swallowed.

"I trust you." She put everything she had into repeating these words for him. "I know you won't hurt me. This you can take from me, too."

"You're sure?" He was almost desperate, a vulnerability in his voice. "This is more than intimate. This is giving me your life."

"I'm strong enough." She was absolutely certain. "And we're giving our lives to each other."

He snarled, his mouth crashing down over hers. His tongue swept over the small hurt on her lip as his hips pressed into her, picking up the pace he'd left off.

Faster, faster, he drove into her. The ecstasy built in her until she thought she could touch the stars behind her eyes. He growled into her mouth, his hands tightening on her, and the pleasure exploded inside her.

She cried out, and he drank it in as he followed her into orgasm, the two of them holding each other in a free fall of ecstasy.

TWENTY-FOUR

BENNETT

Perhaps for the first time in his existence, certainly the first time in decades, Bennett woke gradually rather than snapping into awareness with the waning evening. The sun was setting and with the retreating light of day, he was free to rise. He turned his head to the side, not expecting but hoping to find Peeraphan still in the room. He had told her she didn't have to be, that he would understand if she could not remain in the room with a corpse.

But there she was, within arm's reach, curled up in the chair next to his bed. She had a book from the manor's library in her lap and a small plate of finger sandwiches on the end table near her elbow. Cory and Tobi were playing quietly, tumbling across the back of the armchair and along her shoulders. It was Cory who noticed Bennett was awake first, the sugar glider facing him and giving a short bark before scampering back to his mistress to hide against her neck beneath her hair.

Peeraphan slid the ribbon attached to the book's spine between the pages to mark her place as she closed it and slipped it between the cushion and the arm of the chair. Then she came to the side of the bed and immediately climbed in to tuck herself against him. "Hi."

"Hello." The corners of his mouth lifted and he marveled at the concept of not having to consciously try to form a smile. It just happened. "I imagine Ellery will be going on scavenger hunts for books tucked into chair cushions all around the manor from now on."

Peeraphan chuckled. "Maybe. They don't come into your suites though, do they?"

"Only when they've set aside time with me in advance." He would never deny the fae access to a part of the building they called home when their well-being was tied to the entire structure. "They respect my privacy otherwise."

He hesitated, then added, "There was a time when I wouldn't. Victoria had a long talk with me about the nature of fae like Ellery. Back then, Ellery was less stable and on the edge of becoming a boggart on some days. Thomas, Duncan, and I were more than capable of containing Ellery, but Victoria saw ways of making life better for the entire household. It was Victoria who pointed out that a brownie chooses their home. No one can compel a brownie to live where they do not wish."

"Victoria sounds like an amazing person." Peeraphan might not be perfectly serene when he spoke of his deceased love, but she had never been negative about the memory of Victoria.

Rather than attempt to say something and have it fall short, he wrapped his arms around her and hugged her close. Peeraphan snuggled against him and uttered a happy sigh. Cory and Tobi had abandoned Peeraphan the moment she had climbed into his bed, having opted to remain on the armchair. They sat on the edge, looking at him, so he studied them in turn. "They're quite happy being with you most of the time, but there will be expeditions that would be too dangerous for them to accompany us."

"Us?" Peeraphan lifted her head.

"You might journey on your own to investigate a lead, but given a preference, I would like to join you whenever possible." It was a new experience, this exploration of how to move forward. Deciding on an approach in coordination with someone else was uncomfortable. Not a terrible thing, if he wanted to be clear in his own mind. Simply something he was not yet accustomed to. Victoria had preferred for him to take the lead in planning, throwing herself into supporting him. It was her way, and her strengths had been in executing tasks and providing feedback.

Peeraphan leaned into a different set of strengths, and he wanted to work well with her every bit as much as he wanted to share his life with her. In many ways, the different dynamic in their relationship allowed him to lay his past to rest with no regrets and no more guilt.

Peeraphan was gazing at her small companions. "I have a tall cage at my apartment they use when I'm home. I leave it open so they can wander around while I'm able to supervise. When I can't take them with me, they stay enclosed and safe. But up until now, they've mostly been able to come with me wherever I go."

"Do you still want to keep your apartment?" He would respect her wishes, but he hoped she might be tempted to stay with him. He wanted to say so, but also didn't want to apply pressure.

She propped herself up on one elbow and smiled. "Apartments anywhere in Seattle are expensive. I was barely able to afford it, much less save any money for a rainy day."

"You don't need to worry about finances, if you'll accept my help." He winced. The suggestion may have landed badly. This caring about how a person took what he was saying required much greater precision in his choice of words than he was used to.

"I don't feel completely okay with leaning on you financially," Peeraphan said slowly. "But I do think it's totally fair for you to pay for dinner when we go on a date."

He smiled. "I would be happy to do so."

It was a start. As she grew more comfortable with their relationship, he could ease other burdens and worries so they didn't eat away at her resources. If she wanted to maintain financial independence in order to have the confidence she needed to stand next to him, he would respect and support her wishes.

"Being a part of the Consortium can mean an appropriate compensation package." He leaned forward and dropped a kiss on the space between her eyebrows.

"Mmm." She pressed her lips to his jaw. "Are we still talking money or are we talking about you?"

It was his turn to chuckle. "I meant financial considerations. There are members of various consortiums who have amassed enough wealth over centuries to be self-sufficient. Many, like Asamoah, even provide support for families who are unaware of their supernatural benefactors. But for younger supernaturals, such as yourself, a base salary and certain investment assets are offered in exchange for your work with the Consortium. Some, like Marie, also maintain careers in the human world. I can help you iron out the details, or if you feel it would be wiser to set up your accounts with a separate party, Duncan can connect you with an accountant and financial advisor who handles these things for other consortiums."

"I'd like the latter." Peeraphan settled back against him. "Thank you. I know it's an adjustment, understanding how I want to live. I imagine it's hard to change with the times."

He huffed. "Especially this past century. *Dynamic* isn't enough of a word to encompass the way worldviews change in the minds of humans."

"Which is why I appreciate you." She pressed a kiss at the corner of his mouth. "Thank you for loving me enough to want to understand me."

He pulled her close, taking in a deliberate breath to savor the scent of her as he reveled in her touch. "How can I do any less when you've accepted everything I am?"

He bent his head to kiss her then, and she tilted her face up to welcome him. Things may have escalated if Toby hadn't given a warning bark. Peeraphan pulled away with a gasp, and a moment later there was a discreet knock at the door to the suite.

Duncan's voice came, quiet, but Bennett could hear it through the sitting room and into the bedroom. "Dinner in ten minutes. You may not need sustenance, Bennett, but she does."

Even if Bennett had not been very invested in the well-being of Peeraphan, she was a part of the Consortium now, and Duncan was making it very clear that the rest of the manor residents would be taking a keen interest in her welfare as well.

"Ten minutes to dinner." He said it to her like a challenge.

She giggled. "Think we can make it?"

TWENTY-FIVE

PEERAPHAN

Peeraphan grinned as they entered the dining room. Thomas was waiting for them with a chair pulled out for her. Already picking a fight with Bennett. Over her shoulder, Bennett snarled, but didn't otherwise interfere as Peeraphan took the seat Thomas offered her. The two of them may have scuffled behind her chair as they gently pushed her in, but she was willing to pretend she didn't notice. It was fun, she thought, to have a friendship so good it allowed each of them to burn off pent-up energy. Without each other, the two of them could've been way more dangerous than they already were.

The world really might not survive it.

"Ready to celebrate?" Marie asked. Ashke sat at his own place next to her.

"Sure!" Peeraphan was game for a celebration. "Do you do this every time you retrieve artifacts successfully?"

Thomas snorted. "No."

Bennett started filling her water glass. "We successfully retrieved the red shoes, plus the bonus of the noose of the phayanak, and gained a new member of the Consortium. I'd be interested to hear what was found in the property we neutralized last evening."

Duncan smiled. "Perhaps Peeraphan would be willing to give you a summary, if she hasn't already."

Bennett raised an eyebrow.

Peeraphan blushed. "There was already a lot to discuss."

Bennett settled in to the chair next to hers. "By all means, what did you all find?"

Peeraphan cleared her throat. "Well, I'm not sure if there's a particular format to report this sort of thing."

"There isn't," Thomas said, leaning an elbow on the table and giving her an encouraging grin.

She smiled back. "Duncan had taken care of any security by the time Ashke and I entered the mansion. It was big, with an open plan design and lots of space. It was practically designed for parties and there were art pieces and artifacts scattered throughout the house. They were placed and lit to be admired. To be shown off for guests."

"A few of the items were specifically warded," Duncan interjected. "Otherwise, the house only had a general security alarm system against human theft and a general barrier of salt to negate latent magic. It was fairly simple to disable all of it."

"There were only a handful of actual mythic items," Peeraphan continued. "There was a blood-spattered key, identified by a little exhibit label even. It's supposedly Bluebeard's key, and I'm looking forward to reading up on that folktale. The rest will take some research to identify, but Duncan could sense the magic of them. I want to explore whether I might be able to use my magic to identify them in a similar way."

Nods all around the table. Marie spoke up, "It would be handy if you could, but totally okay if you can't. Not all of us can."

"You'd mentioned specimens at one point." Bennett touched the top of her hand gently. "Obviously, the human thought he was entitled to keep living beings."

Peeraphan's hand curled into a fist under his touch. "There were a few enclosures. None of the beings could speak to us, as far as we know."

"We've relocated them to the island here." Duncan took up the narrative as Peeraphan fell silent. "There was one will-o'-the-wisp in a terrarium that is in the woods near our boat launch for the time being. Two other Japanese spirit-type beings seem to be tsurubebi, based on initial research. They are also in the woods, lingering closer to the stand of conifers near Marie's cottage."

"There were also a pair of karakasa kozo, also Japanese yokai, that have decided to hang out in the foyer here at the manor." Marie waved a hand in the general direction of the pertinent part of the building. "Just beware. They seem relatively harmless, but they like to sneak up on you and give you a lick up the back of your leg or arm or whatever skin might be exposed. It can freak you out."

She shuddered.

Peeraphan made a face. "Noted."

Duncan chuckled. "They all obviously have awareness and a certain level of intelligence, but we don't have a way to determine how long they were held in captivity, how they were caught, or whether they have a home to return to. We're going to need to investigate and reach out to other consortiums in Europe and East Asia to see about the best place for them to live moving forward."

"I might have bumped into someone who might have some pertinent knowledge regarding the Japanese yokai, at least." Marie could have been blushing. "I'll see if I can track them down."

Duncan nodded, looking at Marie curiously, but moved on. "Other than that, there were a few sea dragons in fish tanks, as well as other rare saltwater fish. There are preserved remains of a being that is labeled as a mermaid but looks more like a deep-sea creature, and preserved remains of a coelacanth. We left those in place for the human authorities to find."

"Any follow-up required?" Bennett asked.

Thomas shook his head. "Only the one kill, and you took care of the body. The rest were all rendered unconscious and when they woke, they called the local police themselves. No need to even call in a fixer team for this one. It's just a really daring break-in and theft, as far as the authorities are concerned."

"Francesco was bleeding out and unlikely to have found a safe haven before the sun rose." Bennett wanted to consider the other vampire truly dead, but if he'd wanted that kind of comfort, he should have ended Francesco himself. "It will take him time to recover from the damage and he's not likely to pose a threat any time soon, even after he heals. He'll need more than time to become powerful enough to challenge me."

"Us," Peeraphan said. Thomas agreed quickly, followed by the others.

Bennett nodded and there was a brief silence. It wasn't uncomfortable, but it was there.

Then Peeraphan lifted her water glass and took a sip. "I don't know why you don't always do this—it seems like a relaxed way to do a debrief. We did good things. There's plenty to celebrate."

"And there's good company." Asamoah entered with Ellery, setting out several platters. "We decided to go with a few flavor inspirations from Thai cuisine, but I admit none of us have learned to make traditional Thai food."

Peeraphan inhaled appreciatively. "It all smells wonderful."

"Let's enjoy while we talk more." Asamoah began passing around a platter.

Bennett took what looked like an egg and placed it on Peeraphan's plate, then served himself one as well. He muttered, "I can still taste human food, when I'm well fed. It just doesn't offer me any sustenance."

She smiled. "It's going to be fun learning new things about you every day."

He quirked a corner of his mouth in return. "I imagine I will find the same about you."

She studied the egg on her plate, too curious to wait anymore, now that everyone had one. It was actually a cleaned-out eggshell, piped with delicate crème fraîche and topped with a tiny, lightly battered and fried shrimp, garnished with a delicate tumble of caviar. When she tasted them all together, flavors of creamy coconut milk, zesty lemongrass and galangal, and spicy Thai peppers burst across her palate. It was like her favorite comfort soup, tom kha gai, deconstructed with the essence of the flavors presented in this super fun amuse-bouche.

"What do you think?" Asamoah asked.

He was smiling, seemingly confident in the creation he and Ellery had presented. But Peeraphan thought he also wanted to please her, which was a different thing from knowing a dish tasted good.

She gave him a broad smile. "It's wonderful. I'm betting my mother would love to try this."

Marie sucked delicately on her spoon. "I love Thai food in the city, but I wonder what your favorite dishes are."

Peeraphan shrugged. "I'm not much of one for Thai restaurants. I think they're great, and my dad has several friends who own them on both coasts. But I'm more of a home-cooking kind of person when it comes to Thai food. I lean on the dishes I grew up with as my comfort food."

Asamoah started passing around a new dish, this one filled with fragrant yellow curry and huge chunks of crab, topped with a nest of golden fried noodles. "Maybe I could tempt you into the kitchen with us sometime. If it would be fun for you, you could show us how to make your favorite comfort foods and I could show you how to make some of mine in return."

"I'd love to." Peeraphan clasped her hands together.

"I'd be interested in getting in on this deal." Marie tapped the table. "I've got a few Korean dishes my mother learned from my father and taught to me. I could share those."

Thomas cleared his throat and offered to show them all how he made his Thai fried rice. Ashke piped up that he could share his technique for making dandelion jelly and sparkling berry juice, not to be confused with human alcoholic vintages. Duncan mentioned a few confections he could share the making of to represent his contribution. Peeraphan was delighted with the plans for kitchen bonding and sharing between each of them, but she glanced at Bennett. He had never had a reason to learn to cook. This might make him feel left out.

Bennett reached around her shoulders and gave her a light squeeze. He kissed the top of her head. "I have your time in other ways. This is the closest this Consortium has been since it was founded. I hope it can continue to grow."

Marie cleared her throat. "Once you have a chance to rest and check back in with your life, I'd be happy to show you how I commute to downtown Seattle for client meetings. That will help you decide next steps for settling in to working with us here."

Peeraphan smiled at Marie. "Sounds great. Honestly, it's going to be some kind of chaos at the theater, so that'll take some untangling."

The prospect of dealing with Sirin didn't seem as daunting as it might have even a day earlier. The life Peeraphan was building for herself was so very different, comparisons didn't make sense.

"I'd like to go back with you, the next time you go gathering herbs." It was okay to express a desire, too, right? Peeraphan was getting so much she'd always wanted without ever knowing exactly what to wish for. But this was something more, for her future, and for Bennett's peace of mind. "I'd like to go back with you and learn more about the herbs and plant life there, maybe look for other kinnaree."

Bennett stilled next to her.

Thomas placed his own water glass down on the table with a deliberate *thunk*. "I'd be curious, too, honestly. Any of the times I traveled to Thailand, I didn't encounter major supernaturals. If I want to respect what we were told, I'd have to go with you anyway, Marie, so we could make it a research trip."

Bennett picked up a fork and tapped the tines against the side of the plate. "Coordinating schedules and planning ahead was going to be a necessity as the Consortium grew. I suppose we'll all be making adjustments."

Peeraphan shrugged. "Seems like it was inevitable."

"Past time, really," Duncan said in a dry tone.

"While we're making adjustments, I need a corgi," Ashke announced. "If I'm to properly see to the security of this island, I need a battle steed."

Thomas growled. "Seriously?"

Marie broke into a laugh and Peeraphan giggled. It was still awkward. The humor was kind of strained. But they were in good spirits and they were talking about how to work together more smoothly. Peeraphan was looking forward to when the witty repartee evolved into a natural flow of the camaraderie she was certain was here.

After dinner, they decided on a walk together in the conservatory gardens. He took her down yet another winding path to what seemed to be an impossible spherical construction of smooth wooden branches twisting around glass. It was maybe eight or ten feet at the tallest point and at least as wide in diameter.

"This used to be a butterfly enclosure." He led her inside, showing her the overgrown bushes and miniature trees. There was even a small water feature and a bowl-style seat filled with cushions. "We could clean this up, make certain the plants are appropriate, and make this a home for your sugar glider friends when you aren't able to take them with you."

"Oh!" The enormity of it all crashed around her. Not only was she in the middle of experiencing literally the love of her life, but she had finally found friends who understood what it meant to be other than human. She had the choice of a new home, found a new calling, and had the flexibility to hold on to the parts of her life she treasured: her family, her dancing, her dearest companions. "Thank you."

Bennett pulled her close, kissing away the tears welling up in her eyes. "Did you know? Tears of joy have a different taste from tears of pain or sorrow."

"I can imagine." She gave him a watery laugh. "It's just a lot, and I'm not sure how I deserve all of this."

"Well." Bennett bent his knees and tightened his arms around her thighs, lifting her carefully, carrying her a few steps before lowering her on the cushions. "There are still risks and dangers. Being a supernatural in this world is not easy. Discovery could result in death or worse. You are also rather entangled with a particularly lethal type of supernatural."

Despite his words, his lips were infinitely gentle as he drew kisses in a searing line down her neck and over her collarbone.

She let her head fall back and gave herself over to the sensations. "Mmm. And what would you recommend as the best course of action for survival?"

He teased the straps of her dress over her shoulders and tugged the bodice down until her breasts were freed. His caresses were gentle, and he rubbed the pad of his thumbs over her nipples until they were taut. "I cannot in good conscience say that it is wise to continue your...entanglement. But I admit I'm willing to do every-thing in my power to tempt you."

He closed his mouth over one nipple and sucked while he caught the other between a thumb and forefinger, twisting and pinching ever so slightly.

She gasped. "It's not a bad thing to make unwise decisions."

He released her nipples and nuzzled between her breasts as his hands coasted down to her hips and pulled her skirt up to her waist. She lifted her hips to help and to offer silent invitation, because no one could give her body the sensations Bennett did. He hooked his thumbs in the sides of her panties and drew them down her legs, his ruby-red eyes catching her gaze as he pocketed her underwear.

Somehow, just that act was so incredibly hot, she was wet with need. As if they hadn't enjoyed each other just before dinner and the night prior. He went down to one knee, sliding his hands under her thighs, never breaking eye contact. He had the most devilish expres-sion as he lowered his mouth to her. How he could make her feel so much in one movement was mind-blowing. He chuckled, his lips still touching her most delicate flesh, then he closed his mouth over her and sucked.

She cried out, reaching down and burying her fingers in his hair, unable to do anything but hang on for the ride as he proceeded to alternate between licks and sucking, sometimes darting his tongue deep inside her. He watched her the entire time, and when she looked down her body at him, she wondered how she ever thought he might not want her. His hands gripped the backs of her thighs, just under her behind, as he held her open and he squeezed with each lick until the pleasure pooled low in her belly. Her orgasm tore through her and she flew apart, sending swan feathers into the air around them.

He straightened, undoing his belt and unbuttoning his pants. She breathed deep, trying to clear her head as she realized she'd manifested her wings. As he knelt between her legs again, his erection nudging against her entrance, she reached to wrap her arms and legs, and wings, around him. He slid inside her in one smooth thrust and she groaned with the pleasure of her muscles stretching around his girth.

"Tell me," he whispered against her neck. "Tell me what you were thinking as I came inside you."

She smiled and nipped his ear. "My wings. No one has ever driven me out of my mind so much that my wings appeared."

He made a sound full of smug acknowledgment and flexed his hips.

"Ah!" She tightened her thighs around him. "And I thought, I can fly and you can fly. It was so nice kissing you in flight."

She wanted to know what it was like to make love in the starry sky.

He lifted her up, then, and sat back, coaxing her to unlock her legs so he could lie back with her riding him. She steadied herself with her hands on his forearms as he held her hips. Then he thrust into her, deep, and she gasped, tilting her head back until she was looking up through the glass of the enclosure and of the conservatory itself, up into the night.

"Anything you want to try," he promised as he ground his hips into her. "Anything you want to learn or explore. Any choice you make. I'll support you. I want to see you fly high and far, beloved."

Coherent thought fell apart inside her mind and it wasn't until they lay spent, tangled together with her wings to cover them, that she managed to whisper back, "I love you."

THE END

FIELD NOTES ON THE SUPERNATURAL AND THE PARANORMAL

OBSERVATIONS BY MEMBERS OF THE CONSORTIUM COMMUNITY

KINNAREE

Found in: Himmapan Forest (and the United States ???)*

Category: Sentient

Details: Kinnaree are quite possibly the loveliest of the Himmapan beings, certainly capable of flight should they decide to leave the deep forests and mountains of their home. Descriptions vary from region to region, claiming these beings appear human in the upper half of the body with a human head, torso, and arms, yet below the waist, they have the body, tail, and legs of a swan.

However, many versions of the legend of Suthon and Manora describe seven kinnaree sisters—bird princesses—flying down from the forests of the Himmapan to a lake in human lands. These sisters cast off their wings and tails to play in the waters of the lake under the light of the full moon. It is reasonable to conclude that in the absence of wings and tail at least some kinnaree appear wholly human with head, torso, arms, and legs. How these magical beings remove their wings and tails is unclear from the various renditions of the legend.

Perhaps there is a difference in phenotypic characteristics among kinnaree. A hereditary trait?

While kinnaree seem to have an affinity for air and water, the full extent of their abilities or powers are unknown. They are not natural predators of humankind but are capable of defending their territory if human civilization encroaches on the forests of the Himmapan. At present, the Himmapan has not been discovered by humankind as a whole, though it is possible individuals or small groups have ventured into these forests.

(*) For more information, contact the Darke Consortium

SIDHE

Found in: all regions of the world

Category: Sentient

Details: Often referred to as "The Fair Folk," the sidhe are featured in many tales in west European folklore. Care is taken to avoid angering or insulting sidhe and any humans who encounter one should proceed with caution in their dealings with these powerful individuals. In particular, one should never thank fae as this can be perceived as a dismissal of the effort or work done. Sincerity and thoughtful response is much better received.

Sidhe are generally described as essentially human in appearance with features that vary as much as humans around the world, though they are almost universally faster and stronger. Many have been described as exceedingly attractive, inhumanly so. It is posited that most sidhe use glamour to tone down or completely alter their appearance in order to pass for human.

Though two major factions exist within fae culture, the Seelie and Unseelie Courts, many fae are unaffiliated or far removed from the politics of either court. Some human scholars interpreted these factions to indicate good or evil nature, but further research indicates all fae are morally ambiguous regardless of faction and it is better to proceed with caution, regardless.

Cold iron is believed to repel or harm the fae and direct contact to skin can burn the individual. Large amounts of iron can impede a fae's use of magic. The age and power of the fae may offer some resistance to the effect of cold iron.

While sidhe are not usually predators of humans, they can be considered competitors for the same territory and resources. On the other hand, evidence exists indicating sidhe can be allies and develop mutually beneficial relationships with humans. Sidhe are immortal and reproduce very rarely. There are instances in recorded history of sidhe abducting humans to bolster their population.

VAMPIRE

Found in: all regions of the world

Category: Sentient

Details: Vampires resemble humans and are able to pass as human at night. During the day, vampires are inanimate and can be mistaken for a lifeless corpse. They vary in appearance, most often described as exceedingly attractive. While vampires are stronger and faster than humans, they can exhibit a variety of other supernatural abilities. Such abilities may include flight, shape change, affinity to animals, forms of necromancy, and more. Age may increase power over time, but there is insufficient evidence to validate this theory.

Vampires are natural predators of humans. While vampires can feed off other beings or creatures, humans are their prey of choice and provide the most sustenance. Because of this and their supernatural abilities, they can be considered extremely dangerous to humans.

There are multiple types of vampire propagation. The most prevalent belief holds that a vampire bite can change a human to a vampire. This is an oversimplified misconception in that a vampire must first bite, then drain a human to the brink of death, then offer vampiric blood in return. This exchange provides the mortally wounded human the chance of rising after death as a vampire. It is uncertain what the success rate is for this method of propagation. Vampires are also able to reproduce amongst themselves or with humans. Offspring of vampires and humans can potentially be vampires, dhampir, or fully human in a 25 percent to 50 percent to 25 percent chance, respectively.

Vampires are immortal, in that they do not age and can continue existing indefinitely. They are not, however, invulnerable. Vampires can be, and have been, hunted by humans. The most effective method of destroying a vampire has been to trap them in the open and expose them to sunlight. Another method is to sever the head from the body and burn both with fire. A wooden stake to the heart has been found effective against younger or less powerful vampires, but older vampires can survive. Holy water and other religious objects have not been proven to be a reliable weapon. Young vampires may starve until they crumble to dust. Older vampires may fall into a type of torpor and can be revived with sufficient fresh blood.

WINGED FAE

Found in: all regions of the world

Category: Sentient

Details: Sometimes referred to as fairies, sylph, or pixies, it is unclear whether any of these names are correct. Winged fae appear to be miniature humans with wings resembling those of a butterfly or moth or dragonfly. They are mischievous and rarely give direct answers when questioned about their nature. Like many of the fae in general, winged fae do not lie, but they are skilled in speaking partial truths and allowing the listener to make assumptions or come to inaccurate conclusions.

Because winged fae are significantly smaller than humans, averaging between twenty to twenty-five centimeters in height, some humans have perceived these fae to be childlike even when the winged fae in question is a fully mature adult. In addition to flight, winged fae have the ability to wield magic such as glamour. Their glamour is so powerful, they are often indistinguishable from butterflies or other winged insects and may go undetected when hiding among flowers.

Fairy dust is associated with winged fae, though it is uncertain how they produce this substance. Any humans coming into contact with fairy dust are blessed (cursed?) with a kind of sixth sense for the supernatural.

Winged fae have an affinity with growing things, particularly flowering plant life. They can both encourage such plant life to grow and bloom and derive sustenance from these plants. Arches of flowering vines and hedges seemingly occurring naturally are often the work of winged fey, as are mushroom circles.

As delightful as their appearances might be, a human would be well-advised to remain alert and cautious. Winged fey have a great love of mischief at best and can be frighteningly malicious at their worst. Many have made the mistake of underestimating these beings.

KARIN PUKSA

Found in: Himmapan Forest

Category: Non-sentient

Details: The Himmapan Forest is perhaps one of the few places to observe an elephant-like creature fly. The karin puksa resembles a member of the Elephantidae family with smooth, black skin and the wings and tail of a bird sporting blood red plumage. The wingspan of the karin puksa is quite impressive, at least twice as wide as its body length and despite its bulk, this creature can fly at great speed over significant distances.

The tusks of the karin puksa are used for digging in search of water or roots, for debarking or marking trees, and even for lifting and moving vegetation or obstacles from their path. In fights, the tusks are used in both attack and defense.

It is currently thought that karin puksa are herbivores and generally peaceful unless attacked.

KRAISORN RAJASRI

Found in: Himmapan Forest

Category: Non-sentient

Details: These impressive predators resemble white lions. Their coloring is strikingly contrasted with deep red mane and tail tip, red paws, and red markings around their mouths. They have broad skulls, implying high intelligence, and heavily muscled hindquarters. Their hunting habits include both stalking or ambush, and it is theorized that their preferred prey are large hoofed ruminant mammals such as deer.

Kraisorn rajasri are thought to be solitary, seeking out others of their kind only during mating season. Nocturnal, one might hear a variety of sounds to warn of the proximity of a kraisorn rajasri, including roars or grunts. These may be territorial in nature and intended to warn others off before a direct confrontation occurs.

TSURUBEBI

Found in: coniferous forests, mainly on Kyushu and Shikoku in Japan

Category: Non-sentient ???

Details: These small tree spirits appear as balls of blue-white flames bobbing among the branches of coniferous trees deep in the forest. The bobbing motion resembles the way a bucket swings back and forth in a well. Occasionally, one can get close enough to perceive facial features in the flames. Eyewitness accounts are inconsistent as to whether the face resembles a human or an animal.

These spirits are generally uninterested in humans and seems benign, for the most part. However, some scholars suggest that the tsurubebi is related to another yokai, or supernatural creature of Japanese folklore, called a tsurube otoshi. The tsurube otoshi is found in the same habitats, but is quite dangerous. It would be advisable to approach with caution unless one is certain they have accurately identified this creature. Even then, it is best to observe and leave it be.

WILL-O'-THE-WISP

Found in: United Kingdom and Europe

Category: Non-sentient

Details: A will-o'-the-wisp is a ghost light appearing at night, flickering and glowing like a candlelight within a lantern. They are most often encountered over bogs, swamps, marshes, or cemeteries. Will-o'-the-wisps do not inflict direct harm on those who encounter them, but one should still exercise caution as these spirits are often mischievous and may lead humans deeper into mists or fog until they are lost or fall victim to the dangers of the environment. They are not always malicious and may instead lead a lost wanderer back to well traveled roads or lead searchers to a lost child.

The difficulty in choice for one encountering a will-o'-the-wisp is deciding whether it will lead you to hope or to harm.

BLUEBEARD'S KEY

Region of Origin: Western Europe

Category: Inanimate

Details: One of a set of keys, purported to open a forbidden door within a legendary chateau. The actual location of the chateau is currently unknown. The chateau belonged to Bluebeard, a nobleman of great power and wealth. Bluebeard was known to have married many times, and all of his brides disappeared under dubious circumstances.

The key has magical properties, with the ability to unlock any door under specific circumstances. When exposed to blood, the key's more damning properties are activated, potentially revealing a holder as guilty of transgression or betrayal while also inflicting vivid visions of murder on the holder. Some believe activating these latent powers will curse the holder, resulting in their own death by the hand of a loved one.

It is worth noting that where the most popular French tale of

Bluebeard and his wives depicts the heroine as a damsel in distress, having used the key out of greed and waiting for her brothers to rescue her, older folktales and stories told among the proletariat portray the heroine as having used the key out of curiosity, then being clever and cunning enough to rescue herself.

Noose of the Phayanak

Region of Origin: Kamchanod Forest

Category: Inanimate

Details: First record of the noose of the phayanak indicates this item was given as a gift from a phayanak to a human after the human had saved the phayanak's life. The human had requested this item with the intent to capture a kinnaree. In addition to giving the human the noose, the phayanak also taught the human how to use it effectively.

When dormant, the item resembles a lasso or lariat—a length of rope with a loop at one end, designed to be thrown around a target and tightened when pulled. Once the noose binds its victim, the remaining length wraps around the victim like the coils of a serpent. The harder a victim struggles, the tighter the coils of the noose bind them. The noose is also impervious to being cut or burned and is essentially indestructible by mundane means.

The Red Shoes

Region of Origin: Northern Europe

Category: Inanimate

Details: Cursed items, the red shoes were created by humans. The exact origin of the curse is unconfirmed but is potentially of human origin as well.

The shoes become active the first time a human dances in them. The wearer is then compelled to continue to dance, unable to stop. Eventually, the wearer dies, either from exhaustion or from some mishap as they are forced to continue dancing without surcease.

The shoes appear to be made of red satin and have changed style over time. Descriptions vary across incidents in which the red shoes have been confirmed to have been involved. The nature of the shoes is to be attractive to potential victims. It is possible the shoes themselves compel victims to put them on. The area of effect when the shoes are not worn or are contained within some type of packaging is uncertain, but it is thought that the shoes have greater effect with proximity and visual exposure.

Beings of supernatural or paranormal nature and humans under the influence of magic may have some resistance to the curse of the red shoes. Though folktales and lore surrounding the red shoes indicate religious elements to the nature of the curse, it is theorized that these shoes became cursed first and then became incorporated into religious teachings as time passed in various regions.

Acknowledgments

It takes a lot to work on a project like this one, the beginning of a whole new series. Even before the idea for Mythwoven sparked, I knew who I wanted to work with and it took years before the timing was right.

Thank you to Mary Altman, my editor, for wanting to work with me and for believing in me. For geeking out with me and brainstorming with me. For taking this story from good to a thousand times better with your input and insight.

Thank you to my agent, Courtney Miller-Callihan, for your patience, support, and advice.

They say writing is a lonely endeavor. It doesn't have to be. I have so much gratitude and appreciation for Asa Maria Bradley for her wise words and encouragement, for K Tempest Bradford for her confidence in me when I couldn't quite find my own, and for Josh Storey for knowing exactly what I meant when I tried to capture a specific voice or feel in certain portions of this work. Similarly, my love and admiration to Katee Robert for your thoughts and inspiration.

Shout out to the personalities of Gaming Excuses: Foodie Edition: Dan Wells, Gabriel F. Salmerón, Christina Boekeloo, Kenna Blaylock, Cooper D. Barham, and Miri Grace. Fun in LoL, random chatting, and lots of food pics helped in so many ways, through so many phases of this book's development.

Thank you to Matthew, my partner and my love, for everything. This book was started in 2020 while I was in the middle of burnout and finished in the months after my heart attack at the beginning of 2021. Matthew was there with me through all of it and he never held me back, only ever helped me rebuild and reinvent myself. Daisuke.

Finally, thank you to my readers. I truly hope you enjoy this story and join me for the stories to come!

About the Author

Piper J. Drake is a bestselling author of romantic suspense, paranormal romance, science fiction, and fantasy. Foodie. Wanderer. Usually not lost. She lives in Seattle with her partner and beloved corgi. Visit her online at piperjdrake.com.

Keep reading for a sneak peek at
the next tale in Piper J. Drake's
stunning Mythwoven series

ONE

First impressions are established within the first seven seconds of an encounter.

Marie Xiao had learned this from her father as a child entering grade school. All she'd wanted to do back then was fit in with the rest of the kids in class, be a part of the games on the playground. Back then, those lessons in how to blend had been about having fun and making friends. They'd been the foundation for a lifetime of survival, building a life as a successful woman and a witch.

Three decades later, she'd refined her understanding of what an impression actually was. She'd also become much more intentional about what kind of impression she wanted to give, adjusting for timing and circumstance. There hadn't been a whole lot she could control in the early parts of her life, but she was making up for it now.

She strode into the grand foyer of the brand-new high-rise, projecting confidence with every step. Her custom-tailored two-piece dress suit was a conservative cut blazer over a fitted sheath dress. The hem hit two inches below her knees, allowing her to maintain the standards of even the stuffiest propriety when she sat. It was the color and fabric that caught the eye.

The Thai silk had been a gift from her new friend Peeraphan, otherwise known as Punch. The fabric held color the way few other materials could, wrapping her in the deepest iridescent blue, almost indigo, the color of the night sky just before dawn.

Paired with nude stiletto heels, the outfit made Marie feel powerful without being ostentatious. Eye-catching without being gaudy. It gave her the confidence she needed to accomplish anything she set her mind to.

Perfect for her goal today.

The young person at the security desk blushed slightly as they greeted her and asked who she was there to meet.

She gave them a serene smile. "Rosemary Xiao, consultant. Here to meet with Tobias Mancini."

Minutes later a bear of a man—not literally, but she'd encountered those too—came barreling out of the elevators and headed straight for her. He was still a dozen steps away as he held his arms open and greeted her in a booming voice, "Miss Xiao! Let's take a walk."

The man continued to hold his arms out, like he was herding her to walk beside him. She turned toward him and caught his right hand in her own, giving it a single, firm shake. "It's a pleasure to meet you, Mister Mancini."

Brown eyes flickered with surprise, then narrowed as the man smiled. "Of course." His right hand tightened around hers. "Call me Toby."

She kept her smile, but brought her left hand to join her right in their handshake and returned the pressure of his grip with her own. "You're too kind. My family name is pronounced a bit more like sh ih ow. I appreciate you making the effort."

He laughed and the sound came out a bit more like a series of barks, like a sea lion making himself heard. She just continued to smile until he eased his grip on her hand and she let the handshake drop on her own terms.

When he swept his left hand out ahead of them, indicating the direction in which he intended for them to walk, she fell in step beside him. He did not place his right hand at the small of her back as he initially had tried to do, before she'd maneuvered him into acknowledging her with that pointed handshake.

It was all posturing and in those few seconds, they'd both established their impressions of each other. She knew exactly how to handle him, and he was aware she wouldn't be the kind of business associate he could steamroll into doing whatever he wanted.

So far, so good, as far as she was concerned.

He led her to the far end of the foyer, where a set of stairs curved up to the second floor. The building had an airy, open design and a portion of the second floor looked out over the foyer below.

"As you can see, Miss Xiao," he began and his pronunciation had improved a little, "our building is a recently completed construction. We had plans to enhance certain areas with greenery, but we weren't happy with the designs proposed by the original builder. We heard you are the best in the Pacific Northwest, so when we decided to contract an external resource, you were at the top of our list."

Well, at least he was making some effort to respect her, and she wasn't immune to compliments, especially when they were in regard to her expertise and not her looks. She could probably work with this person.

"Many of the top employers around the world recognize the benefits of gardens in the workplace. They become places to provide a bit of respite, build camaraderie, encourage collaboration, and improve morale." This part of the discussion flowed easily for Marie, mostly because she believed in what she was saying. "Designed properly, people love where they work, even if the work they do is challenging. Environment could make the difference between high-performing employees flourishing and unhappy workers burning out."

Toby nodded, grinning broadly. "Exactly. Yes. What you said. Glad we're on the same page. We need our people at the top of their game. We're not just making potato chips here."

He laughed and she gave him a brighter smile so he'd feel she had appreciated the joke. They continued walking as he showed her more of the common spaces she would be including in her design work. They took the elevators to a few different floors, as well as the roof, then returned to a different set of elevators to reach the subterranean floors.

"This area is where more of our research and development happens." He led her out of the elevators to a security checkpoint. "The original builder left a lot of plants in one of the storage rooms down here to be used in the greenery design. Waste not, and all that."

She nodded, offering her visitor badge to the camera as she stepped alone into the revolving door. It locked in place as she stepped in, holding her while security confirmed her identity and visitor status. While she waited, she glanced around, mildly entertaining herself with calculating the chances she might catch sight of an umbrella logo. Really, they could do anything to her in here—gas, lasers, flooding. The possibilities were disturbing.

After a moment, a voice sounded from somewhere above her. "Please step through."

The revolving door turned, letting her out on the other side. She'd done freelance consulting for a lot of companies and only one or two big pharmaceutical companies had that kind of extra layer of security inside the building.

"It's a fuss, I know," Toby said as he joined her, tugging at his shirt cuffs. "But the storage room has lights and all, good to keep the plants alive until you're ready to place them up in the rest of the building."

"It's no problem." Or at least, she didn't think it would be so long as security had the appropriate notification to allow her to come and go as needed.

Toby reached for a door. "Here we go. We've also got any diagrams you'll need for the areas of the building we want you to set up with garden things. If you have additional recommendations beyond those, we're open to your proposals, but we'll want estimates on budget and time required. We'll need to approve your designs as well before you get started."

Marie didn't step into the room yet, taking in the rows upon rows of cuttings under plant lights. Some specimens were in buckets of water and others were in seedling pots. The life energy of these plants was faint, yet there was a determination there, in the way nature tended to persist. She could help these plants flourish. Would enjoy it. It was one of the reasons her mundane day job complemented the not-quite normal aspects of who she was.

"There are some unusual specimens here." She let a little awe creep into her voice.

Toby's chest puffed out with pride. "Of course. Can't have those glass balls over on seventh avenue be the gold standard for innovative urban workspaces. We want you to be sure to incorporate these plants into your designs."

Marie stared at one plant, then looked around at several others. None of these were native to the Pacific Northwest, but one or two of these in particular had no business in this part of the world.

She turned to Toby. "If you have an inventory list of what's in here, I'll be sure to include all of these in my designs."

"Ah. Ahem." Toby cleared his throat, handing her a flash drive. "I don't know if there's an inventory list in there, but the diagrams you'll need are. If you need to, you can come back to do an inventory yourself when you show us your first draft."

Obviously, he hadn't put whatever files were on the flash drive on there in the first place, or he'd have known if they included an inventory list. Not a surprise. People as high-placed on a company org chart as Tobias Mancini tended to focus on strategy, rather than tactical details. He'd probably left the task to an administrative assistant. It wasn't a particularly good or bad sign. She ought to avoid making him feel awkward about such things in the future, though. Independent consultants got the best repeat contracts from clients who felt comfortable working with them.

"Of course." It cost her nothing to be agreeable.

This particular contract gave her plenty of time to confirm exactly what varieties those plants were. Besides, she needed to figure out if anyone at this company knew what they might have down here in their storage room. Because at least one of those plants could induce a mental state that was absolutely not what would be considered safe for work.

"I'll look forward to it," she murmured, and it was truth. This contract had suddenly gotten a lot more interesting.

If no one at this company realized what they had, she could always propose to swap the plant samples out for something that looked similar and cost less. Clients usually agreed and she had peace of mind that her designs incorporated plants with far less potential danger to anyone or anything coming in contact with them. Too often, people underestimated plants, choosing them for appearance or scent without understanding what a plant was capable of.

They returned to the hallway. Toby shut the door to the storage room and turned to her, opening his mouth. Before he could say whatever it was, someone came through the security check and brushed past her and Toby.

Marie stepped back quickly, managing to avoid both the man in the lab coat and Toby.

Toby, on the other hand, let out a disgruntled huff and called after the man. "You. Who is your supervisor?"

The man kept walking.

Toby followed after him, catching up in two or three ground-eating strides, and grabbed the man's arm. "I asked you who your supervisor was."

The man turned, blinking down at Toby's grip on his upper arm and then up at Toby, his gaze resting finally on Toby's employee badge.

"Oh." The man removed an ear bud from his ear. "I'm sorry. I didn't hear you."

"That doesn't explain why you just blew by us in the hall-way," Toby snapped. He proceeded to give the man an earful about common courtesy and recognizing the executives in the company anywhere, anytime.

Marie let most of it wash over her, since it wasn't directed toward her anyway. The man's lab coat was opened wider because Toby had a hold on his arm and a flash of gold caught her attention.

The man was wearing a serious piece of jewelry, intricately carved with accents of blue and green and yellow. The central stone was an unusual, green-tinged yellow, carved into the shape of a beetle. Maybe a scarab? It definitely had an Egyptian feel to it.

She had several friends and acquaintances who wore amulets and carved pendants, either for fashion or for faith. This was maybe the biggest she'd ever seen though, as big as her open hand with fingers spread wide. It seemed large enough in height and width to be impractical for someone working in a lab—more like a chest plate. But then, who was she to say what someone ought to wear? It wasn't her business.

No. The amulet had her attention and fashion choices were not at the forefront of her mind as she studied it.

The man had extracted his arm from Toby's grip and straightened his lab coat, hiding the amulet from view. He glared at her and she kept her features schooled to an expression of polite curiosity. She might have even widened her eyes a little to lean into the cute clueless appearance.

"I'll be having a word with your manager," Toby was finishing up. "Be glad I don't speak with HR about your attitude."

Honestly, she wondered how often HR got feedback about Toby. The man was too tactile, in general. She had avoided it today, but she thought the way he'd stopped this employee was crossing a line.

She made a mental note to include it in her feedback at the end of this contract. She didn't want to walk away from this project, yet.

After another minute or so of listening to Toby, the man in the lab coat was able to go on about his business.

Marie made sure to study his features, his build, even the way he walked. She wanted to be able to recognize him again, even if she couldn't see his face right away.

"Sorry you had to witness that." Toby didn't sound at all apologetic. "People just don't have common decency these days. Rudeness in the office place is just not acceptable. Doesn't make for good team building. I see behavior like that and it's like waving a red flag in front of a bull."

Marie wondered how often his metaphors got him into trouble with Human Resources too. She only offered a pleasant smile in response to Toby's grin and allowed him to usher her back up to the grand foyer. As she left, she assured him she would be in touch by the first draft deadline, or before. Then she left the building at a brisk pace, her heels clicking across the floor in a staccato beat.

She had research to do. There were plants in that room that shouldn't be allowed anywhere outside of Egypt and there'd been power coming from that amulet. Old magic. Either one would have warranted her returning to deal with them.

The presence of both? Probably not a coincidence.